RETRIBUTION AND THE BIROBIDZHAN OPTION

STEVEN LEE MILLER

Acknowledgments

I want to express my gratitude to the many of you that have supported me in this adventure. My wife Judy, son Cory and daughter Erin for the encouragement, feedback, and needed space. Joe R. (different real last name) and Steve B. (the real Paul ... had too many Steves!), both former SEALs but served at different times, never knew one another. My rescue lab mix Nicky, who died this year at age fifteen. She would quietly hang out and rest on the floor as I typed away. Monica Dannas, Lori Appel, Bill Vosen, and Don Kay.

DISCLAIMER

FURTHER INFORMATION, COMMENTS, MAILING LIST

Feel free to email the author any comments or questions. Or if you would like to join his mailing list, email: stevenlmiller@sbcglobal.net

ISBN-978-1-7358912-0-0

There is no time limit. Those that seek out this deed, do not always ask permission. They do not need to. They just do it.

Retribution

—————

Joseph Stalin created the Jewish Oblast of Birobidzhan (pronounced, "Biro-bid-zhan") in 1928. It was later considered as the official Jewish Autonomous Region by the Union of Soviet Socialist Republic in 1934. This was fourteen years before the establishment of the State of Israel.

Shortly after World War II, Birobidzhan experienced its peak of Jewish inhabitants: thirty thousand. Since then, due to immigration to the United States and Israel, there are only two thousand Jews remaining. The region keeps Yiddish as its official language.

Today in 2020, there are changing political trends, including a deteriorating chill in Israel's relationship with the United States. Israel's population is experiencing an explosion requiring them to obtain more land to expand and accommodate its people.

A solution to these issues is under current consideration by Israel and Russia:

Introduction

"The Birobidzhan Option"

OPTIONS:

General Option: A thing that may be chosen; a right to choose.

Stock Purchase Option: Gives investor the right, not obligation, to buy a specific **stock** at an agreed price and date.

Real Estate Purchase Option: Gives investor the right, not obligation, to buy a specific parcel of **real estate** at an agreed price and date.

Chronological List of Characters

HEROES OR DESPICABLE SCOUNDRELS? (1978-2015)

1. Tyler Short
2. Thornton Howard III
3. David Miller
4. David Miller's parents both College professors
5. Per Dennis
6. Rosendo
7. Señor X
8. David Miller changes name to Steven Lancaster
9. Dr. Schlomo
10. Randall Tucker
11. Pablo Escobar
12. Cantor Eric Weinberg
13. William Weidemann
14. Stephen J. Weinstein
15. Sergeant Smith
16. Major Godfrey
17. Michael Green
18. David Berman
19. Wally Spencer
20. Buddy Wilson
21. Claire Arscht
22. Ashley Arscht
23. Dr. Saliba
24. Dr. Said
25. Juan Sanchez

The Birobidzhan Option (2019)

1. Steven Lancaster
2. Joe Reid
3. Sheila Reid
4. Paul Dos Santos

Chapter One

BY TWO A.M. THE PARTY WAS IN FULL SWING. THE MULTI-colored lights seemed to go off and on in time to the beat of the music. The DJ, wearing dark sunglasses and a set of head-phones, another set hanging around his neck, was moving to the beat of Gloria Gaynor's *I Will Survive* mixed with *Count-down* by Snoop Dogg. The hundred-plus twenty-somethings were dancing, drinking, and having a great time. The party's host, known as *Benny the Blast,* had bars set up on both his kitchen island and on the large deck overlooking the three-quarters moon that shone on the beach and waves in the Dana Point community. Benny had invited all his neighbors to attend the party, thinking that way he would not be reported to law enforcement for disturbing the peace in the neighborhood.

Zoe Reid, a friend of one of the invited guests, was dancing inside the house, holding a martini glass and still high from the line of cocaine she had ten minutes prior. Her friend Whitney, who knew Benny, invited Zoe to come with her to his party at the Cove gated community in Dana Point. There was not any particular event being celebrated, just a Saturday night of fun at a rich guy's house—lots of laughing, storytelling, and people looking to get hooked up. It was loud with wall-to-wall people. Zoe was having a lot of fun, as any single twenty-four-year-old would. Home on a quick break after finishing flight attendant school in Atlanta, she was visiting her parents, and saying goodbye to everyone for a while, as the company was going to base her out of New York. This visit would also include an awkward meet-up with Dennis the next day. She was going to tell him the relationship was just not practical for her anymore. She hoped they could still be friends. They had both thought they could work through issues before flight attendant school started.

The endless alcohol and loud music of Benny's party numbed Zoe's discomfort and was giving her more courage for visit. She was looking forward to this new adventure in her life but would deeply miss her parents.

Carlos, nobody knew his last name, was an uninvited guest. He mingled with some of the party-goers, danced a bit, walked around with a margarita, but his real reason for being there was to have a word with Benny.

The party was very loud. Engaging in any conversation required either yelling in one another's ears or going to a part of the house that was quieter.

Carlos grabbed a steak on a skewer from the kitchen island counter and walked in the direction of Benny who was leaning up against the wall near where the sliding glass door separated the inside from the back deck. Standing there without the music blasting, one would hear the crashing of waves and seagulls' squeals. At least the noise did not stop the smell of salt air and the cool breezes.

Carlos put his right hand alongside his belt line just above his hip. He wanted to make sure his 45-caliber pistol was still there and covered up by the oversized dress shirt. Due to the crowd of people, his route was not a direct one. He had to go in and out and around just to get where he wanted to go. Benny was engaged in conversation with two female guests, with another female and male guest standing just behind them as if they were waiting for their turn to speak with Benny.

Another uninvited guest entered Benny's house. He too was looking for Benny.

When Carlos finally made it over to the host's location, the female and male guests were now engaged in conversation with Benny. Out of the corner of his eye, Benny noticed Carlos standing behind them. This was not a good thing. He knew why Carlos was there.

Benny quickly excused himself from the conversation and looked up at Carlo. "What's up?"

"You know what's up. Where is it?"

Benny tried to shake Carlos away by saying he was in the middle of a party, he had the money, but could not get at it right now.

Then, out of nowhere, the other uninvited guest, David Bellini, appeared beside them. "Where is my money, Benny? This was due two weeks ago."

"Guys, I need a little more time. As you can both see, I am a little busy right now." A couple of girls walked by and waved at Benny. They were both wearing sexy cleavage-exposing cocktail dresses and clutching expensive purses.

Benny had one bodyguard somewhere at the party but he had no idea where he was. Feeling intimated by the two, he walked briskly away, seeking to get further into the dense crowd, thinking that would deter the two from continuing their demands. But they followed.

Carlos caught up, panting slightly. "I want the money now." Carlos lifted his shirt, making sure Benny saw the large semi-automatic pistol. He clearly did.

"I can't pay you now."

"Benny, you have been jerking me around every week for two months. I said last week, that was your last extension." In a stone-cold, matter-of-fact manner, Carlos slowly took out his 45, and execution-style shot Benny at point-blank range. Traveling through Benny's skull, the bullet exited, striking Zoe Reid in the chest. She would not survive the incident. David Bellini watched the whole thing.

Chapter Two

LESS THAN FORTY-EIGHT HOURS AFTER THE SHOOTING, both Carlos and Bellini were located and arrested by a joint team of the Orange County Sherriff's Department and the United States Marshals office. This rare cooperation between these two entities was the result of a warrant issued by the United States Justice Department, Santa Ana office.

Lancaster was assigned the Bellini prosecution, another U.S. attorney the case against Carlos. They were both brought down to the federal justice center, where they would await bail and preliminary hearings.

Bellini was seated in a private conference room and met with a disturbed Steven Lancaster who wanted to investigate further by asking him questions. Before that, Lancaster gave him his Miranda rights. Bellini, a sophisticated person, told Lancaster he understood his rights, and that they had the wrong guy. It was Carlos, not him, that pulled the trigger. Bellini claimed that had he known what Carlos was going to do, he would have stopped him. It was by pure coincidence they both attended the party looking to get paid.

"I know you didn't pull the trigger, Carlos did, but we can still charge you based on the felony murder rule. You were both there to rough him up and force him to pay. Even if Carlos was heavy-handed, you are still on the hook."

Bellini was arrogant but he was not completely aware of the felony murder rule and how or why it should apply to him. However, he already had the top Orange County Criminal defense attorney on retainer just in case something like this might happen.

"You can't charge me with this. You have no evidence I did nor directed anything. I am having my attorney come down here soon, and he would advise me not to say anything, so I won't."

"Do you feel any sense of responsibility for the deaths of Benny and the young woman behind him, Zoe Reid?"

"Not really. Carlos did that on his own. Certainly, that was without my permission. He is the guy who did all that. Besides, the stupid girl that got whacked: I am sure she was aware of Benny's reputation. She took a risk just being there."

"So, Bellini, you are saying it was her fault for dying because she happened to be there?"

"Hey. It is the risk one takes in a world full of drugs."

"Are you kidding me? She was invited to the party by a friend. She had never met Benny before. She had just graduated from flight attendant school and was about to start her career."

The non-remorseful, arrogant, cost-of-doing-business Bellini did not care. She was just some anonymous somebody. "Too bad for her. Anyway, my lawyer should have me out of here soon."

What a cold ruthless asshole, Lancaster thought. He was reeling on the inside. This poor girl probably had a family. He was determined to get justice. His own father had been murdered years ago by a drug trafficker and Lancaster was never able to get justice. He vowed to himself, he would not let this victim's family down.

The next day was Bellini's bail hearing. Lancaster argued he should remain in custody pending the trial. Bellini's smooth-talking defense lawyer, with his puffy designer handkerchief and fancy suit, convinced the judge that since he did not pull the trigger, and there was no evidence supporting a conspiracy of any kind between Carlos and Bellini, Bellini should be granted bail. It was at a high price of $200 million, but Bellini was out in two hours.

Chapter Three

Sneaking on to the guarded, gated community on Lynda Isle in Newport Beach was not that difficult to do at night. Only a five-minute swim from the shore, Joe found the physical exercise easy, even with two knees that both needed replacing, a bad back, and his sixty-six years of age. He had done much longer swims years back under far worse conditions.

Joe did his homework ahead of time. He knew where the guy lived. Knew where the target's house was relative to the boat dock he'd swum to. He knew this was where the gangster would return to the day he was released on bail. What he didn't know was the sophisticated laser security system the island's wealthy homeowner's association installed.

Getting up on top of the dock, he took off his fins and mask and went through the backyard of a neighbor's house up to the street out front. He crossed the street, water dripping, and went into the thick shrubs, where he could take a short break and see if there was any movement inside the target house. He was still very wet he wasn't too bothered. He would have preferred to have accessed Bellini's house through Bellini's own boat dock, but that would have required swimming around the entire island and taking an extra hour.

He had his Glock attached to his wetsuit, in a small waterproof pouch. He also had an extra clip of bullets, just in case the ten already loaded were not enough. He neatly laid down the mask and fins at the base of the oak tree in the middle of the shrubs, ready for him to retrieve when he finished the deed.

With what must have been the flip of a switch, several floodlights emanating from Bellini's home lit up the entire outside all at once. Joe was not sure how or why this happened, as he knew he had been incredibly careful and silent in getting to where he was. He considered Bellini might have a wireless security system, which was not a good thing. Joe had to either move forward or retreat. He was there, this might be his only chance, so he decided to move forward.

He decided he was most likely discovered anyway so, instead of seeking an open window to sneak through, he took his six-foot-seven-inch body and went to the front door and kicked it in, setting off the house's alarm just as a police siren approached from down the street. Not a wonderful thing, he thought, but at this point, he didn't care much about the consequences to himself. He just wanted to finish his job. Joe remained calm and confident even with these challenges, no doubt from his military training.

The lights inside the house were completely turned on, at least on the first floor. Joe was looking for the staircase, thinking his subject's bedroom was upstairs.

He then heard at the front door the loud command, "Police officers. Come out with your hands raised."

It was too late for Joe, he had to move on. He found the base of the stairs and was about to run up when two of the resident's private security guards rushed to the upper railing on the second floor and the one with the shotgun fired. Lucky for Joe, it was a terrible shot that missed him completely. But Joe knew at that point there would be no way he could make it up the stairs. He quietly considered his options. Try to go out back then jump in the water? Surrender? Run upstairs without cover and die? He opted for the go out the back and jump into water, figuring the police would not shoot him in the back. He was right about that, but when he realized the entire house except for the front door was bolted shut, he knew he had to move on to the next best option ...

Surrender to the police!

Chapter Four

His jail cell had a harbor view, but so did most of them in the Newport Beach Police Department. His breakfast that morning was brought in by officers who would pick up from one of the many great restaurants in the area. Joe was able to enjoy, from *Charlie's Chili* on the peninsula, a delicious chili and cheese omelet, hash browns, sourdough toast, coffee, and orange juice for breakfast. That would be Joe's one and only meal at the jail.

At 9:30 a.m. the Newport Beach Police Department had a unique first-time visitor. While many prosecutors had come to the jail in the past to interview those in custody, this time was different. Steven Lancaster was the first Federal prosecutor to come to visit the jail in recent memory. All the others were state court prosecutors. Lancaster was the assigned prosecutor to the Bellini murder and wanted to speak with the victim's father.

He was escorted by officers back to the holding cell where Joe was. The two spoke in private for a while. When Lancaster was done, he called out for the jailor guard to come back and open the cell so he could leave.

He asked the guard, "Is the watch commander around?"

The jailer took Lancaster to the other side of the police head-quarters, knocked on the watch commander's door, was told to enter, then introduced Lancaster. The watch commander, instead of wearing a uniform as Lancaster had expected, was wearing a beautiful suit and tie. His office was much nicer than Lancaster's; maybe the most high-tech office he had ever seen. He never knew there were so many security cameras within Newport Beach.

The commander asked Lancaster what he could do for him. The two spoke for almost an hour, then Lancaster left, heading back to his office in Santa Ana.

An hour later, the watch commander went to Joe's cell, issued him a citation for a trespassing violation, gave him back his Glock, and told him he was free to leave.

Lancaster knew what Joe wanted to do. He also knew Joe was the father of the female victim. Joe Reid was a decorated former Navy SEAL; he was simply told by the police not to do that again!

———

Later that night at their home, Claire asked Steven, "Did you get that guy out?"

"Yes. He was cited for trespass and released."

"I am a defense lawyer; you are the prosecutor! This is not something I have ever seen you do before."

"What are you trying to say, Claire?'"

"You only did it because you were living vicariously through him. His daughter was murdered by a drug dealer. Just like your father was."

"And?"

"I am trying to say that you saw what this guy did as something you wish you did but didn't."

"I don't need to answer you."

Chapter Five

"I didn't even know he was there until after I shot Bellini and of course, the woman that was behind him."

"Really? And I remind you, your testimony is under oath."

"Yea."

Lancaster turned around, walked away from the witness box, back to his counsel's table, reached underneath, and grabbed the Nike gym back. He sat it on his chair, pulled out what looked like a two-foot-wide, six-inch-tall black fishing tackle box, and placed it carefully on top of the table with the large padlock facing both the witness and jury boxes. The tackle box was labeled, *"BOX OF TRUTH"* in one-inch stenciled letters. There was also a two-inch stenciled question mark above that. Lancaster walked back to the witness.

"So, it is your testimony that you had no idea Mr. Bellini was even there up until the time of the shooting?"

"Correct."

"And you have already pled guilty to your crimes and are serving life in prison?"

"Correct."

"And Mr. Bellini did not pay you to testify in this manner?"

"No, of course not."

"He didn't pay you $150,000 last week for you to testify that you had no idea he was ever there?"

"No."

"And this is your testimony under oath?"

"Yes."

Lancaster knew he'd backed Carlos into a corner. Wanting to play this effectively, he glanced at the jury, then back to Carlos, and strutted over to the *BOX OF TRUTH*. This is great, he thought to himself. Bellini is so fucked.

He did an about-face and, with a flourish, pulled a key from his coat pocket. He unlocked the box, pulled out a single envelope, which also had a distinctive looking question mark on the outside, and opened it up. There were three sheets of eight and a half-inch by eleven-inch paper folded inside.

He gave one piece to the defense, one to the judge, then with the remaining sheet of paper, walked back to the witness.

"So, Mr. Carlos ..."

The lead defense counsel interrupted, "Objection, Your Honor."

Lancaster paused.

The judge spoke. "Just a moment, Mr. Lancaster. Counsel for the defense, what is the basis of your objection?"

"Your Honor, the document was not exchanged or disclosed to us prior to trial as required by the rules of Federal Criminal Procedure."

"Mr. Lancaster, care to respond?"

"Your Honor, the document is being used for impeachment purposes only. I have no requirement or obligation to disclose or exchange this ahead of time."

"I agree, Mr. Lancaster. The objection is overruled. Mr. Lancaster, you may proceed."

Lancaster's confidence grew on the inside, even though he showed no emotion. *I love doing this.* He continued his examination of the witness.

"Sir, this is a copy of a bank wire transfer dated one week ago from Mr. Bellini's Wells Fargo bank account to your wife in the amount of $150,000. Could you please exam this document?"

Carlos studied the document for thirty seconds. The courtroom was quiet in anticipation.

"Okay, I've read it."

"And you have never seen this document before?"

"No."

Lancaster's confidence grew. This should all but guarantee a victory.

"Can you explain the $150,000 transfer?"

"I can."

Oh shit! He can explain this? But how? Maybe it was he who had just been trapped. He would find out very soon.

"What was this for?"

"This was for my wife. She is an interior designer. She did some work for Mr. Bellini recently."

"Yea, right," said Lancaster. He paused, confirming he had been had. *They set me up. They saw this coming and had a bullshit story ready. But how? I must look like a fool with the Box of Truth. If the jury doesn't see it this way, I am so fucked.* Claire always warned him that someday the Box of Truth would backfire and bite him on the ass. "I have no further questions."

"Re-direct?" the judge said to the defense.

"Yes, Your Honor."

Lancaster looked at Smith seated next to him, tapped him on his knee to get his attention, then shook his head slightly.

The lead counsel stood up with three sets of documents. Each set was held together with alligator clips. He gave a set to Lancaster, the judge, and walked forward to the witness.

"I don't have a *BOX OF TRUTH* like the prosecution," he began, "but this may help clarify some things."

Lancaster skimmed over the set of documents and then showed them to Smith and his co-counsel. "Oh fuck," he hissed.

"Mr. Carlos," said the lead defense lawyer, "What are these documents?"

"They appear to be billing invoices from my wife to Mr. Bellini for design work and furnishings. They total $151,100 and are dated two weeks ago."

"I have no further questions," said the defense attorney.

"Mr. Lancaster?" said the judge. "Any more questions?"

Lancaster paused. He looked silently down at the documents. He knew this was a planned and it was he who had been set up, but he couldn't prove it. He would have to wait until final argument to try to address this new problem. Hopefully, the jury would see this as a fake set-up too. How had they known he would be producing this wire transfer document?

"No, Your Honor."

Chapter Six

STEVEN LANCASTER ADJUSTED THE POSITION OF HIS HEAD from facing the left side of his pillow where Claire was sleeping, opened his eyes slightly to the right side, and glanced at his alarm clock. It was 2:50 a.m. His alarm was set to go off in just over three and a half hours. He rolled his sleepy eyes and thought how lame this was. Over his career, he'd tried over three hundred cases but trials still made him extremely nervous.

Getting a good rest the night before closing argument of a murder trial was important. Despite taking an Ambien at 11 p.m., he was not sure if he ever actually fell completely asleep or not. Sure, he was at least daydreaming about nonsensical things, but he doubted that earned him the sleep credit his body and brain needed.

Steven and Claire went to bed at the same time every night, usually around 11:15, as soon as the sports report was over on the television that sat across the room on the dresser. As was typical, they would talk for a few minutes, then she would pass out and he would remain staring at the moon-illuminated ceiling fan. He played a game with himself every night, trying to count the revolutions of the fan. It was not always due to a trial. He told his friends he had always had an active monkey-brain. No matter how late it was at night, relaxing and falling asleep was a problem for him.

Tonight, though, it was about the trial. Lying there on his back, he couldn't stop thinking about it—trying to predict what his opponent or the judge might do, and how he would respond. What if this, what if that? Lancaster's thoughts were all over the place: Why can't I sleep? Was the drug Propofol, administered to Michael Jackson every night by his private doctor, necessary for him to fall asleep? It must have been powerful. Perhaps Steven needed that!

After about forty-five minutes of trying to fall asleep, even after taking the Ambien, the itching would start. First around his nose area. He would scratch. Then almost immediately after, his cheeks, his arms, then legs. He was itching all over. Now he was even more awake than when he initially lay down. On top of that, there was another sleeping challenge. Steven was one that could only sleep lying on his back with none of his limbs crossing over another limb. He was fearful that by crossing any limbs, he would cut off the circulation in his underneath limb, which might cause it to become numb, uncomfortable, or even lead to gangrene causing his premature demise. He had his problems. Being paranoid and obsessive were just two of them!

He looked over with envy at Claire who could fall asleep so quickly. On top of the paranoia and obsessive tendencies, he had issues with anxiety and depression, and his inability to fall asleep would exacerbate those feelings. When that happened, he would sometimes get out of bed and do ten to twenty push-ups on the floor, hoping that would tire him out. If he had Xanax, he would take one.

CLAIRE KNEW WELL OF STEVEN'S SLEEPING ISSUES. OVER the last couple of years, she'd suggested several remedies he should explore, including cognitive therapy, self-hypnosis, having a glass of wine, reading in bed, or uploading an application on his phone that would play soothing white noise sounds such as rain or waves. It did not matter. Nothing worked.

Steven had promised Claire he would seek out help from a functional medicine practitioner. That was over two years ago, and he still had not made an appointment. He recently promised her again he would do it when the trial was over.

The morning's court appearance would be closing arguments for the three-week-long murder and drug trafficking jury trial. When this was over, maybe this would stop the itching, take his mind off the crossed limb dilemma, and allow him to relax and get a good night's sleep.

Chapter Seven

WHEN HIS ALARM WENT OFF, LIKE MANY MORNINGS AFTER little sleep, he did not know what was going on. Then he realized it was time to wake up. After a quick shower, he made the ceremonial twenty-ounce cup of coffee for the ride into the office. He pressed the garage door on the wall next to the door and thought to himself, for probably the one-hundredth time, he must clean the place up and organize it. He would save so much space if he hung up the old bicycles.

He unplugged his white Prius Prime and glanced outside—another June-gloom foggy Southern California day. The drive in was twenty-five minutes, give or take, depending upon traffic. He was listening to Sirius radio, Watercolors, soft jazz music.

As was typical during trial, by 8:15, Lancaster was inside the courthouse cafeteria at his usual table, reviewing his notes and re-writing his outline of major points he would argue to the jury. Some of the notes were ideas he jotted down in the middle of the night. As usual, he had handwritten the thoughts without the lights on. His scribbling resulted in the inability to read his own writing. It was very frustrating to have written down something that might have an important impact on the trial, yet now be unable to read his own writing. He tore up his illegible notes, made a crumpled ball of the paper, and threw it in the direction of the trash can. He missed. Nothing seemed to be going right at the moment.

He took in a deep breath.

He reminded himself that, except for Claire, his boss, and his mother, nobody else knew the post-trial announcement he was going to make. He'd had enough dealings with wealthy defendants paying for the best lawyers and experts to put up the best defense.

Conversely, he knew well how the poor were assigned inexperienced public defenders who were overworked and did not have the necessary resources. It was not an even playing field. It was not fair. He heard, *ad-nauseam*, the same boilerplate arguments made by criminal defense lawyers—my clients are innocent, he made a stupid mistake, he was framed, mistaken identity, prosecuted because the defendant was a minority, poor, was entrapped, illegal search and seizure, blah, blah, blah. He heard these defenses so many times, that he began to question his own values and sense of reality, finding himself buying into their arguments.

Drinking now his third cup of coffee, he started daydreaming about the judges he had appeared in front of over the years. Lancaster thought most of the judges had egos that were out of control. The lifetime appointment of Federal District Court Judges to the bench gave them a God-like sense of power and entitlement. Nonetheless, many judges were angry because they felt they were paid merely a fraction of what the lawyers that appeared before them made. They were angry when lawyers were unprepared, late to court, or did not do what they were asked; angry when they did not like the lawyer's work product; angry when a lawyer would take a position on an issue that conflicted with the judge's own political agenda. Many judges were quick to sanction lawyers with fines, threaten them with jail for contempt, or make referrals to the state bar for what they saw as unethical behavior.

He finished his coffee and stood up, picking up the crumpled piece of paper as he did so, and bussed his tray. Plastering on a fake smile, he nodded to a couple of defense lawyers he knew from other cases as he made his way out of the cafeteria. He walked back toward the courtroom, where he expected to find a lot of people in the audience. The Bellini murder and drug trafficking case had been in the system for close to three years. The defendant, David Bellini, had been out on bail all this time. In a few hours, the case would be in the hands of the jury to decide. *Oh, fuck!*

Wearing his lucky blue pinstripe suit and the Family Guy socks his daughter Ashley had given him for Father's Day, he entered the courtroom. He glanced over at Joe who stood beside his wife Sheila in the front row next to the center aisle. They had become close personal friends of both he and Claire. Lancaster nodded to them with a straight face, trying to offer some reassurance, then he continued past the bar gate to the counsel's table. As he sat down, both Smith and his second chair, Assistant U.S. Attorney Rawlings, were already seated and busy organizing some of the exhibits they thought Lancaster would use during closing. Smith, a forensic accountant employed by the Justice Department and a disabled Army veteran, was there to keep Lancaster organized. It was amazing to watch him use his one prosthetic arm and hand as he sifted through documents faster than most people could do with a real limb. Lancaster would miss Smith after he left the Department.

At the other end of the table, defendant Bellini was wearing a modest suit and watch. Modest, because his lawyers wanted to understate to the jury his personal wealth, otherwise it might be used against him. He sat next to his two private lawyers. The judge in her black robe and large hula-hoop earrings entered the courtroom from her chambers.

The bailiff stood up, faced the packed audience, and said in a loud and commanding voice, "All please rise, this Department is in session. The Honorable Melissa Chang presiding."

Her Honor looked in the direction of her bailiff. "Please bring the jury in."

The bailiff went to the jury room, gathered the panel, and escorted them back to the courtroom, where the parties and all attorneys stood out of respect.

Once everyone was seated, the judge continued: "Counsel," looking at all attorneys and the defendant, "I recognize we rested just prior to lunch yesterday and I thank both sides for behaving ... at least, most of the time." She smiled at the lawyers. "I know cases can sometimes get heated, so I appreciate your civility. Before we get to closing arguments, I want to ask both sides if there are any issues we need to discuss at the sidebar?"

"NO, YOUR HONOR," SAID STEVEN LANCASTER.

"No, Your Honor," announced the lead defense counsel.

The court reporter was recording all of this on his stenograph machine. One or two people in the audience, most likely press, were seen taking notes. Lancaster's mind drifted for a moment as he pondered why courts did not simply use tape recorders instead? A court reporter may have made sense in the 1930s, but now? What a waste of taxpayer dollars.

The judge looked at the jury panel and said, "This next stage is called closing argument. Both sides will have the opportunity to present their respective positions, and what they believe the evidence proved, including why the defendant is guilty or not guilty. The prosecution will go first, followed by the defense, then if Mr. Lancaster requests, he may choose to have the final say, and rebut the defense's position.

"At the conclusion of the closing arguments, I will verbally instruct all of you on the duties of applying the laws to the facts; the bailiff will escort you back to the jury room where you will begin your deliberations.

"Mr. Lancaster, you may present your closing argument."

"Thank you, Your Honor."

Chapter Eight

CLOSING ARGUMENTS BY THE ATTORNEYS ENDED BY MID-afternoon. After, the judge gave the jury their instructions about deliberation, she told those left in the courtroom that since it was getting later in the afternoon, they would adjourn for the day, and informed the jury to return to the jury room by 9 a.m. the next morning.

Steven sleepily surveyed the jurors, observing their clothing, hair, jewelry, purses, reading books, and anything else that might give him further insight into their political or personal biases and hint at which way they would cast their guilty or not guilty vote. How had the defense known he had the wire instruction? They must have, otherwise, how could Bellini's attorneys have known to have those invoices ready to explain the cash transfer?

Does a man with long hair translate into having a liberal bias? Short hair conservative? Does revealing a tattoo signify a liberal? Does being well dressed mean they are conservative? Does a twenty-something wearing a tie-dye shirt with a peace sign suggest being a liberal? Harley Davidson shirt? Someone reading John Grisham? People Magazine? Do these factors provide us any clues?

His thoughts continued. What does it mean when a juror takes notes during final argument? That he or she is a good listener and wants to be very thorough? A bad listener, because why the necessity of writing it down if it was already addressed? Conversely, what does not taking notes suggest? That they do not care. Are they bored? Have they already made up their mind?

Sometimes, Lancaster thought nobody cared. The jurors only received $10—$15 per day for their service. Many of their employers would not pay them to attend jury duty and would become resentful. Many just wanted to do the minimum possible and get the hell out of there.

Lancaster looked back at Joe and Sheila. They looked worn out. The closure of their daughter's death had taken so long. They both hoped and prayed the jury would come back guilty. Sheila reminisced how she used to walk Zoe in her stroller down at the Huntington Beach Pier and sing songs to her. She remembered the videos she'd enjoyed as a child—Aladdin has been her favorite; the high school plays she performed in; the costume Sheila made for her when she was the Good Witch in the *Wizard of Oz*.

Joe was a basket case on the inside, doing his best to cover up his emotions. He would never walk Zoe down the aisle nor dance with her at her wedding. She would never work a day as a flight attendant. She would never move to New York. Her hopes and dreams had been taken away from her when she was so young. It was not fair.

Sheila's world was still turned upside down. Even though it had been three years since Zoe's death, the trauma of somebody taking away the life of her baby girl—her friend; her pride and joy—was just not fair. And the person who was just prosecuted seemed completely unapologetic, devoid of any empathy. He even had the nerve to say to Joe, during a break when the jury was not present: "She got what she deserved." His eyes had glistened when he said it—he knew that Joe had tried to kill him at his home.

The jury was escorted by the bailiff out through the rear door behind the judge's bench, as the attorneys, defendant, and people in the gallery all rose. Once the final jury member had left the courtroom, many in the audience remained standing and began to shuffle out toward the exit doors. Joe and Sheila sat back down. Joe was six foot seven inches and always had to finesse his knees and legs due to the small seats and lack of room in front of him.

"Okay, counsel," said the judge. "As usual, I have no idea how long they will be deliberating, and whether or not they will have any questions. If you would like, there is no sense waiting around here, so you may leave, as long as you remain within thirty minutes of the courtroom and keep your cell phones on."

Both sides nodded in the affirmative.

"That will be fine, Your Honor," replied the lead defense lawyer.

The judge stood up, picked up her notes, and went out the back door to return to her chambers.

Lancaster shook hands with the two defense attorneys. Like him, they had worked hard on this case and had shared a journey of close to three years. And now it was almost over ... At least before any appeals started. Lancaster did not bother reaching his hand out toward the defendant. He pressed his lips together and gave him a short nod. He privately wanted to tell the defendant to enjoy his last day of freedom, but he knew that would not only be inappropriate but also not a given. The defense had done a respectable job. He knew the *Box of Truth* stunt had been a disaster. He shouldn't have done that. Nonetheless, there were holes in the prosecution's case and that their client should be found not guilty.

Lancaster gathered his papers, organized them into his briefcase, and turned to walk back through the aisle where Joe, Sheila, and now Claire, were waiting to walk out with him. Lancaster hugged all three. Joe was holding back tears; Sheila and Claire were visibly crying. This was an emotional trial. Behind them was Lancaster's boss who wanted to be there for the closing argument.

He congratulated Lancaster, and said, "I will see you in the office tomorrow morning?"

"Yes, I will see you there," said Lancaster.

Chapter Nine

AFTER LEAVING COURT, THE FOUR OF THEM AGREED TO meet for an early dinner over at Baggio's next to South Coast Plaza. The two couples had been there together before. It was about a fifteen-minute drive from the Santa Ana Federal Courthouse, halfway between where the Lancasters and Reids each lived. Lancaster drove his car, Claire hers, while Joe and Sheila drove together.

The time between the completion of closing argument and the verdict was never easy for Lancaster. His anxiety and depression were bad but he did an excellent job of covering his emotions so Joe and Sheila wouldn't notice. It was hard for Lancaster. Claire knew this reality: waiting for the unknown; wondering if there would be justice.

Lancaster, Joe, Sheila, and Claire were all seated in one of the restaurant's red booths. The red and white checkered table-cloth was underneath a glass protecting top. The menus were in between the two, to ensure they would remain clean if patrons dropped food or spilled liquid.

Lancaster spoke first after letting out a trial-ending sigh. He was ready for an adult beverage. He said to the server, "I'd like a Heineken with an IV."

"I will have the same thing," said Joe. "Only, you can bring me two IVs. One for each arm." The server smiled, as did Lancaster.

"What kind of white wines do you have?" inquired Sheila who looked like she needed a drink; maybe two.

The server finished a yawn with her left bicep covering her mouth. "Sorry, my son was up most of the night. We have Chardonnay and Pinot Grigio, by the glass. If you would prefer a bottle, we offer several more choices."

"A glass of Chardonnay is fine." Zoe was Sheila's only biological child. This guy destroyed her life. What she really wanted was not a glass of wine, but more like five shots of tequila.

"Just tap water for me please," announced Claire. She was a recovering addict and did not allow herself any alcoholic beverages. But her feelings were in line with the others. Especially her husband, who really wanted the victory. She knew not only would it give the Reids a sense of justice, but also her husband. He had prepared, gone through the emotional rollercoaster, and treated this case as if he were seeking justice for the assassination of his father.

The four quietly studied their menus for a few moments.

"How do you think it went today Steve?" asked Joe, placing his menu on the table.

Steven hated these kinds of questions, but they always came up. He cleared his throat. "I would love to tell you we won, but I've gone through this exercise too many times. Any trial lawyer will tell you they lost cases they should have won and won cases they should have lost. After over thirty-five years of doing this stuff, you think one would have a good idea, but I do not. Even if I did, and even if I felt confident about it, I would not say anything to you, because I do not want to set you up for disappointment. Plus, I am not always good at reading juries."

"I understand," Joe nodded. He hoped there would be a murder conviction and that this Bellini would get the death penalty or life in prison. "What happened at the crime scene seemed so clear to me. Yes, I know Carlos pulled the trigger, but come on, Bellini knew what was going down. Yet Bellini's defense lawyer tried to create confusion for the jurors."

"Yes, he did. Welcome to my life, Joe. That is the job of defense lawyers. The only predictable thing was that Bellini's high-priced attorney is very experienced and knew what he was doing. I can tell you, he got paid more in this three-week trial than I make in a year. He is a smart guy and creating confusion in the jury is what he was paid to do."

Claire chimed in, "I know Bellini's attorney fairly well through the county criminal bar association. He used to be our president and spoke during many of the Continuing Legal Education Seminars."

"At least you never had to go up against him," responded Steven as he stared over at Claire.

"That is because I also do criminal defense, unlike you, my husband Mr. Prosecutor."

Sheila asked, "Is his high-priced lawyer known for pulling certain legal tricks?"

The server returned with their beverages and took the food orders.

Lancaster shook his head and grinned. "The main thing he is known for, does it on virtually every case, and did it again here, is to play word games with the most important jury instruction."

Claire set down her water glass and interjected, "He used to joke to us at previous Bar Association meetings, that he could almost sleep through an entire trial, not even cross-examine witnesses, call his own witnesses, and could still either win or get a hung jury, simply by playing word games."

"What is a hung jury exactly?" asked Sheila.

"In order to get a conviction," Claire explained, "the jury has to be unanimous in their decision. Conversely, for the defendant to get off completely with not guilty, he also needs a unanimous verdict. If they are deadlocked and not all in agreement, the judge usually encourages them to go back into deliberation and work hard to gain consensus. Many times, it works, but not always. With a hung jury, there is no conviction and the prosecution either has to try the case all over or dismiss the portion of the case the jury was hung on."

"Was his strategy that the jury could not meet the beyond a reasonable doubt standard?" asked Joe.

Lancaster told him, "Yep," as he sipped on his green Heineken bottle.

"What does that mean?" asked Sheila.

The food was served, and they began eating.

"The court gives the instruction to the jury that all the crimes the defendant is accused of, the prosecution has the obligation to convince the jury that the defendant is guilty beyond a reasonable doubt and to a moral certainty."

"And that is when the defense lawyer went to the whiteboard and did that confusing moral thing?" commented Sheila.

"Yes," said Claire, "he tries to scare the jury, and he is pretty successful at catching at least one to get them hung."

Sheila's eyes teared up for the fiftieth time that the day.

"So, what did the defense attorney do?" asked a fatigued Joe. "I was obviously there, but by that time I was so dammed tired and probably not listening as well as I should have."

"That is typical of what happens," responded Lancaster as he chewed. "The jury is burned out too. Statistics from surveys show that many times after just a witness or two, plus the body language of the defendant sitting at counsel's table, they have made up their mind. But the game his lawyer plays is surprisingly good and sometimes even confuses *me*."

Lancaster continued, "If you recall, he jumped all over the moral certainty thing, suggesting to each juror that if they are not morally certain of his guilt, they must vote not guilty. He breaks down his view of what the word *moral* means. He gives the example of the philosophical concept of Nihilism and says if you are a Nihilist, you are one who does not believe in morals, because morals are not scientifically based or provable. Therefore, you cannot be morally certain in this case. Nihilist must then vote not guilty. Then if you are moral, he asks the question, where did you get your morals? Then he answers on your own, through church, religion, or ancestors. That we as individuals are personally responsible for our decisions, and if we choose to make an immoral decision, there will be consequences for us, specifically that our souls would be in danger of going to hell. So, he questions whether, as jurors, in this case, they are so morally certain that they are willing to take that chance, and if not, they must vote not guilty to protect their souls."

"I got that," said Sheila.

"Oh my God," agreed Joe. "Nobody can ever be totally certain." Joe felt at that moment the case was lost. "And what about the wire transfer and invoices?"

"I think it was bullshit," said Lancaster. "I don't have any proof, but it certainly feels to me that they knew it was coming and were ready for it. Nobody keeps invoices standing by to prove the basis of a wire transfer. How did they know? I would like to say they had a bug hidden somewhere." He sighed. "We have done what we can do. It doesn't have to be total certainty. Keep in mind that group pressure within the jury is a good thing. Hopefully, they all had previously made their own decisions. We will just have to see what happens."

After the four had finished their early dinner, Lancaster noticed, without saying a word, something he did during every meal—a bad habit. But why did he only ever recognize this after he ate?

During every meal, Lancaster would unconsciously wad up his napkin and crumple it into a little ball. Most people might fold their napkin here or there, but Steven always destroyed his.

His daughter Ashley once asked him, "Why do you do that with your napkin, Daddy?"

He told her, "No idea, Ashley," but privately, he always felt embarrassed and ashamed.

Lancaster would never be mindful of his behavior before a meal would start, only afterward when he was finished, and the napkin was already crumpled up. When he was eating in public and it was one of those rare times, he would catch himself; he would stop, look around, and see if anyone else was doing it. His non-scientific observations were that one out of ten people did this. It was a habit he was not proud of.

Chapter Ten

A FEW MINUTES AFTER 9 A.M. THE NEXT MORNING, Lancaster pulled out his magnetic card, juggling his crème-only first cup of morning coffee and briefcase, slid it into the security slot, then input his code to enter the Justice Department's office. He walked down the hall and knocked on his boss's door, which was partially opened.

Sitting behind his desk and sounding as if he were on the phone with some big shot in Washington D.C., he gestured for Lancaster to come in and grab a seat. Lancaster's boss was the kind of guy who, if he was on the phone with his door open, everybody within five or six offices on both sides of his could easily hear him. His boss knew that, from hearing others comment throughout the years, but did nothing about it. He told Lancaster one day at lunch that his loud voice on the phone was simply a display of his enthusiasm and excitement. Plus, he didn't care what others thought.

Sipping his coffee while waiting, Lancaster glanced around the office at the different photos, diplomas, art, and awards, not noticing anything new he had not seen before. He always liked the autographed Angeles baseball his boss had on display atop his desk. Maybe his boss would give it to him as a retirement present.

"How do you feel the trial went?" asked his boss who had just hung up the phone.

"Jesus Christ, what do you ask me that for? You know the game! Who knows how it went?" exclaimed Lancaster. "I thought it went well until the *Box of Truth*. What can I say?"

His boss responded, "You can say you changed your mind about retiring. By the way, I never like your *Box of Truth*."

"I could but won't."

"Oh, come on Lancaster. Look, if you want, I can take you off trials and have you reassigned to supervise the cases. You would probably sleep a lot better at night."

"That's not it. I have this love-hate thing with trials. They are exciting but I admit, can be frustrating and stressful. You know that. It is what being a lawyer is all about. I would be bored being a supervisor and not going to court."

"But you would have less stress."

"That's true. Maybe I just need a one- or two-year sabbatical."

There was a pause, then his boss said in a calm and empathetic tone, "Well guess what Lancaster, me too. Unfortunately, with all the cutbacks, we just cannot do that. Ever think about becoming a judge?"

"I have thought about that, but think I need an entirely new adventure."

"Anything specific on your horizon?"

"I have a lawyer friend up in Ventura County. I have always had a good relationship with him, and he says he wants to talk."

"A lawyer?"

"Yes."

"But you are burned out and say you want a new adventure."

"He is a civil lawyer. Maybe that would be more refreshing for me."

"I doubt it. I think you would be bored. Besides, you must learn Civil Procedure and will be fighting over money."

"That's true. I don't know what I want."

"Any update from the court concerning your trial?"

"Nope, just waiting for the call from the clerk."

LATER THAT MORNING, WHILE SITTING BACK AT HIS OFFICE desk, his cellphone rang. "Lancaster," he announced.

"This is the clerk in courtroom B. The jury has reached a verdict. The judge has ordered counsel to be back at 1:30 today."

"That was quick. Okay, I will see you then," he said with a big sigh. He thought to himself, with a slight sense of optimism, that quick verdicts were usually beneficial to the prosecution.

He hung up then immediately called Joe. "The jury has a decision, and it will be read at 1:30 today. Obviously, let Sheila know, and I will see you there."

Joe told him, "My fingers are crossed."

Lancaster texted Claire to inform her of the court clerk's call.

Claire text back that she had her own 1:30 court appearance at the state courthouse across the street, but that she would ask for a priority and get there as soon as she could.

Even though it was a quick verdict, the tension of the expected decision was ever-present. "I hate this," said Lancaster aloud, but only loud enough for him to hear.

He stood up from his desk and walked to the second-floor cafeteria for a sandwich before heading over to the courtroom.

Chapter Eleven

As Lancaster walked across the courtyard toward the courthouse, he was approached by a television reporter and cameraman.

"Do you have a prediction, Mr. Lancaster, about what the verdict will be?"

"Sorry, I cannot comment due to the gag order. Speak to me after."

Lancaster entered the courthouse through the special entrance reserved for federal employees, not having to go through the screening and X-ray machine as was required for members of the public.

Lancaster opened the door to the courtroom. It was precisely 1:31 p.m. The gallery was packed with no seats available. As he walked toward counsel's table, Smith and second-chair Rawlings were already seated, as were the defendant Bellini and his attorneys.

As Lancaster took his seat, one of the bailiffs went out the back door to get the judge.

The bailiff soon thereafter reopened the door from the other side, and Her Honor walked in and took the bench. The judge asked the bailiff to bring in the jury. He stepped out, brought them back, and they were at once seated.

The bailiff announced, "All rise, face the flag; recognize and consider the principles for which it represents. The honorable Melissa Chung of the Central District of California, presiding."

She did not skip a beat. Turning to her right, the judge looked toward the jury box and said, "Mr. Foreman, has the jury reached a verdict?"

"Wait, wait," said the court reporter, who seemed to be loading paper into his stenograph machine. "Sorry, Your Honor, I wasn't quite ready. I am good now."

"No problem. Has the jury reached a verdict?"

"We have, Your Honor," said the foreman.

"Please hand it to the clerk."

The courtroom was void of sound. One could hear a pin drop. Steven smiled to himself as he recalled a joke at the Department of Justice that was always told. It related to this specific moment of dead silence at the end of a trial where the foreperson hands over the decision to the clerk:

What would happen if someone right this second, blew out a huge loud fart?

. . .

THE CLERK WALKED UP TO THE JUDGE, TOOK THE FOLDED written verdict, handed it to Her Honor, who carefully read it to herself, looked back at the panel, then handed it to the clerk.

"Would the defendant, Mr. Bellini, please rise?"

He stood up along with his two attorneys. All others in the courtroom remained seated, except for the bailiff who stood near his desk, not too far from the defendant. Lancaster thought that if this trial were broadcasted live on television, this would be the perfect time for the network to sell an expensive commercial.

"Would the clerk please read the verdict?"

"As to the first count of drug trafficking: Guilty. As to the second count of murder in the first degree, the jury is still deadlocked with a split decision of ten guilty, two not guilty."

Judge Chung looking at the entire jury panel. "Do you believe that reconvening and deliberating some more to consider the murder charges would be useful?"

All jurors shook their heads.

Sheila Reid was immediately heard gasping and crying. Joe consoled her, as did Claire who was sitting on her other side. Joe was tearing up but tried to show little emotion. Lancaster put his hands and face flat on the counsel table. Smith, missing three of his limbs due to a helicopter crash while serving in the Army in Iraq, along with Rawlings, tried to comfort him. A hung jury on a murder charge was not something he wanted to end his career on. He felt horrible for the Reids. He felt as though he had lost the case, partly because the defense had been spying on him the entire time.

The defendant and his counsel tried to appear disappointed, but one could not help looking at the defendant's lead counsel. He gave the impression he was serious and stoic, but he was happy and celebrating like hell on the inside. A hung jury on a murder charge was considered a quasi-win by the defense. If the defendant owed his lawyer any money, there would not be a problem getting paid. Even a bonus.

As to whether the prosecution would retry Bellini on the murder charge; that would be determined later. If they did, Lancaster would not be the one doing it. Putting that issue aside, there would still be sentencing on the drug trafficking conviction in the next week or so. The defendant could also choose to file an appeal.

Chapter Twelve

AFTER HE GOT HOME THAT NIGHT, HE TOLD CLAIRE, "THEY had to have known I knew about the wire transfer. I bet they had a bug."

"Well, let us look," said Claire. "I would start with your briefcase. That is with you all the time, both here and at the office."

The two of them looked carefully inside the brown tan leather briefcase. Other than his papers, it appeared empty. Claire placed one hand on the inside and one on the outside of the case and felt around. Just below one of the handles, on the inside of the briefcase materials, she felt a loose bump. It felt like a quarter-inch rectangular shape but when they both inspected the area, they couldn't see anything. Lancaster grabbed an X-acto knife from the garage, and carefully cut the stitching that held the bag together, just below the handle where they felt the object.

Once opened, they felt for the piece, found it, and it came right out. It was a piece of metal; some sort of electronic device. Lancaster took the piece out to the backyard.

"I wonder how long that has been sitting there?" he said when he came back in.

Claire responded, "If this was at home with you, and have no reason to think otherwise, besides discussing a bit about the case, we also talked about a lot of other things, and if people heard that, it can't be a good thing."

"No, it can't."

Lancaster called the FBI.

———

Two days later, Lancaster received a letter at his Santa Ana office. The envelope, with a Colombian stamp on it, was addressed to David Miller a/k/a Steven Lancaster. It was short and read as follows:

Dear David (Or I guess now Steven):

Long time, no speak. After all these years, we still have unfinished business. Meet at Rosendo's bar this Saturday night at 10:00 p.m.

Sincerely,

Senōr X and Rosendo

The letter included a thirty-year-old picture of his mother, with a target drawn over her.

Claire, knowing well about her husband's past, suggested he inform the FBI about the threat. But Lancaster, who was scared, was not willing to do so just yet.

THAT NIGHT, OR MORE ACCURATELY, EARLY THE NEXT morning, Lancaster was lying in bed watching the ceiling fan go round and round. He couldn't sleep. He was thinking hard about all these coincidences. The defense had known that he knew about the wire transfer and they had been able to prepare for it to make them look good and the prosecution look bad. But that was nothing. The letter from Señor X was the first he'd heard from the guy since before his father's assassination. He was scared for his mother. He needed to protect her somehow. He couldn't tell the FBI because if he did, he was not sure where that would lead. He didn't want to take the chance. Were these two coincidences related?

Chapter Thirteen

THAT WEEKEND, THE REIDS HELD A SMALL GATHERING OF friends at their home in Long Beach. Steven, Claire, and their daughter, Ashley, were among the thirty or so guests. The Reids wanted to show their appreciation to Steven for his efforts.

Over beer, Joe, Steven, and Joe's friend, Paul, stood in the corner of the living room, talking.

"This is my friend, Paul Dos Santos," said Joe. "He lives in San Diego."

"Nice to meet you, Paul. How do you two know each other?" Lancaster felt a bit shameful not being able to get a murder verdict and forcing himself to engage in conversation with a stranger.

Finishing a swig of his Stella Artois, Paul, with small squinty brown eyes was moving his head to the beat of the background music of Led Zeppelin. "We served together in the Navy."

Looking over at Joe then back to Paul, Lancaster asked, "You were stationed with him at Coronado in the SEALs?"

"Yeah. We were in SEALTeam 3."

"I was Joe's commanding officer," said Paul.

"Oh, bullshit, Paul!"

Paul kept a straight face and had another swig. His squinty eyes stared at Joe. Blood pressure and pulse didn't move at all. "Maybe in rank and pay only. I never called you Sir."

"Yes, you did."

"Maybe once or twice when we were in front of more senior officers who didn't know us."

Lancaster, again forcing words out to make conversation, asked, "Really? I thought you were supposed to call officers, Sir?"

"In our team, we called whoever, whatever the hell we wanted."

Paul nodded. "True."

Lancaster, intrigued by Paul's answer, asked, "What did you call each other? Did you have nicknames in the Navy?"

Both Paul and Joe let out a little laugh. The corner of the living room was away from most of the party guests, who were hovering primarily in the family room and kitchen.

"Don't tell him, Paul—there are ladies and kids present!"

"Fuck you, Joe. His name was Erection, or sometimes we just called him Erect, Erect One, or Weenie."

Joe and Paul smiled as Lancaster let out a single chuckle.

"Why?"

"Do you really want to know? This was a long time ago."

"Yes, I really want to know. In fact, given your nickname, I have to know."

Paul said, "Well, just look at the guy. He is, what, six foot seven? He is tall and straight up. Very erect. We called him Erection. Seemed to fit. Still does."

"Okay, I ... see that. And did you have a nickname too, Paul?"

"They called me Easy."

"Easy? How did you get that nickname?"

Joe and Paul looked at each other, looking puzzled for a moment, and both shrugged.

"I remember now," said Joe. "When we were in BUDs together, he was an ensign and our team leader. Paul gave a speech to our platoon team at the beginning of our training. He said our training was going to be hard and gave us an idea to make our getting through together a bit easier."

"What was that?"

"He wanted all of us to specialize in certain responsibilities since we were limited in time. By doing it this way, we could be more efficient and do a better job. So as an example, we would have inspections of our rack, locker, equipment, and living area. Most all sailors, of course, would do each chore. Easy said our time was always limited. We were going to save time, energy, and be more efficient. One guy would square away everyone's boots, another the racks, while another swept the entire hutch, and another made sure our lockers were perfect. We were able to enjoy a little more sleep doing it that way, as we could do things faster and more efficiently."

"I felt each sailor, specializing in just one task, would save us each a lot of time and make things easier, hence they called me 'Easy'."

Joe shook his head in agreement, then said, "And it really got all of us through, especially during Hell Week."

"Everyone in our platoon made it. I think forty percent of all others rang the bell and quit. I was enormously proud of our guys."

"So, Easy and Erection?!"

"Joe is fine for now. I am out of the Navy."

Looking in the direction of Paul, Lancaster commented, "I take it you are out too?"

"Oh, yes. I have been for some time. Run my own business now."

"Tell me, Paul, is your business as unique and creative as Joe's?"

"Easy's business is probably more creative, but more boring than mine," said Joe. "But I am sure he makes a hell of a lot more money than I do."

"Really? What do you do, Paul?" asked Lancaster.

Looking at Joe, he asked, "Do I want to tell him if he is a criminal prosecutor?"

"I don't think he is anymore. That was his last trial."

"Sort of," said Lancaster who technically felt he still had an ethical obligation to enforce laws. "We still have to go back for sentencing next week, but that is it. Unless what you do is outrageous, I am too tired of it all to care."

"Just tell him, Paul. I am sure it is fine. If not, I'll just beat the crap out of him."

"I'm kind of in the wholesale food distribution business," said Paul. "You know the expiration dates you see on food packages? Like, purchase by a certain date?"

"Yes."

Paul responded, "I buy food in bulk with a day or two left prior to expiration. At ten cents on the dollar, sometimes less. Then I load it up into trucks, cross the border into Tijuana, and wholesale it there."

"You are selling expired food to the Mexicans?"

"No. It is not expired when I bring it down there. As to when they sell it, I have no idea. Not my business. I'm not even sure those expiration dates are relevant in Mexico." Looking to change the subject, Paul asked, "So, you are retiring as a prosecutor?"

"I have been doing it a long time, and I am burned out now. I am not ready to stop working altogether, but I want to do something else."

Joe grabbed a chip from the counter and dipped it in some blue cheese dressing. "Have you decided what you want to do? Are you going to take that other law job with your friend?"

"I don't know. He has not offered me a job yet. I was talking to my life coach and—"

Paul interrupted: "A life coach? What the fuck is that?" He squinted at Lancaster and looked him up and down a couple of times. "He coaches you on how to brush your teeth?"

"Listen to this, Easy," Joe said, smiling.

Lancaster was not sure how to react but he continued: "Actually, he kind of does. I credit him for saving my life. He certainly prevented me from having a nervous breakdown earlier in my career. He suggested I go on his upcoming retreat to seek inspiration as to what to do in the next chapter of my life."

"A retreat? Is that one of those touchy-feely things?" asked Paul. "And you pay money for that? Give me a dollar and I will tell you what to do."

"I think Lancaster likes to do things like that."

"Alright, so tell me, what is this retreat thing?"

"He explained the retreat to me, Paul," said Joe. "Not sure you really would want to know. Plus, you may think it is bizarre and that he needs his head examined."

Paul finished the last of his beer. "Okay, I am interested in hearing about this," he said with a straight face.

Lancaster knew the subject matter of solo nature journeys was considered weird by many and felt a bit uneasy. "Do you want to answer him, Joe?"

"No, this is your deal. You own this one."

"You asked for it, Paul," responded Lancaster. "You meet with a group in nature somewhere. Usually like national parks, monuments, or in the wilderness. The leader is an expert in Qi Gong, and Native American spiritual practices. After you arrive, there is the first phase, which is the training. This goes on for the first two or three days. After the training, each person goes off to their selected sacred space—"

"Sacred space?" said Paul. "What the fuck is that? I'll give you a sacred space right here, right now," as he pointed toward his crotch.

"Haha," said Lancaster. Joe smiled. "A sacred space is where you remain in a predetermined designated circle, maybe fifty yards in each direction, for the next four days or so. During this time, you do not see anyone, speak to anyone; there is no radio, writing, fire, no nothing."

"Sounds a little boring," Paul said.

"That is part of the point. The boredom challenges you to be in the present moment, and simply be. Or simply consider things. Nothing there to bother you. It is very peaceful I am told."

Lancaster paused as Paul looked over at Joe and raised his eyebrows. Paul grabbed another beer, twisted off the top, and took another swig.

Lancaster continued, "So we are by ourselves, alone, using these tools and practices, and just sitting with nature. This journey allows one to get inspired, gain clarity, and get rid of bad thoughts we hang onto."

"And you want to get clarity on what you are going to be when you grow up?" asked Paul with a grin on his face.

Joe laughed as Lancaster smiled.

"Maybe."

"So where is this solo nature journey going to take place?" asked Paul.

"El Salvador."

Paul was stunned. He dropped his half-full beer bottle on the warm and thin carpeted living room floor, where it broke into pieces, and splattered beer all over. Joe knew why Paul reacted that way.

Chapter Fourteen

LATER THAT EVENING, AFTER HALF THE GUESTS HAD already left and a few more consumed beers, Joe and Lancaster reconnected, this time in the kitchen. The light was much brighter in this part of the house than the darker living room. The kitchen had an island with light blue two-inch by two-inch tile bordering mortar. Lancaster, who not too long ago used to wear white short-sleeve dress shirts to work with a clip-on tie, and who was certainly no expert in fashion or design, thought the place could use a little updating. Joe and Sheila's place was about a half-mile away from the port of Long Beach.

Lancaster said, "I am so sorry we didn't get the conviction on the murder charge. We knew it would not be easy, but Bellini would not agree to more than ten years total. That was not going to work for us, so we went to trial."

"I appreciate it. I know you did the best you could."

"It isn't necessarily over. We can decide if we want to retry the murder charge."

"Will you?"

"My boss, who is the decision-maker, told me that if Bellini and his lawyer will agree to a minimum thirty-year sentence, we will drop the murder charge. If he does agree to this, he will be into his seventies before he ever gets out."

"Think he will go for it?"

"The guy has an exposure of twenty to forty years on the drug trafficking charge alone that he was convicted of. Agreeing to thirty years in prison would end the death penalty risk for him. I think it is a good deal at this point for everyone."

There was silence for a good sixty seconds. The chatter of others mingling in the background drifted toward them, along with the music of Bill Withers singing *Just the Two of Us*.

Joe, in a very deliberate voice, started to tear up a little. "In the Navy, much of what I did was secret, and technically still is today. But a lot of my work was to neutralize threats of drug traffickers, primarily in Central and South America." Joe's eyes turned red. "I, I, I devoted a large part of my career going after drug dealers. We had a lot of success. Yet in the end, I couldn't even protect my own daughter." He was sobbing now.

Lancaster wasn't ready for that. It was like a stab in his own heart. He draped his arm over Joe's towering shoulder and upper back and tried to hold it in, but he soon began to weep too. Joe's trauma was too painful.

Joe continued. "I know we never had a conversation about this as I didn't think it was appropriate. After Bellini made bail, I know you did me a little favor on that trespassing problem. I never told you thank you. I really appreciated that and I feel I owe you a debt."

"Yes, the Newport Beach Police Department called me after your arrest while you were in custody."

"I figured. So, you asked them to release me, because you told them it was minor trespass, at least that is what the officer told me."

"I did."

"Why did you do that? I sneaked into Bellini's gated community on Linda Isle in the bay and was caught red-handed on his property with a Glock 9MM."

"I felt your pain. You just wanted to take care of business yourself. I told my wife Claire later that same night, if I were in your shoes, I would have tried to do the same. That's why I asked the police to release you."

"But why?!" Joe asked again.

"I am so sorry about what happened to Zoe, Joe." Lancaster took a pause, breathed, and in an exceptionally faint voice, began, "There are probably less than four or five people in the world that know what I am going to tell you, so please keep this to yourself." There was a pause for another several seconds. "My father was assassinated by a drug cartel. It was all my fault. They killed him because I wouldn't do something for them."

Joe blinked. "They did?!"

Lancaster put his lips together and nodded.

Joe did not ask Lancaster any more questions. He wrongfully assumed it pertained to an earlier drug prosecution. Unbeknownst to Joe, Lancaster had not even been a prosecutor by that time.

"I sometimes regret never going after my father's murderer. Perhaps when you tried to kill Bellini at his home in Newport, I was living vicariously through you. I was also thinking about what I would have done if it had been Ashley. There is more I would like to tell you, but right now I can't. I wish I could. Maybe later."

They both teared up some more as they held one another, recognizing this horrible connection they shared. They'd both lost love ones at the hands of drug traffickers.

A FEW MINUTES LATER, CLAIRE AND SHEILA CAME OVER TO Joe and Steven.

SHELIA ASKED BOTH STEVEN AND CLAIRE, "SO CLAIRE, HOW is it you do criminal defense work, and you, Steven, are a criminal prosecutor? Doesn't this make for arguing with each other at home?"

"No, not at all. I would say for both of us, at this point in our careers, we recognize we are simply both advocates, trying to see that our clients' rights are protected. My client, of course, is the government, and Claire's clients are 'scum bag' criminals. Just kidding!"

"I would agree but not the scum bag part," added Claire. "For me, I went into criminal law because I like the subject matter. I always thought it was interesting. I think when I started doing criminal defense, I was more idealistic. That feeling has faded a bit over time."

"The same was not completely true for me," said Steven. "I went to work for the Justice Department because not only did they offer me a job, but I tend to lean more toward the prosecution side of things. Even though, today, I am burned out a bit. prosecuting is still my personal bias. I also went through a phase when I wanted to make a difference by doing what I saw as the right thing. Today, Claire and I round-table certain criminal law scenarios, and play devils-advocate with one another to get a perspective of what our opponents might think."

Claire added, "Yes, I often lie to Steven as I don't want to give up our defense lawyer secrets! We have fun. I still enjoy it. I know most of the judges and prosecutors here in Orange County. It is a nice community overall. Steven is mostly in federal court. Less than ten percent of my cases are there. I am mostly in state court."

"We have better carpeting and decorating inside federal court than state court. We are also kind of arrogant to the state court lawyers as well," remarked Steven.

"Sheila, did you ever get a new job?" asked Claire.

"I am still looking. I do a little bookkeeping for Joe."

"How long have you two been married?" asked Steven.

"Around twenty-four years," said Sheila. "This is my second marriage and Joe's fourth or fifth."

Joe at once responded. "Excuse me, Sheila, my dear. If you exclude my annulment to the psycho-bitch, which only lasted three months, you are my second as well. What about you two?"

"Five years for us. We were both married once before. Both of us had practice spouses," said Steven.

"Do you like it here in Long Beach?" asked Claire.

Sheila responded, "We do. It is close to and convenient for Joe's work. I have some family not too far away in the South Bay area. I tell you what, though, if I were a young person just starting out, there is no way in the world I could afford buying a house around here."

"It's really a hardship on our budget. But we love the beach," agreed Joe.

"Yes, we do," said Claire, as all four raised their glasses. "To the beach."

"Any plans to retire soon, Joe?" asked Steven.

"Retire? I would like to retire now. I would love to play golf, travel, and read more. I get a pension from the Navy and will start taking social security in around five years. That will be the time. But until then, I get to ride my Wave Runners daily and take people out to the Islands."

"Sounds like a lot of fun. I cannot imagine traveling faster than forty miles per hour in Southern California. I mean, with all the traffic and everything."

"No traffic to speak of in the ocean," said Joe.

"Honey," Sheila interrupted, "I want to get the coffee started."

"Sounds good," added Joe, as Sheila and Claire walked toward the other side of the kitchen.

Chapter Fifteen

PAUL WALKED OVER TO JOE AND LANCASTER WITH A plastic water bottle in his hand. "So, when is this nature journey thing in El Salvador?" he asked.

Looking at Paul with a serious face, Joe responded, "Are you thinking of going because of ..."

"I might."

"It's in a few weeks," said Lancaster.

"Do you know any other people going?" asked Paul.

"I do. Besides the leader, Buddy Wilson, I am taking this young kid. He is not really a kid anymore. He is a young neuroscientist named Juan Sanchez, a friend of mine, that I met several years ago in El Salvador during a criminal investigation. He used to be in MS-13 but turned his life around. I have become a bit of a mentor to him. He is going."

"Paul, do you want to tell him about it?" asked Joe.

"If he can keep it secret."

"I am already keeping one of your secrets. I can just add this to the list," Lancaster said with a smile. "I promise."

"Obviously, when you mentioned El Salvador it affected me. It brought back an unpleasant memory. Back around 1988, during the civil war in El Salvador, we were told of this target. A guy who was both a senior Farabundo Marti National Liberation (FMLN) rebel and a drug trafficker. He was living in the coastal community of San Diego. And yes, there is a San Diego in El Salvador—much smaller than the one here in California. It's on the Pacific ten miles south of the city of La Libertad."

Lancaster jumped in, "La Libertad is actually the city where I met Juan. Sorry, go ahead."

"We were ordered to go down there and neutralize him. My team, including Joe, parachuted down a mile offshore at around 4 a.m. one day. We jumped with a couple of rubber rafts and motored quietly into shore a few clicks from San Diego. We went down to where we were told his house was and were given intelligence that he left the house at 7 a.m. each morning when a driver picked him up and drove to the rebel hideout.

"I was trained to use the rocket-propelled grenade launcher. I was pretty accurate from a couple of hundred yards out. As we were in position, locked and loaded, ready to go, the target came out of the house, right on schedule. I had him in sight and fired. At that exact second, a little girl ran out of the house. They were both hit. I never got over killing that little girl. She was wearing a pink dress, the kind you see little girls wear to make them look like a ballet dancer."

He was trying to hold it all in. His beer helped give him the courage to tell this story. "She was no more than five or six years old. I killed her."

Paul paused. There was silence for some twenty seconds as Joe calmly nodded his head up and down.

"I haven't stepped foot in El Salvador since. Yet, I think about that little girl every day. Some days, all day. Maybe getting back to El Salvador and participating in this nature journey could be of benefit to me to get this monkey off my back."

Lancaster nodded his head with a sympathetic and encouraging smile. "It just might."

Joe and Lancaster met in the court cafeteria before the sentencing. Since Bellini was going to agree to the deal, Sheila felt she did not have the desire to come down. They would be putting him away for thirty years that day.

Joe said, "I hope this will go smoothly and be all over soon."

"Yes, me too. I doubt he will harm anyone else anymore."

"Was the guy that murdered your father ever brought to justice?"

"Nope."

"And do you know who he was?"

"I don't think I know the guy who actually pulled the trigger, but I'm pretty sure I know who ordered it."

"Can you tell me more?"

"I am trying to figure out some things, including something new. Let me get Bellini sentenced, complete my resignation, and have a few beers. Then I might just tell you everything."

BACK IN COURT, BELLINI AGREED TO THE RECOMMENDED sentencing. The court imposed the thirty-year federal prison term with no possibility of parole. He was taken away at once. Both Steven and Joe were relieved.

By the afternoon, Lancaster was no longer employed by the Justice Department.

Chapter Sixteen

SOUTHERN CALIFORNIA IS HOME TO SIX HUNDRED thousand motorcycles and another ten million cars. There is a lot of traffic and it is hard to get anywhere. It is just not a fun place to drive around.

Joe's business was the first of its kind to address the traffic problem in a unique way. His business took guests out on personal watercraft, such as Wave Runners and jet skis out of Long Beach Harbor to go island hopping around the Channel Islands. He kept a fleet of about twenty watercraft. The eight Channel Islands sat between twelve and seventy miles off the California coast. Except for Avalon, a small town on Catalina Island, fewer than five people lived permanently on each of the other islands. The Islands were part of the National Park system and supplied campsites and trails for those who could figure out how to get there.

Joe told Paul and Steven, "When we have a full group and all my watercraft are operational, we can take up to nineteen guests. Our mothership, an old fishing trawler, leaves hours prior to the group to the planned destination. The ship travels at around eleven knots. It serves as our hotel, bar, and restaurant. Our Wave Runners can go up to fifty-five miles per hour. The guests are split into three groups of four to six. Each group includes a high-speed chaser boat that follows closely behind and stays in radio contact with the riders. In case of a maintenance problem or other emergency, the trawler staff is trained to taking care of such things. The safety and comfort of our guests is our top priority."

"Do the weather and seas look okay today?" asked Lancaster as he finished putting on his wetsuit on the floating dock next to the three Wave Runners.

"Conditions look great. Sunny. Little to no sea chop. The Coast Guard said it will be calm for the next two to three days. Couldn't be much better," answered Joe.

"Will we need to still wear wet suits?"

"I am," said Paul. "I am sure if you don't want to, Joe won't require you to wear one."

Joe responded, "Water is sixty-one degrees Fahrenheit, about average for this time of year. You will want to wear a wet suit. We have a two- or three-hour ride to Santa Cruz Island, not including our stop along the way at Anacapa Island."

The trip included Lancaster, Paul, and Joe, plus a chase boat driven by one of his employees, which carried their supplies including food, water, and camping gear. The mothership would not be used for this small group.

They left the harbor just after 7 a.m. with the chase boat close behind. They headed northwest and would stop to take a bathroom and refreshment break at Anacapa Island, a little more than halfway to their destination.

When Lancaster headed out with the others, he considered how wonderful and revitalized he felt. The air was so clean. Water splashed his face as he rode over waves, the sun beat down, primarily from behind, and there was that salty sinus-clearing smell, which could only be attributed to the ocean. Southern California felt strangely empty and free.

When they arrived at Anacapa, Joe had the ship-hand from the chase boat fill the gas tanks on the Wave Runners. After their morning break, the trio fooled around the island's rugged coast, motoring in and out of the many inlets and jagged rocks. It was a lot of fun.

Joe led them to Potato Harbor on Santa Cruz Island. The Wave Runners drove right onto the beach. The chase boat was moored offshore where the ship-hand transferred the equipment onto a rubber boat, then brought it into shore.

The cove they entered fanned out in a semi-circle and had the most amazingly clean white-sand beach extending some fifty feet. The group traveled up a trail to a hill, which took them to the empty campground about a quarter-mile away.

"There is nobody here," said Lancaster. He saw some fifteen picnic tables and vacant campsites, including several hills and valleys covered with oak trees and brush, plus a handful of dirt roads. There were no structures of any kind other than the small toilet in the campground. He imagined this was what much of Southern California looked like before anyone lived there.

"Should we set up camp?" asked Paul.

"No. That is what I pay my chase boat guy to do. Let us unwind and then go for a short hike. By the time we get back, he should have all our hammocks set up for a little siesta."

"Sounds good to me," said Paul.

"What's for dinner?" asked Lancaster.

"It depends on what you catch," said Joe with a straight face. "Sometimes fish, sometimes wild boar."

"Whaaaat?!" said Lancaster.

"Just kidding! Don't get so worked up," grinned Joe. "We have steaks, salad, potatoes, fruit, and lots of beer. I have this dialed in."

Paul nodded. "He does."

The three of them went for a short hike. They climbed a hundred feet above the campground and walked across a ridge that provided a panoramic view of the California coast some twenty miles away toward the east. Joe pointed out the distant cities of Santa Barbara, Ventura, Oxnard, and the general direction of where Malibu would be.

All three were within five years in age of one another, with Lancaster in the middle. They talked about growing up, high school, and how their lives had evolved since. Lancaster was not comfortable telling the complete details of his past; at least, not yet.

Joe was raised in Indiana and was offered a basketball scholarship by the famed coach Bobby Knight. After two years, he just could not handle the coach's temper tantrums so he dropped out and joined the Navy.

Paul, on the other hand, went to San Diego State, where he received a Navy ROTC scholarship. When he entered college, he wanted to fly jets and land on aircraft carriers. That never happened.

Paul and Joe met at Basic Underwater (BUDs) training in Coronado. Paul was a commissioned ensign for less than six months; Joe was already in the Navy six years. Those two bonded and had been great friends since. They credited each other for not just getting through BUDs but for saving each other's lives more than once. They were both Type A personalities, displaying confidence that they could do anything and nobody would stop them. A rational human being would not want to mess with either one.

They took the trail back toward camp, and as they started down their final descent off the hill, they saw the ship-hand speaking to a park ranger and two Coast Guard sailors, while a helicopter circled above. They also saw a small Coast Guard speedboat, plus a private speedboat in the bay below. The Coast Guard boat anchored in the small bay, the private boat had its front end beached and appeared to be stuck in the sand. A Ford pickup truck, with a National Park emblem and activated blue and red police lights on top, was parked next to where the men were gathered.

The ranger and sailors were wearing bulletproof vests and carrying M-16s. Joe's ship-hand did not look happy.

As Paul, Joe, and Lancaster approached, the park ranger said, "Hi, Joe."

"Hi, Jimmy. What's going on?"

The ranger said, "The Coast Guard was chasing the other boat you see down there on the beach. They have not searched the vessel yet but have a strong suspicion they were smuggling drugs. Their boat was carrying two male Hispanics who jumped off. One had a semi-automatic rifle, the other a high caliber pistol. They took off running up here. Coast

Guard radioed my office, so I came down here and met them."

To Lancaster's surprise, both Joe and Paul immediately pulled out pistols from behind their lower back waistbands. Joe had his Glock 9MM; Paul a SIG 40 caliber.

The ship-hand pointed to a dense area of vegetation about three hundred yards away, and said, "See that tree forest over there? Both ran into that. Neither has come out. They have to be hiding in there."

The dense forest area covered some three or four acres and was made up of large oak trees and brush.

"Okay, let's go get them out," said Paul.

"We have a cutter that just left Port Hueneme," said one of the Coast Guard sailors. "They should be here in forty-five minutes to an hour."

Joe responded, "Too much time. We will get them out. This shouldn't be too difficult."

Paul, the career team leader, went automatically into decision-making mode. "Let us set up a perimeter. I want you," (pointing at the ranger), "to take the south end, you guys," (pointing at the two sailors), "one on the east, other on the west. Joe and I will go to the north and insert ourselves in from there. If they were smart, they would voluntarily come out and surrender."

"You two," Paul looked to the ship-hand and Lancaster, "just wait here. In fact, if you like, feel free to take naps in the hammocks."

Lancaster responded in disbelief. "A nap?! You want me to take a nap while you may be in a firefight right over there?" He pointed to the trees.

"Yes, a nap. A little rest."

"Hahaha! You think we could sleep right now?" asked Lancaster.

Paul said, "I could. But suit yourself. Stay here."

The other five, with their weapons locked and loaded, safeties off, took their positions, creating the perimeter around the forest, as Paul had suggested.

Joe had a suspicion he knew what Paul was going to do. After taking up their position on the north side behind a couple of large boulders, Paul, in a loud and commanding voice, spoke in Spanish, seeking to get the attention of the two fugitives.

"Gentlemen, my name is Lieutenant Commander Paul Easy, retired U.S. Navy SEAL."

"Your last name isn't Easy," Joe whispered.

"It's all I could think of. Besides, who cares?" Then once again raising his voice and continuing in Spanish: "You are surrounded by others with high-powered automatic rifles. I am ordering you to lay down your weapons. Come out of the forest with your hands up right now."

There was silence for two or three minutes. No movement from the two from inside the forest.

Paul, still speaking Spanish in a loud voice, went on, "I don't know you. You do not know me. You are not listening to my order. Let me give you both some further thoughts to consider. There is a Coast Guard cutter that is going to be here in the next half hour. They will have fifty sailors, all with automatic weapons. They are anxious to fire them."

Paul paused for a moment, then continued. "In addition, when I mentioned earlier we are retired SEALs, what that means is, since we are retired, we are no longer governed by any rules of engagement. Let me translate that a little more for each of you. What we are going to do, so the boys from the cutter will not be stealing our fun, is to sneak up on the both of you. You will not see us or hear us until each of you are stabbed with our twenty-one-inch knife blades. Then, after you are both stabbed, and assuming alive, we will cut both of you into little tiny pieces and throw your meat into the harbor like chum to see if we can attract some sharks. So, I am going to count to ten, and if you are not out and surrendered, we are coming in after you."

By the time Paul got to seven, they both exited the forest with their hands up. The Coast Guard sailors handcuffed the pair and began walking them back toward the trail that led to the beach. The park ranger went back to where they had been hiding to recover their weapons.

Lancaster and the ship-hand, who watched and heard the entire operation, looked at one another. "Holy shit," Lancaster breathed, "these guys are good!"

Chapter Seventeen

THAT EVENING AT THE CAMPGROUND ON SANTA CRUZ Island, the four were all relaxing, drinking beer, and bullshitting around the campfire.

Joe asked, "Are you ready to tell us your secret growing up story Lancaster?"

Lancaster responded, "It is as good a time as any. It is a thirty-year story. I will try to keep it brief."

"You can take as much time as you like," said Paul.

"So kind of you, Paul. I graduated high school in Los Angeles in 1978. Van Nuys to be specific. Birmingham High School. On graduation night, every high school graduate in the Los Angeles and Orange County area goes to Disneyland."

The ship-hand interrupted, "I went to high school in Cerritos. When I graduated in 2012, I did that too."

Lancaster nodded his head in the affirmative, then resumed. "So, all the kids take buses to Disneyland. We would be there all night. I graduated number two in my high school class, got into Harvard, and was going to attend there in the fall. During the bus ride, they were playing music through the speakers up above the seats. They played a song, which changed my life forever. It was a song, I think, by Bob Dylan, which included the lyrics, 'If you want an education, don't go to college but hitchhike around Mexico'."

Joe asked, "You followed the advice of a song you never heard before and didn't go to Harvard?"

There was a pause. Lancaster took a small branch from a tree and stirred the campfire, trying to allow more air to get to some of the unburned wood.

"If you put it that way, Joe, I guess the answer is yes."

Joe cracked a smile, showing his teeth, as he shook his head.

"I told my parents early the next morning I wasn't going to college. We compromised by agreeing that I could take a year off and would start the following year. Harvard would not give me a deferred admission. I went to Mexico, Central America, and South America. While spending some time in the small town of Armenia found in the coffee region of Colombia, I was introduced by the owner of a bar named Rosendo, to a guy who was a big-time drug trafficker. They called him Señor X. He exported cocaine for a major cartel, and figuratively speaking put a gun to my head, along with this other guy named Per. He flat out told us we are going to help him smuggle coke up the United States. Even though he put guns to our heads, he said he would pay us each $1,000,000.

"We had no choice. We had to do it. So, we did. We sailed from Buenaventura, Colombia in a little over two weeks, until we arrived in Oxnard, California, which Joe pointed out to us from up on the hill earlier.

Suffice to say, the drug trafficker actually paid the $1,000,000. I became a millionaire at eighteen years old by force."

Paul said, "Not a bad payday." He took a swig of beer. Paul always had a poker face. It was hard to detect, especially for people that did not personally know him, whether he was serious or simply kidding.

"That's not really funny. It turned out it was." Lancaster's expression turned serious. "The guy had long-term plans for me, which I was not interested in."

"You got paid a million bucks? And they wanted you to do more jobs, I assume," responded Joe.

"You're right. After I got back to the states, a week later, the drug trafficker who referred to himself as Señor X wrote me a letter, telling me to do another job. He had my parents' address and their photos. I ignored him. I did not hear a word. Nothing happened. So I thought that was the end of it. Then six years later, while in finals week during my last year at U.S.C. law school, he wrote me another letter, demanding I do another job, this time sending me the same photos of my parents he had from before, but drawing targets across their faces. Once again, I ignored the letter. They murdered my father by shooting him point-blank in the face shortly thereafter. He was a college professor, and the hitman killed him in front of his forty students while he was teaching."

Paul asked, "Was this that Cal State Northridge Professor?"

"It was. He was my father." Lancaster paused a few seconds. "I graduated from law school, moved my mother out of her home, and got her to quit her job as well. She had been a professor too, teaching at U.S.C. We had our names changed."

The other three were all stunned but wanted to hear more.

"So, Steven Lancaster isn't your real name?" asked Joe

"It is now, and that is what I go by. My earlier name before he was murdered was David Miller. Then about three years after law school, I got a job with the Justice Department as a criminal prosecutor. I had to keep what happened a secret. I experienced tremendous guilt, depression, and anxiety that got worse every passing year."

"Why?" asked Paul.

"You ask me why? I was more guilty than many of the people I prosecuted. Imagine: I worked for the Justice Department as a criminal prosecutor, yet I was a former drug dealer, and, at that time, I was still hiding several hundred thousand dollars in cash. It was my fault my father was murdered.

"The other guy I mentioned before who also was forced by the Colombians to do this drug deal, his name was Per, was also threatened at gunpoint. I was never a hundred percent sure whether Per was a victim like myself, or just pretended to be one to keep an eye on me, so I avoided him for years after. It saddened me. I had become friendly with him. We shared a common experience. He kept me sane and calm on our drug-smuggling operation, but when it was over, I just panicked and ran, never even saying goodbye. It took me twenty-five years to reunite with Per. Today, we are friends again.

"It was creepy for me when you pointed out Oxnard earlier since that is where we sailed into with the cocaine. That was in 1978.

"Years later, I was married to someone before Claire, which only lasted a couple of years. After getting divorced, and for the years before meeting Claire, I had intimacy issues. I was all fucked up. I questioned whether I was a hypocrite, prosecuting people for lesser crimes than my own. I had guilt about so much stuff. I was depressed and not doing too well."

Joe responded, "You mentioned to me the other day about your father being killed by the drug dealer. I am so sorry. What did you do after he was killed?"

"I did nothing to seek justice against the drug dealer because if I had, I would be at risk of going to prison myself. They would have learned I was a drug dealer too. I also had issues with the money. I wanted it but felt guilty every time I spent some of it. Yet, I really was not prepared to let that go."

He looked over at Joe. "Then when Joe told me how he spent a career fighting drug dealers and how he couldn't protect his own daughter, that was a stab in my heart. It still is. I couldn't protect my own father and, unlike him," he looked at Paul but pointed to Joe, "I was too much of a pussy in my role as a prosecutor to go after the responsible parties, Señor X and Rosendo. And here is the worst part: after not hearing from these assholes for close to thirty years, they recently sent me another letter, demanding I meet them in Colombia. They sent me an old picture of my mother with a target drawn over her face. This is what they did to me with my father. And they carried out their threat. I did nothing, and, well, you know the rest of the story."

"Did you call the police or one of your prosecutor friends this time?" asked Joe.

"Yes, but no. As you know, Joe, during the trial, I believe the defense team set me up on the bank wire issue. They had to know I had discovered it, so they produced the alibi. I also think they created phony invoices. I mean, come on. Nobody brings invoices to trial to support a wild alibi unless they knew what I had planned ahead of time. I concluded it had to have been a bug they planted somewhere on me."

Lancaster looked at Joe.

"And I didn't tell you this, Joe. After the trial, Claire and I found an electronic bug sewn into my briefcase. That act I *did* report to the F.B.I. But then I thought further about it. Bellini, a big drug dealer in Southern California, had to give the cartel the ability to listen in as well. I assume now he did business with them. You may wonder, Joe: did Claire and I talk about my experience when I was eighteen during Zoe's murder trial? I did. Of course, I did. I told Claire that Joe's story was in some ways like mine. So, they figured me out. I did not report the recent letter by Señor X and Rosendo to the F.B.I. because then they would figure me out."

Lancaster paused for another moment. He stirred the fire some more as Joe handed him another fresh cold beer. Being a little buzzed from the beers he had consumed and feeling foolish for telling his story to others that would have had the courage to do something about it, Lancaster turned quiet.

"So, what do you plan on doing now?"

"There is not much I can think of other than going to El Salvador and maybe trying to figure things out."

Paul asked, "Does this stuff have anything to do with that nature journey?"

"Yes ... no ... probably not. I still have never been on a nature journey. I did promise my psychologist that someday I would go on one. He is the one that hooked me up with Buddy Wilson, the Nature leader. That someday is this upcoming trip to El Salvador. Paul's going, do you want to go too, Joe?"

Joe said, "No, thanks. Not for me. I have been in nature plenty times alone but would not consider it a relaxing spiritual experience. When you and Paul get back, tell me about it, and maybe I will change my mind and do it someday."

The next day, they rode the Wave Runners back to Long Beach. Back at the dock, Paul invited Steve and Joe down to San Diego for a tour of his wholesale food business operation.

Chapter Eighteen

TWO DAYS LATER, LANCASTER GOT INTO HIS CAR AND drove to San Diego. Joe was unable to attend due to a Wave Runner island trip, which was previously scheduled. The drive from Irvine took about an hour and a half.

Lancaster turned his Prius into the industrial building's parking lot, located a few blocks from the San Diego harbor in National City. He saw Paul outside speaking to a driver in a Penske rental truck. As Paul finished his conversation, the driver started to leave. Paul then noticed Lancaster walking toward him. Lancaster cracked a smile as they met up and high-fived one another.

Lancaster said, "I like your uniform, Paul." Paul was wearing dark green pants and a long sleeve shirt with a patch over his left chest pocket with the inscribed words, "Pablo Discount Foods."

"Who is Pablo?" asked Lancaster.

"Me. It's my Spanish name."

"That makes sense. Why don't you show me around?"

Paul took Lancaster inside the thirty thousand square foot warehouse, saw stacks of food items organized mostly on industrial shelves, plus giant refrigerator and freezer rooms.

"So, this is your operation. All these items are expired?"

"No. Nothing is expired. Now, some items may have only a day or two left, but these are U.S. standards, not Mexican. Many Mexicans are poor. If they can buy food at seventy percent off the price that is sold in stores, it is a great deal for them. In fact, here is something crazy: the prices are reduced so much over in Tijuana, many Americans drive across the border, just to buy the stuff over there."

"Are there other companies, besides yours, that do this as well?"

"Yes, I have some competitors."

"Do you sell to the same stores they do?"

"Doesn't exactly work that way. There is a big wholesale marketplace in Tijuana. We drop our items off, and there is an ongoing auction where food retailers buy the merchandise. There are no retail buyers that go there, just the stores and they bid on bulk lots. Several stores from all over Baja California come up and take part in the auctions.

"An auction? The type of auctions we have up here in the states?"

"Yes, almost exactly. In fact, want to hear something funny?"

"Sure."

"So, I take it Lancaster, you have been to an auction before?"

"Not lately, but I see those car auctions on T.V."

"You know when the auctioneers speak really fast and nobody really knows what they are saying? You know, like I have fifty, looking for seventy, seventy, seventy, and sometimes you can't understand them at all?"

"Of course. And people in the audience are afraid they will raise their hands by mistake and be forced to buy the stuff."

"That is true, but what I want to say is, the Mexican auctioneer, like the American auctioneers, have the exact same style, and just like here, nobody knows what they are saying either. The only difference is, they are speaking in Spanish."

They both chuckled.

"And it is legal, Easy, for stores down there to sell food that is expired?"

"I don't know. Why do you keep bugging me about the food being expired? I do not know if it is expired at the time they sell it. I don't ask, and they don't tell me."

Paul continued to give Lancaster the tour through his plant, showing the operation, how everything was organized, including where the food arrived, and where it was shipped out from.

"When you were telling us about your past and your father's murder, I can't tell you how sorry I was. I understood your predicament. I am sure I would have done exactly the same thing as you. I don't know what else you could have done, without getting hurt, killed, or put in jail. I would have done the same thing."

Lancaster glanced away from Paul, looking at the ground to gather his thoughts. Changing the subject, he said, "Are you married; have kids?"

"Married? God, no. Kids? Yes. I have been married four times. I have six kids from six different women. Not good at relationships. Two of my kids live with their mothers in the Philippines. After my last child was born, I got a vasectomy."

There was a pause. Lancaster did not know if Paul had his eyes closed, or whether that was just his nature. His narrow, staring eyes were barely visible through his eyelids.

"Doubt Sheila or Joe mentioned this to you. Sheila was my first wife."

Lancaster hadn't known this.

"Zoe's older sister, Teresa, is my daughter. They are technically half-sisters."

"Joe is married to your ex-wife?"

"Yes. No problem though. I am happy for both. Hell, they have been married a lot longer than Sheila and I were. Besides, Sheila and I have always remained friends. Joe is the stepfather of my daughter. Zoe was Joe and Sheila's daughter."

"And you are good with all this?" He thought this was a little odd.

"Oh, yes. I love Joe. Couldn't think of a better person to be her stepfather."

"So, obviously, you knew Zoe?"

"Since she was born. She called me Uncle Easy." Paul got a bit of a lump in his throat.

There was a pause in the conversation.

Lancaster smiled, changed the subject, and said, "You were pretty amazing going into action on Santa Cruz Island, going after those bad guys in the forest. You and Joe work well together."

"I think we do."

"When I think of what you did there, plus God knows whatever you did while in the SEALs, I am in awe. You certainly have risked your life so much. What motivates you?"

Paul smiled and said, "Maybe a couple of reasons. Contrary to widely held belief, it is not because of mom, apple pie, or the kid next door. Frankly, it started out and remains to a certain extent, that it is fun for me. An adrenaline rush. Didn't have to sit around a desk.

"There was this mission—Joe was on it too ... a terrorist threw a hand grenade that landed right next to several of us. A member of my platoon threw his body on top of it. He absorbed all the fragments and kept the rest of us safe. As you would expect, he died instantly. That guy's courage and selflessness broadened my motivation. Since that event, I feel an obligation to carry out his memory by protecting others."

"Sorry about your friend. That was quite heroic."

"It was. Because of acts like that, I still find the lure of missions which get my fun juices flowing."

"Grab a bite?"

"Sure."

The Prius headed north where they would drive toward Little Italy next to downtown and the San Diego airport. Even though it was only a bit after 1 p.m., there was traffic starting to back up. Lancaster pulled into the diamond lane to avoid it.

The two started to talk about the Chargers and their move to Los Angeles, when Lancaster glanced in his rearview mirror, "Is that what I think it is?"

"What are you talking about?"

"That car behind me. I think he is trying to pull a fast one in the diamond lane. He doesn't have a passenger."

Paul twisted around and looked for himself. His eyes were momentarily not squinty.

"No, it's not," he smiled. "I've seen people putting Madigan's in the front passenger seat, but this is a first. Doesn't even have the decency to put clothes on it." Lancaster looked into his passenger side-view mirror for a better peek. "I think it is one of those life-like sex dolls."

"It is," replied Lancaster. "Actually, a love-doll." He paused a second, then continued. "It is the Bambi model with blonde hair."

"The Bambi model? How do you know that?"

Lancaster, thinking about how to skillfully answer the question, said, "Just do."

"Seen them on the Internet?"

"No."

"So, from where?"

"If you want to know, my wife."

"Claire has one?"

"No, she has two. A male and a female."

Paul was amazed. He'd never have thought Lancaster was the kind of guy to have a connection to those things. "I guess that is a good thing, Lancaster?"

"She enjoys it. But we had a problem not too long ago. I walked into my bedroom and saw my twelve-year-old daughter and a friend of hers playing with the male doll."

"Playing?"

"Not that way. I should have said, inspecting. Still, not something you want to have to explain to both your daughter and the parents of her friend."

There was a pause as Paul was at a loss for words. Lancaster got out of the diamond lane and started pulling over to the right. "If you are looking for a job," he said, changing the subject, "and are willing to commute from Orange County, I'm looking for a couple of drivers, and a graveyard shift manager."

"Thanks for the offer, but no thanks. Not my kind of thing. I do find your operation and business model quite fascinating, though."

Chapter Nineteen

STEVEN, PAUL, AND JUAN SANCHEZ, THE YOUNG neuroscientist, all met at Los Angeles International for their Avianca flight to San Salvador. Their El Salvador base camp and solo sites would be about ninety miles north of the San Salvador Airport along the Pacific coast. By being in that region, they would drive a part of the Pan American Highway to avoid the stop and go San Salvador city traffic. Driving up the coast would take them past San Diego, El Salvador, the town where Paul had that unfortunate experience while in the Navy. Buddy Wilson would meet them at the base camp-site later that day to begin the training.

Juan Sanchez wasn't proud he was a former MS-13 member who was brought to the United States by his parents as a young child, then deported back to El Salvador with his family in his late teens.

After his deportation, the El Salvadorian government put him into a state-sponsored rehabilitation program, where he worked at an animal rescue kennel in La Libertad. As it turned out, and unbeknownst to Juan, the kennel was a drug-smuggling operation where cocaine was sewn inside dogs and exported to the states. Lancaster met Juan in El Salvador as a result of an investigation of this crime, including his interrogation. He found Juan very credible, not involved in the con, and instrumental in bringing down the entire operation.

Lancaster became personally empathetic to Juan's circumstances. He believed Juan became a member of the MS-13 gang, the result of an unpleasant environment growing up in Los Angeles. Juan had a terrible stutter and obsessive-compulsive disorder. He was supposed to get treatment in Los Angeles but was deported back to El Salvador just prior. He was honest. During the investigation, Lancaster learned both he and Juan attended high school in the San Fernando Valley part of Los Angeles. Thus, a connection between Lancaster and Juan was formed.

Lancaster sponsored Juan and his family to get back to the United States, paid for his special educational needs, removal of tattoos, and even college education. Today, Juan had a master's degree in Neuroscience and was a researcher at California State University, Fullerton.

Juan's decided to join Lancaster for the nature solo to help him better reconcile his past and his relationship with his home country. He trusted Lancaster's recommendation to join him. During the drive from the airport to the base camp, the two spoke with one another.

"How have you been, Juan?"

"I have no complaints. My family is well. Dad is still cooking. Right now, he is working at a restaurant in Eagle Rock. My mom is driving for Uber."

"Uber?"

"Yes. She can work when she wants and makes good money. I moved down to North Orange County and am a research assistant to one of the professors at Cal State, Fullerton."

"Finish your degree?"

"Yes, I got my bachelor's and master's in Neuroscience at Cal State Los Angeles."

"You also got rid of the stuttering and don't see you tapping the walls anymore."

"Haven't seen you in a while. That is all gone. I am just busy with my research."

Juan seemed pleasant, a little quiet, and certainly more intro-verted than Steven recalled. "What are you doing exactly?"

"Neuroscience, of course. I am working in cognitive behavior as it relates to memory."

"Tell me about that?"

"I forgot! Just kidding. The science is pretty new, but we are testing data to see if human memory is a reproduction of one's past, or if it is based more on a generative, constructive and dynamic process, like sleep."

"So my memory is not really my memory?"

"We think your memory is still your memory, but whether one recalls data from a storage bank inside your brain or not, that is not completely clear. We may actually construct our memory in a unique way."

"Not to sound too stupid, Juan, but I assume there are applications to your research?"

"Oh, absolutely!" Juan's energy suddenly woke up. "It will help us to treat those with distinct types of dementia. More interesting is that the largest financial supporters of these types of studies are not from the healthcare industry but from those seeking to develop further the field of artificial intelligence."

"As in computers and robots? They invest more in this research than in the healthcare industry?"

"This may seem a bit bizarre, but artificial intelligence and how the human brain works, the lines between the two are becoming more blurred."

Lancaster shook his head. "This is what the world is coming to?"

"Yep."

———

THERE WERE TEN OR TWELVE ATTENDEES TAKING PART IN the nature journey retreat, which included Buddy Wilson, as the leader, and one assistant. The base camp was found on a high bluff overlooking the Pacific, some three hundred feet above the empty shoreline. Looking from the bluff, there were no people, no structures, just pristine sandy beaches, and the thick green jungle adjacent. Buddy's guiding first principle: *the world is both interconnected and interdependent.* There were eleven principles in total.

During the basecamp training for the retreat, Buddy shared many Qi Gong practices with the group. He showed them how to deeply ground themselves, cultivate energy, and relax more deeply during their solo time. Teachings of Mama Bear, Papa Bear, Swinging Dragon, the Bone Marrow Cleanse—all great. He taught them about the five elements of Water, Fire, Metal, Wood, and Earth, along with the corresponding vibrational chants.

This was truly Buddy's passion: integrating these wonderful teachings and having the students immediately go out for three days in the wilderness. By themselves. No human contact. No fire. No writing.

"When we get out there, I suggest twice a day, the eleven directions of gratitude. Do this and it can provide a substantial positive impact on anyone suffering from depression, or even posttraumatic stress disorder."

After two days of training, the participants went off into their sacred solo spots for three nights and then came back to the base camp, where they shared their own unique experiences. Everyone was amazed by their newfound connection to nature. There were no negative incidents reported, and everyone made it through.

Paul seemed finally to be at peace about his earlier unpleasant experience in El Salvador. He told the group how he used many of the five-element verbal exercises to create the right vibration to rid him of his years of pent-up guilt and sadness.

Juan was deeply moved by the multi-directional gratitude practice. He knew if it were not for the earlier efforts of Lancaster to get him out of El Salvador and aid his family, things would have turned out far worse.

Lancaster enjoyed the solitude of the journey. He had his moments of boredom, fear, and being hot during the mid-day, but he became quite relaxed. Unfortunately, there weren't any magical moments where he got new clarity about his future, with the one exception he was glad he left the Justice Department.

Chapter Twenty

When Lancaster arrived back in the States from El Salvador, he had an interesting phone message from someone he had not spoken with in years. It was Cantor Eric Weinberg from Temple Valley Har Shalom in Encino. He called the cantor back.

The cantor had related to Lancaster, that he had followed his career over the years after his first encounter with Dr. Schlomo, his later arrest years later, the Bellini murder trial, and the fact he was recently retired.

An interesting part of the phone conversation included the following exchange:

The cantor told Lancaster, "A friend of our congregation, a Mr. Michael Demsky, has one of the most interesting opportunities I have ever heard of. It pertains to international affairs, requires some travel, and does not pay very much. The potential this opportunity offers has world-changing implications. I told him about your career and how you previously dealt with an important ethical dilemma. He was impressed. I cannot tell you the specifics of this opportunity over the phone, but he would like to meet you in person to talk about this, plus answer any questions. Is it possible for you to come to Encino in the next few days?"

Lancaster's interest was piqued. "I have to be up in Thousand Oaks next Tuesday morning. What about early afternoon that same day?"

"I will make it work," said the cantor. "See you then."

Chapter Twenty-One

ON TUESDAY, LANCASTER DROVE THE FIFTY MILES FROM Irvine to David Berman's Thousand Oaks office. Having to drive up the gut of the infamous 405 Freeway along the Los Angeles Westside, it took him just over two hours in bumper-to-bumper traffic.

Lancaster thought to himself, there was no way he would commute every day from Irvine to Thousand Oaks and back again. David would have to either open an Orange County office, allow him to telecommute, otherwise Claire and he would have to move up this way, where their daughter Ashley would have to change schools.

As he was getting out of his Prius in the parking lot, he immediately felt the sun. It was at least ten degrees warmer here than in Irvine. No morning fog here. He entered David's office and informed the receptionist he was there for his appointment. David came out three minutes later to greet him.

"So nice to see you, Steven, and thanks for driving up."

David was wearing boardshorts, flip flops, and a short-sleeve button-up silk shirt that said L.A. Dodgers in handwriting across the front, much like the team uniform looked. He also wore a gold Rolex watch with diamonds along the edges. It was typical for David to wear something like that. On the other hand, Lancaster wore a blue pinstripe suit and a tie, along with a Citizens Eco-Drive watch.

"Nice to see you, David. It has been a while." Lancaster put out his hand to shake, as David began to spread both arms for a hug. They did an awkward combination of both.

"Other than bumping into you in Federal court once or twice, probably not since your wedding with Claire at our ski house in Park City."

"No, we skied with you guys a couple of winters ago in Park City."

"Oh right, I forgot," answered David who always seemed to be spinning too many plates. "That is when we got stuck on the Orange Bubble lift while on the canyon's side. It has still been some time. Let me give you a quick little office tour. Obviously, this is the reception area, over here," (pointing), "is one of the conference rooms," (now pointing ahead), "an attorney office, paralegal office, clerical pool, another couple of attorney offices, library, kitchen, other conference room, photocopy and supply room, two more attorney offices, my office there in the corner, and next to me, possibly your office someday. Over there, our firm's award wall with various memorabilia from different cases and charitable organizations. That is my Gavel they gave me when I was president of the National Privacy Lawyers Association."

"These are you in the pictures, David?" asked Lancaster, who was pointing at the wall.

"Yes. President Obama: here is me with Governor Newsome, Governor Brown, Senator Feinstein, Representative Pelosi, the Clintons, and a few others."

"I didn't know you were a Republican."

"Actually, I am."

"You are?"

"No, just kidding."

"So, come on in my office."

They went into David's office where he had a panoramic view of the Santa Monica Mountains. His office was ultracontemporary, with lots of metal, glass, light wood, and a colorful carpet.

"Let us sit over here on my Roche Bubois couch. Would you care for anything? An Expresso, Latte, tea, water?"

"Do you have just regular coffee? Maybe with a little cream?"

"Absolutely."

David got up, opened his door, and asked one of the staff for a coffee with cream, and a Latte for himself.

Then he continued. "How does it feel to be unemployed?"

"It has only been a little more than a month, but so far it is nice to have the time off. Went camping with Buddy Wilson in El Salvador. It was fun."

David smiled, as he knew Lancaster was mocking his favorite saying: "It was fun."

"Are you guys still doing primarily Consumer and Privacy Class Actions?" asked Lancaster.

"Yes, we experiment occasionally in Securities and some employment class cases as well. But certainly, Privacy Law is still our bread and butter. I have to ask you, although I am sure I probably can guess the answer, how was your drive up here?"

"Oh, not great. There was lots of traffic, especially on the 405. Things finally cleared up somewhere around Tampa on the 101."

"Yes, I know. It sucks. The 405 can have traffic in both directions twenty-four hours a day, seven days a week."

"You would think, David, when they added more lanes to the 405, to, what, eight or so on each side, that would ease things up? I do not think it did. At least I have a plug-in Prius, so I can use the diamond lane, but there still is traffic."

"I find myself using Uber most of the time, especially if I have court in Los Angeles," said David. I can do some work and let someone else deal with it. But that is okay; if you do not want to move up here, I would consider opening an office, probably near you by the John Wayne Airport."

"I like that idea. Claire still has her practice in Tustin, and Ashley has all her friends in school down in Irvine."

"I figured as much. Plus, my idea for you, would best be suited working out of another address. I would of course take care of all the expenses, your salary, malpractice insurance etcetera, but thinking of having the firm being the Law Offices of Steven Lancaster."

"Okay, but why is that?" Lancaster felt a little hurt that he wouldn't officially be part of the David Berman firm.

"The vision I have for you could be interpreted by some as maybe a conflict of interest. It is not, but I still do not want to confuse people, even irritate some colleagues. You know how class actions work?"

"But not all the specific ins and outs of class certification, the approval process. I certainly have no idea how to go to trial on one of these cases. Obviously, the general concept is you find a wrongdoing that is happening not just to one individual, but everyone. So, you get a class representative, file a lawsuit on behalf of all class members, seeking to change the way the company is doing business and get them compensation."

"That is true. My idea for you is kind of a unique niche associated with class actions. Almost nobody does what I have in mind. You would champion a compelling cause where everyone would hate you."

"Hate me? What are you talking about?"

"Normally, in class action cases, after the dust clears in the litigation, most cases are settled. Many times, through a mediation process. If the case is resolved, there is both a preliminary approval then final approval process by the court. Again, just like we had in the Child Burn case you were part of."

David continued. "You ever get one of those postcards or letters in the mail, inviting you to participate as a possible member of the class action?"

"I just got one in the mail, as a matter of fact, about the one stock I own."

"Exactly. Did you read it?"

"Normally, I would not, but I read that one, and did a little research on the subject prior to coming here. I figured doing so would help prepare me better for today. Frankly, I never paid much attention to those class notices before. Often just throw them out. I sometimes get checks in the mail, sometimes never hear again."

"Well, most of the time, as a member of the class, you would have to send in a proof of claim to get money. In a handful of cases, you do not have to do anything, unless you object or option-out."

"Whatever that means. I probably should pay better attention."

"What I have in mind for you, Steven, is under the guise of your own law firm, your niche would be to represent class members who want to object to a proposed settlement, essentially arguing the settlement should be denied as unfair."

"I represent objectors?" thought Lancaster with a blank expression.

"Yes, representing class members that want to object. It can be very lucrative. You will be doing a particularly important public service, and everyone will hate you."

"You are going to have to explain this, especially the everyone hates me part."

Chapter Twenty-Two

JOE AND PAUL WERE MEETING AT THE SEA NET Restaurant down at the end of the San Clemente Pier for their monthly beer and lunch. Located about halfway between San Diego and Long Beach, it was a convenient and beautiful place to get together.

As they were each served a Coors Light, Joe asked, "When is the last time you did a mission?"

"I know which one it was; it had to have been over ten years ago."

"Want to do another one?"

"You thinking what I am thinking?"

"Not sure."

"Does it involve helping Lancaster?"

"You bet your ass it does. I cannot tell you how much I appreciate him going to bat for me. Not just because of the trial but convincing the Newport Beach Police to release me when I was caught on Bellini's property with my Glock. He told me to not do that again. But then he said, if he had the guts and opportunity to do things over again, he would have tried what I did to avenge his father's murder. While that dick fuck Bellini did not get the death penalty, he is not going to see the outside of prison until at least his mid-seventies. I am happy with that. As to Lancaster, they never got the guy that ordered the hit on his father. And now with his most recent threat, I want to … get involved, shall we say?"

"I know, Lancaster was never able to get justice for himself."

"No, he didn't. It is sad. From the story he told us, he was in a tricky situation because of his job. He didn't know who pulled the trigger, but he knew it was Señor X that ordered it. I have some ideas about payback."

"What are you thinking?"

"The town Lancaster mentioned in the coffee region of Colombia, Armenia, you can fly there from Bogota. Lancaster told me the Rosendo guy owned a bar in town, which had a distinctive neon sign. I would bet the bar is still there, hopefully still owned by Rosendo. Rosendo had obviously some kind of a relationship with that Señor X. I am confident if we find Rosendo, we can find both. Rosendo set Lancaster up, Señor X ordered the hit on Lancaster's father. I want them both."

"Lancaster, I have to admit was wonderful in encouraging me to go with him to El Salvador on the Nature Journey, and that is after I busted his balls and teased him over it. I credit him. The retreat was mentally challenging at first. I have been living with that nightmare for years. I think with the Nature training it helped me come to peace with all that."

"Give me an example of one thing you did."

"All of sudden, Mr. Erection, you are curious. Promise not to laugh?"

"Hey, if it helps, I am in favor."

"Okay, well, solo leader gave me this recapitulation exercise. Carlos Castaneda wrote about Don Juan who could give the *dark sea of awareness* what it was after, the life experience. I had to bring back the incident with the little girl, then through a series of inhales and exhales, purge the bad energy from my system."

"Did that help?"

I still do that practice every day. I also found the house where the El Salvador mission went down. Still looks the same. I laid a wreath and teddy bear in front, with a simple note, 'I am so sorry for the death of your little girl wearing the pink ballerina dress from 1988.'...

"I am okay now. I am fine. So, when do we go to Colombia?"

Chapter Twenty-Three

"Here is how representing an Objector works," David continued. "I will use as an example of a consumer case. A cell phone carrier has been screwing its customers by not crediting them the correct amount of money when an account is closed. This really happened so it is easy to illustrate. A Class Action was brought against World Mobile when a customer noticed that, when he canceled his contract, the company did not pro-rate his bill properly, causing him to be overcharged. The company should have not charged the remaining days of this billing cycle. But they did. They charged him for the rest of the month, even though he canceled his contract in a proper manner.

"We did some research before the case was approved by the court, and found World Mobile was doing this to all their customers. Billing for, and collecting money for, services they did not earn. The class representative personally paid around $22 more than he should have.

"World Mobile has in the United States some thirty million customers (about the population of Texas), of which it was determined that four million had canceled their contracts much like this guy did, and were overcharged anywhere from $1.50 to $35 per person, the average being around $17.

"The class representative filed, through his attorneys, and after two years of litigation, tried to settle with World Mobile for $8 million."

"I kind of see where this is headed," commented Lancaster.

"So, pretend this person comes to you. He comes to you for advice, thinking the class action settlement proposal he read about in the notice was unfair. He tells you they want to settle for $8 million, but he did some math. He took the $17 average customer overcharge, and multiplied it by four million customers, and said the $8 million, while a lot of money, is not fair when you consider how much the company ripped the class off. Instead of eight million, it should have been a lot more—closer to $68 million, in fact. They were only paying their ripped-off customers $2 each.

"So, you decide to represent the guy that comes to you as an objector asking the court not to approve the case because it was not enough money?" David concluded.

"And because I represent this objector trying to make the settlement fair for the class members, everyone hates me?" asked Lancaster.

DAVID SMILED BACK. "JUST ABOUT EVERYONE. THE LAWYER representing the class hates you because you want to prevent him from settling ... preventing his big payday in the next thirty days. The defense lawyer and his corporate client hate you, as they think you are a troublemaker. They just want to end this case as cheaply as possible, and they see the $8 million settlement as getting out on the cheap when compared to their $68 million exposure. Plus, your involvement is going to cost the company more in attorney fees because those lawyers are paid by the hour. The judge many times simply wants to clear the court's docket and get rid of cases. He or she is tired and just does not want to be bothered. The objector only makes the judge work more. So yes, everyone hates you."

"How does a lawyer representing an objector make any money?"

"The law allows you to be paid a multiple of your usual hourly rate, called a loadstar. Probably like the formula the plaintiff's lawyer is getting paid. Class action lawyers tend to charge high hourly rates. My billing rate today is $700 per hour. So, if you object to the settlement and, because of your efforts, force the parties to settle for a higher amount, you are rewarded in this manner."

"What if nobody, including the judge, agrees with my objection? What if they won't readjust the settlement amount and approve it anyway?"

"No problem. If the court overrules or denies your objection, you file a notice of appeal with the court of appeals."

"Can I do this? And even if I could, would this not hold up the payment to the class members?"

"Yes! And BINGO!! This can be your leverage if the trial judge or parties do not agree with you. The settlement will be tied up for another one or two years unless they work out a deal with you. Remember, you are doing this because the lawyers are settling for too little. The defendant corporation and plaintiff lawyers must spend more on attorney fees, risk a settlement that was made at $8 million with a new liability exposure of $68 million. A lot of uncertainty and everyone else just wants to get the case done."

"And that is why they hate me? They think I am shaking them down?"

"Yes, they do. But can't you see that if the basis of your objection is reasonable, it is not a shakedown?"

"You're right. And is this what actually happened in the World Mobile case?"

"It did. As soon as the notice of appeal was filed, and before there was any briefing by the various stakeholders, there was a meeting and a new settlement reached closer to $20 million. The objector's lawyer made for himself just over $1 million and was able to get the consumers over twelve million more."

"So, the consumers benefited as did the objector's attorney? I see that. So where do you find these objectors?"

"Advertising. Almost nobody does this niche of law. You would have no competition. You pick out only the cases you think are legitimate, make a lot of money, and help a lot of people. You can do well by doing good. It's fun!"

"Seems like I have heard that doing well by doing good line before. And your answer of advertising ... of course. When I first started practicing law, and before the Justice Department, I did a little bit of Workers Compensation law. I would advertise in the newspaper and phone book back in those days. There was no Internet then. Okay, but even if we did open up an Orange County office, we can't use your firm's name?"

"I would be uncomfortable. I have too many friends that engage in class action law. While there are not many lawyers that represent objectors, the few that do, are frowned upon, given a bad rap, and considered shakedown artists. Again, I do not think they are, but it is better for all of us if we did this through a separate entity. I would be your partner, mentor, give you a great salary, plus a piece of the action. You would probably make more with me in five years than your entire career with the Justice Department."

Lancaster responded, "That seems remarkably interesting. You know, I have always admired and respected you, and obviously, I can never thank you enough for hosting our wedding in Park City."

David smiled. "Come work with me. It will be fun."

"It would be, David. Let me chat with Claire."

Chapter Twenty-Four

ON THE FLIGHT FROM LOS ANGELES TO BOGOTA (THEY would have to transfer and take a domestic flight to Armenia), Joe complained as usual about the legroom.

"I would have been happy to fly business or first class with you, but you're such a tightwad, Joe."

"You can afford that, Easy, by selling expired rotten food. I can't."

"Fuck you, Erection. Work harder then. Come work with me."

"Fuck you back, Easy. I'd rather make my living driving jet skis in the ocean, thank you very much. Anyway, this mission is going to be fun; just like the old days, provided I don't need to see a chiropractor when we land."

"Yes, it will. Can't wait."

They both fell silent for a moment.

"You know, Paul, you didn't have to do this with me."

"Oh, come on. You didn't need to do it either."

"Yea, but this is personal. Lancaster helped me get justice for Zoe. I would love to get justice for Lancaster. As I see it, this Rosendo and Señor X are just like Zoe's murderer. They don't give a shit about anything but themselves. It would warm my heart to get Lancaster justice. Bellini and these two are all the same to me."

"That's true. I am doing it pretty much for the same reasons. Zoe was my niece. Plus, you cannot do it alone. You need a swim buddy like me. Besides all that, it's kind of fun."

"You are a sick fuck, Easy."

They both smiled and chuckled.

Chapter Twenty-Five

LANCASTER WAS DRIVING EASTBOUND ON THE 101 FREEWAY after his visit with David Berman. As he approached Parkway Calabasas and started to go down the hill and into the valley, he saw brake lights ahead. His car's outside thermometer hit ninety-five degrees and he thought he certainly couldn't live with this commute. He was grateful David had offered to open an Orange County office. He continued his drive back in the direction of Orange County, where he would stop off for his afternoon appointment in Encino with Cantor Weinberg and Michael Demsky.

Lancaster exited at Balboa Blvd., the street where his parents got off when he was a kid growing up and going home. He turned left and headed east on Ventura Blvd. and drove by his old office building. He had not seen it in twenty years. Encino had changed so much: there were a lot of taller buildings, and other places he recalled did not seem to exist anymore. Except for Benihana, the Japanese restaurant! That was still there on the south side of the street. It had been there since he was a kid. More traffic.

All different. Temple Valley Har Shalom was just ahead on the left.

Lancaster entered the synagogue's beautiful spacious lobby. Lovely green plants were hanging from the walls. He was greeted by the Temple's receptionist and invited back to the office, where Cantor Weinberg was already waiting, along with Michael Demsky.

Both gentlemen stood up. The cantor reintroduced himself by telling Steven it was nice to see him again, and then presented Michael Demsky. After the initial greetings and offering of tea or coffee, the three sat down.

"I was telling Michael," said the cantor, "how I have followed your career for probably close to thirty years. That we met early on when you had that first encounter with Dr. Schlomo, his later conviction, and then your last trial against the drug dealer."

With a thick accent, either Russian or Israeli, Michael, who was a bit on the chubby side, especially in the waist, and who had a thick but neatly tapered beard, said, "Steven, if I may call you that, I was born in Russia but immigrated to Israel in the early 1990s. I spend about a third of my time here in California, a third in Israel, and another third in Russia. Things in Israel seem to be changing rapidly. When Obama was in power, many in Israel felt the United States was ignoring us. Then when Trump got into power, policies reversed. Jerusalem became our capital; we began to thrive more economically and had more Jews from around the world make Aliyah, and Israel their home.

"Unfortunately, opponents of Trump, both here in the United States and frankly the world, seem to be returning to power and have less favorable views about Israel. Your Democrats seem to want to appease the Palestinians, make friends again with the Muslim Brotherhood, and get back on track with Iran and the earlier nuclear deal. They also want Israel to give back much of their land, including East Jerusalem, the Golan Heights, and more of the West Bank. The same is true for much of Western Europe. The treatment of Israel and Jews, especially in France is horrible.

"So, Israel, whose population has exploded just in the last five years—its economic health never has been better—feels a sense of pressure they have not experienced since probably the 1970s. On top of that, we have run out of space to accommodate new immigrants."

"Michael, feel free to call me Steven, Steve, or Lancaster. I answer to all three. But back to the Israeli problem you are presenting: how do I fit into this?"

"I think, Steven, Michael, and I see you as a noble person. Obviously experienced in the law. I told Michael your mother is Jewish. Your father was Catholic, but in the eyes of Israel you are legally Jewish."

"But I don't practice very much. In fact, close to zero. My wife and I actually celebrate Christmas with our daughter."

Michael responded, "It doesn't matter. A person born to a Jewish mother has a Jewish soul. We do not necessarily need someone with a political or religious bias toward Israel. We need you more for your sense of ethics and legal skills."

"Remember, Steven," said Cantor Weinberg, "I told you this opportunity could have an impact on world affairs?"

"Yes."

"From the Lebanese border, all the way down to Eilat and the Red Sea, it is as if Israel is one giant city. There is no more room. Yet we find ourselves unable to morally turn away those that have a legal right to return, and this includes many in France, and other parts of Europe, South America, and the United States that are seeking to immigrate."

"So, I fit in with my ethical and legal maneuvering skills?"

"For this project, yes. Did you know that Israel is not the only autonomous Jewish region in the world?"

"By autonomous, you mean a country that is a specifically dedicated homeland for Jews?"

Michael said, "Yes."

"I agree. There is no other exclusive or autonomous Jewish country."

"Wrong! There is," responded Michael with a smile, as Cantor Weinberg, also displaying a happy grin, nodded along. "Check it out on the Internet."

Lancaster looked skeptical. But then again, he always did.

"In 1934, the Soviet Union actually created an Autonomous Jewish region in Eastern Siberia. It is called Birobidzhan. Pronounced, Biro-bid-zhan. Way out east, toward the Pacific Ocean, China, and Japan. It still exists. They have a news-paper that is in Yiddish. Many of their street names are in Yiddish. Yiddish is still taught in some of the schools. It exists still today, although many of its Jewish inhabitants emigrated out of the area in the 1990s, mostly to Israel or the United States."

"The world is different today, Steven. Given the changes in world politics, who is friendly to whom, and the lack of space and opportunities going forward, Israel is in talks with the Russian government to redevelop and expand this same autonomous region. They want to create a new strategic relationship, improve the economics of that area, including with the Chinese neighbors, and making this a safer and more secure world."

Lancaster seeming confused and seeking clarification, said, "The Russians want this?"

"They do. The Russians, especially Putin, loves the Israelis. He considers Israel a sister country of theirs, with the second most Russian speaking people in the world. The customs and much of the Israeli culture, especially in the Russian Israeli community are similar. Many Israelis still have family and businesses in Russia. The Russians think that by offering this opportunity for the Jews to come back, this will benefit both parties."

"The Israelis are looking for a handful of select people to serve on a transitional negotiation team, to explore the possibilities and decide whether this can, in fact, be done. As to you, your position would be to make sure any treaty or agreement would be legal under United States and International law. You are on the Israeli short-list of people they want."

"Let me add to what the cantor is saying," said Michael. "A model of this possible Israeli–Russian relationship, some of the insiders suggest this could be something like creating the new Hong Kong of Siberia. With free land, little to no taxes, the Russians and the Chinese are excited about the economic and development opportunities in this part of the world. Besides that, it offers a solution to minimize the population growth burden on Israel and allows her to expand into this new frontier. I think this autonomous region could become a part of Israel, much like Alaska or Hawaii is part of the United States, even though not connected by land. You would be taking steps to reduce the possibility of future wars, increase the prosperity for millions, if not more, and bring back to life a forgotten Jewish autonomous region."

Lancaster seemed to be taking this all in with a sense of amazement. It was something he never would have remotely considered, but it seemed well-thought-out and logical. He was in awe of the basic concept. And in awe that he was being considered for something so potentially historical!

"Wow. I do not know what to say. I am trying to absorb all this." Lancaster himself had quite the smile. His juices inside were alive. This to him was unbelievable, but he wanted to play down his display of excitement as much as he could.

Michael added, "While Israel and Russia have already engaged in some preliminary discussions, including basic framework, they want to be careful. We, including you, would visit the leaders of the Jewish Russian Community in Israel first to get a better sense of their views, then some Israeli politicians, then Moscow to meet Russian politicians, then off to Birobidzhan. Making this deal is not going to be so simple. In fact, quite difficult. But if you go with me on this fact-finding mission, I think you may be impressed with the possibilities."

Chapter Twenty-Six

AFTER STEVEN LEFT THE TEMPLE, MICHAEL WENT OUTSIDE to the parking lot in the rear. He made sure nobody was looking, then discretely took out his cellphone and called the 310-area code number.

Another person answered on the first ring, as if waiting for the call. "Yes?"

"It's me. Steven just left. He liked the idea."

"What's your next step?"

"I want to set up a meeting at the Los Angeles Israeli consulate with Steven, myself, and somebody from there. I want the Israelis to tell him in their own words, the scope of the project."

"Steven is most likely going to be required to register as a foreign agent."

"I am sure he probably knows that already," agreed Michael.

"How much more does he know?"

"Other than that he would be involved in the Birobidzhan project, nothing."

"We will keep it this way for a while. He is a smart guy and I feel he will be of tremendous value. Let us just hope not too smart, Michael."

"I understand," said Michael.

Chapter Twenty-Seven

LANCASTER PRESSED THE AUTOMATIC GARAGE DOOR BUTTON on the wall to shut it, then entered his Irvine, California home.

"I'm home," he announced. He already had his coat off, tie loosened up, and briefcase in his hand.

"Hi, Daddy," yelled Ashley from the family room.

"Hi, Ashley," he called back, smiling to himself. Ashley was becoming a young teenager. She gave Lancaster so much pleasure.

Lancaster could smell something that had garlic in it; most likely dinner.

"Hi, Honey," said Claire, as Lancaster entered the kitchen area. She was standing at the stove with a large wooden spoon, stirring something. "How did your appointments go?"

"My appointments both went great," he said with a smile as he set his briefcase down on the small counter next to the house phone. "I was presented with two amazing opportunities. Both completely different. David gave me an interesting law offer and would even set up an office down here. No need to move or commute."

"That is encouraging," said Claire as she mixed marinara sauce with meatballs. On another burner, she had mixed vegetables cooking. "I will have dinner ready in five or ten minutes. Can you please hand me the salt from over there?"

Claire knew without him even saying, that this was a good day for Steven. She knew he was in a good place.

"Here you go. Do you want me to bring the parmesan cheese to the table?"

"That would be good. How did that other meeting in Encino go with the cantor?"

"No big deal. Just an opportunity to save the world." Lancaster smiled again. "It is good to be home."

He gave Claire a little kiss on the lips and she whispered into his ear to make sure Ashley could not hear, "Maybe when you wash up, you can take that special pill, if you know what I mean?" She winked at him.

He winked back. "I think I know what you mean."

She moved over to the refrigerator and took out some almond milk for Ashley to drink with her dinner. "Saving the world is great Steve," she said, closing the refrigerator door. "Does it pay anything?"

"A little bit. I am sure not as much as David's opportunity. Not as much as you make."

Claire looked at him with an expression that told him not to put pressure on her. "And the Encino Saving the world opportunity? You would have to commute up to the Valley?"

"No, this is an international travel job. Not really law. More of an advisement role."

"Go wash up, put your things away, and we can sit down to dinner? Ashley!"

"Yes, Mom."

"You need to turn off the television, wash up, and get ready to eat as well. Did you finish all your homework?"

"Mom, why are you bugging me about that stuff?" Ashley was sitting on the carpet in front of the television, wrapping her left leg and knee behind her neck until she looked like a pretzel. "I have a little more math to do, plus I have to write a poem. But the poem isn't due until day after tomorrow."

Claire finished preparing dinner. Steven and Ashley sat at the table, and the food was served.

"So, Dad, are you going to get a new job?" Ashley always came off upbeat, positive, and excited.

"I might. I want to talk to you guys about it."

Ashley felt great that her adoptive father wanted to include her.

"It's not exactly what I or you might imagine." He explained to Claire and Ashley the unique niche of David's proposal and how he would be located down in Orange County.

After hearing the explanation, Ashley commented, "That sounds dull and boring, Daddy. I like criminal law better."

He was always amazed how Ashley could immediately cut to the chase and get to the heart of the subject.

"I can see the need for attorneys representing objectors. I can also see how no one specializes in that field." Claire paused to have a couple more bites of her food. "And your other ... I think you called it, 'save the world' option?"

"This is more complicated, and I should probably talk to you about this later."

"Why can't I hear about it, Daddy?"

"I just don't have all the information yet, Honey. Hopefully soon. And when I learn more, I will tell you about it."

"Okay."

Lancaster asked Ashley, "So what did you do in school today?"

Ashley turned toward Claire, took a deep breath, and said with enthusiasm, "Oh, yes, I forgot to tell you, Mommy. You know that boy named Andre Collins?"

"The tall boy whose family just got the new puppy?"

"Yea. He asked me to marry him today."

Lancaster and Claire looked at one another before turning back to Ashley.

"And ... what did you tell him?" Claire asked slowly.

"I told him no way. I am too young for that. Besides, he hasn't even kissed me yet."

LATER THAT NIGHT, AFTER ASHLEY HAD GONE TO BED, both Steven and Claire retired to their room to wash up and get ready themselves. They had the television on in the bedroom with the 11 p.m. news playing.

"So, what about the save the world opportunity?"

"I think I told you that the cantor was the same individual I met with years ago when I considered getting Workers Compensation referrals from Dr. Schlomo."

"I remember that story. He is the one that said you shouldn't do it because the doctor was a fraud."

Claire walked out of the closet wearing a very sexy outfit, which gave Steven a huge ear-to-ear smile, not to mention a tingle elsewhere.

He continued the conversation. "Yes. The man is still the cantor at that same Temple. He told me he has followed my career, was aware when I busted Schlomo, and most recently the Bellini trial. He learned I was retiring from the Justice Department and thought I would be a good fit for this project."

Claire smiled playfully at him. "A good fit? What does that mean?"

"I assume," Lancaster replied, his own smile deepening, "the good fit comment pertained to my possible position on the project."

Claire nodded, still smiling as she rubbed some lotion on her arms.

"So, he introduced me to this Russian Jew, Michael Demsky. He is active in the Russian Jewish community and is involved at some level with Israeli politics. He also had a lot of connections with Russian politicians."

As she took a short pause from brushing her teeth, keeping the toothpaste in her mouth requiring a bit of an inhale, Claire said, "So what does this have to do with you?"

"The Rabbi, I mean cantor, thinks I am this highly ethical person."

"You are ... kind of. By the way, can you please grab the red toy off the shelf for later? It is next to the Nordstrom shoe box."

"If I have to." He smiled some more, as did she.

Steven reached up high onto the top closet shelf above his suits. "But I digress. As to the project with the changes going on in the world, including the political climate here, you know, the new sentiments and directions some are wanting to take. Less pro-Israel. Plus, the fact that Israel has so little land for all their new immigrants, they want to further secure themselves, and if possible, get more land. They want me as part of their advisement team."

"More land? How is that going to happen?"

He told her about Birobidzhan along with what the cantor and Michael had told him.

"So Israel would move their entire country there?"

"Not at all. At least I do not think so. They would keep Israel as it is today, I assume, and just expand their state with this land, and of course with the blessings of Russia. The specifics of any deal have not even been established yet. And both the Israelis and Russia want to explore if this will work. They told me that the number of people looking to immigrate to Israel is enormous. They said it is all because of the DNA results they are seeing from WhoWeR. Everyone in the world seems to be getting tested from that company."

"I never even thought about that. So, does this pay or is it a volunteer position?"

Lancaster smiled. "I was frankly so captivated and honored to be even considered for this, I didn't even bother to ask. I get the sense that it is a paying position but will not pay as much as David's opportunity. But this project is potentially world-changing. What is more, besides not even asking about the salary, I have not even reconciled if this is the right thing to do. I am an American and I do not know that I want the Israelis getting too close to Russia. How will that affect our country's relationship and security position? I might be half-Jewish, but that does not make me Israeli. Oh, shit Claire, the red toy's batteries are dead."

"There should be some in the second to top dresser drawer on the right. There better be, or I am sending you out to Walmart immediately." They both smiled. "Where do you go from here to make a decision?"

"The batteries work."

Both Lancaster and Claire got goosebumps.

Smiling but continuing, Lancaster went on, "My first step is to get feedback from you, my large-breasted wife. I want to study the Internet more about this Birobidzhan region. Learn the history, including why the Jews moved out of the region in the first place. Whoever knew there was a second Jewish Autonomous Region, which was established even before the State of Israel? I think it would be helpful to set up a little Face Time appointment with Wiedemann."

Claire got into bed, turned off the lights, and said, "Give me the toy."

Chapter Twenty-Eight

JOE AND PAUL LANDED IN ARMENIA, COLOMBIA AFTER
their short domestic flight from Bogota. Armenia had a small
airport serving the coffee region. Neither of them needed to
stop by baggage claim since they each traveled with only a
backpack.

"We will grab a cab and get over to the FINCA and check-in,"
said Paul. "You know, this is the same place Lancaster stayed
when this whole other thing went down in 1978? After we get
situated, I want to do some recon of the bar and the
surrounding area."

"Sounds good to me. I specialize in doing recon in bars.
Maybe we can have a couple of drinks while we are there?"

"I think to fit in and not be detected, that will be required.
Which shirt will you be wearing? Your blue t-shirt or brown t-
shirt?

"I haven't decided yet. I would ask you the same question,
but you probably only brought the black shirt you are wearing
now."

Paul grinned, nodded downward, and squinted his eyes, suggesting Joe was right.

"I heard the FINCA has a pool. I wouldn't mind jumping in after we get there, to help shake off the long flights."

"SEALs always love the water," responded Paul.

Chapter Twenty-Nine

MICHAEL HAD JUST GOT OFF THE PHONE WITH LANCASTER and confirmed the meeting at the Israeli consulate the next day at 11 a.m. Lancaster thought it was moving so fast, it would be interesting to hear what they had to say.

The two of them met at the Israeli consulate on Wilshire near La Brea, not too far from the Tar Pits. It was a little before 11 a.m. There was security screening on the outside of the building, and a secondary check on the inside. Both Michael and Lancaster wore suits. As they entered the building, they were initially greeted by a man in a security guard uniform, who was, judging by his lack of any accent, American. He asked them both for their identification, and what the purpose of their visit was.

Lancaster handed over his driver's license. Michael gave him an Israeli passport. The guard input their information into a computer, and like TSA protocol, they were quickly approved and sent to the next station. They got past X-ray, and whatever the other machine was, and walked up to a window that was protected by bulletproof glass where they were greeted by the receptionist.

"May I help you?" asked the receptionist who seemed to have an Israeli accent and had a small red flower pinned to her hair on one side.

"I am Michael Demsky, and this is Steven Lancaster. We have an appointment with your External Affairs Department."

She typed something into her computer, waited a few seconds, and said, "Oh, wow! You will be meeting with Mr. Herzog the assistant Israeli Ambassador. I did not even know he was here. Please take a seat, and someone will be out in a few minutes to escort you back."

As Lancaster and Michael headed toward the empty brown leather couch in the waiting room, he said to Michael, "The assistant ambassador. I am impressed."

"Yes, I had no idea who we would meet with," said Lancaster. I figured it would just be some random consulate representative. Think they will serve us lox and bagels?"

Michael looked at Lancaster, smiled, and responded by mouthing no, as he simultaneously shook his head. "I got to tell you," he smiled, "from what you told me about your upbringing, I am surprised you even know what a bagel is."

"What do you think I am, a shagetz?"

Demsky almost fell forward laughing. "A shagetz? Okay, I believe you."

Michael rose and walked back to the receptionist. "Where is your restroom, please? Do I need a key?"

"It is out the door behind you, turn left, walk about five more doors down, and you will see it also on the left-hand side. You don't need a key."

Michael walked back to where Lancaster was sitting and told him in a quiet voice, "I have to take a pee. I'll be back in a couple of minutes."

"I think I will join you. I have to go too."

Michael pushed open the men's bathroom door and headed for the private stall, while Lancaster opted for the bank of urinals. As Lancaster began to relieve himself, he observed something a little odd. He heard Michael's pee and, for no real reason, glanced over in that direction. In the space between the bottom of the door and the floor, he could see Michael's black dress shoes pointing away from the toilet. He must have been sitting instead of standing up.

Not a big deal, he supposed. People were weird. Hell, *he* was weird for even looking and thinking about it.

They both finished, washed their hands and Lancaster didn't say anything about the incident as they returned to the reception area to wait.

The electronic security door next to them made a buzzing sound. An elderly woman called out their names and asked them to come back and follow her. The two were escorted down the hall to a conference room where a man in a suit was sitting down, reviewing a file of documents. There was a large rectangular glass table with several ergonomically designed fabric swivel chairs, and two Israeli flags: a little one in the middle of the table; a larger one on a six-foot pole that rose from a platform on the floor. On the wall hung pictures of Ariel Sharron, Benjamin Netanyahu, Golda Meir, and Itzak

Rabin. The elderly woman asked if they wanted tea or coffee. Michael asked for a black coffee.

Steven said, "Nothing for me, thank you."

"Mr. Lancaster, Mr. Demsky nice to meet both of you. I am Assistant Ambassador to the United States, Itzak Levitz."

The three exchanged greetings as they sat down at the table.

"Sorry if I appear a little on the sleepy side. I took the red-eye in from Washington and arrived at Los Angeles International Airport, probably two hours ago."

"Thanks for meeting with us," said Steven.

Levitz replied, "I understand Mr. Demsky has given you a basic briefing about what this project involves."

Both Steven and Michael nodded as Michael said, "Correct."

"I wanted to give you some more information. This project is considered a secret by the state of Israel, although I would not be surprised if many countries knew bits and pieces about it. You will have to register as a foreign agent with your former employer, the Justice Department, make certain disclosures, and update them every six months. You knew that already. I also suggest you seek outside counsel to get your own independent opinion, to make sure the activities you are going to be involved with do not violate any laws or your fiduciary/ confidential status with us. My government will, of course, pay your legal bills."

"Sure. Why all these formalities?"

Levitz responded, "The United States of America is always concerned about any influence a foreign agent, such as your-self, may try to assert against it. I can assure you that will not be the case. Their concerns are you acting as a lobbyist, spreading propaganda, undermining United States policies, etcetera. You will not be doing any of that. In fact, your primary duties are merely to ensure that any actions we may take, treaties we may sign, are consistent with and in compliance with United States and International law. You are retired from your Justice Department. We are confident you have some knowledge about the law. We also are confident you are ethical, as represented by Mr. Demsky, and verified by the cantor at Valley Har Shalom.

"The United States is our most trusted ally, but given Israeli's political, domestic, and security concerns, we must consider all our options, including relationships with other governments. This project, of course, includes the determination as to whether a new policy or treaty can be worked out like between Israel and Russia. We would want you to sign an engagement letter, where the state of Israel will be your client. You will serve as a fiduciary in your counsel to Israel."

There was a long pause as Lancaster took all of this in. "Assuming the position interests me, I meet with independent counsel, register as a foreign agent, and all is kosher, where do we go from there?"

"You and Michael will fly to Israel where you will meet others on this project, along with some from the Israeli–Russian community. You will then shuttle between Israel and Russia. You will not be the only lawyer. In fact, there will be several —not just Israeli or American, but a few from Europe as well. You will get to know and work with all of them. At some point, I anticipate you will meet with both Russian and Chinese attorneys."

"Chinese?" Lancaster said. "I can understand Russia, but why Chinese attorneys?"

"The Autonomous region sits on China's northern border," responded Levitz, gesturing to his associate who had just walked into the room.

The assistant ambassador pulled out a map and showed Michael and Steven exactly where Birobidzhan was located, including the adjacent Chinese border, Pacific coast, and where the area was compared to the rest of Russia.

"This concept we are exploring could include a significant three-party economic or trade deal with China. But we need to deal with Russia first and see what they want from us."

Michael acknowledged this with his eyes wide open and a slight nod. "Pretty fascinating. Never did I contemplate, after leaving Russia, that I might someday return as a permanent resident and be comfortable about it. The world is changing."

Levitz said in a voice that was a complete exhale: "It is. And Israel needs to explore this option."

Chapter Thirty

STEVEN HAD DIALED UP WILLIAM WEIDEMANN ON FACE Time and was waiting for him to answer. William still had the same small, no-window office on Market Street in San Francisco.

"Hi, Steven. Can you see me?" asked William.

"I can," said Lancaster.

"No short-sleeve LDS mission shirt today?"

They both smiled.

"I don't think I have worn a short-sleeve white shirt since George W. Bush was President. You are the one who suggested I should not. That was prior to coming down to Orange County on my first date with Claire. Do you still keep all those books in your office?"

"Let me move my computer around and I'll show you. Can you see them? Are you still in Orange County? Do you miss San Francisco?"

"I see your books, along with two or three flyers on the bulletin board. As to San Francisco, I miss the restaurants, culture, and diversity. I miss needing a car. The weather I like better down here. The beaches here are great for hanging out, walking around Balboa Island, and playing golf. I also like the more family-friendly environment in Irvine, especially since I have a daughter."

"You, Claire, and Ashley are doing alright?"

"I would say we are doing great. I recently retired from the Justice Department. Claire still has her criminal law firm practice in Tustin."

"I am not sure if you told me that before, or whether I saw a post on Facebook; but yes, I knew you retired. Are you enjoying that?"

"That is why I made this appointment. I am glad I left. I do not miss the everyday court fights. But I'm not ready to stop working. I get a pension now; that is nice. But I could still use a little more money. I would not mind paying off our house and getting rid of all our credit card bills. We are not hurting—Claire does well—but I still have the desire to keep doing something to stimulate my brain. Besides, I am not ready to play golf every day just yet."

"I don't personally like golf. I never understood spending half a day chasing a little ball in the grass. Any job ideas or prospects?"

STEVEN SAID, "I THINK GOLF IS SOMETIMES OKAY. AT LEAST when I don't have a meltdown. As to job prospects, I do, and would like your input."

"So tell me what is going on?"

"Remember the house I got married at in Park City?"

"How could I not? I officiated it. Did you forget? I married you and Claire."

"Duh! Stupid for me to say that. You recall David Berman, the lawyer that owned the house?"

"Oh, sure. The wealthy lawyer. Mr. 'It's fun'?"

"That's right. He does say that everything is fun all the time. I wonder if he really means it. Anyway, he offered me a very lucrative job. I would make more money than I did with the Justice Department right out of the gate. I would not be doing criminal law anymore, but something that has to do with class actions. He would set up my own office down here in Orange County, so I wouldn't have to move or drive the two hours each way up to his office in Thousand Oaks."

"That sounds good, if it is an area of law you like."

"I guess I probably would enjoy class actions. I would really like to work with him. He is, like, half my age, and about as smart and creative as any lawyer I have known. It would be kind of fun being associated with him. There, I even said it's fun!"

"Fun can't hurt at all. Having a fun job is something most people would love to have, and few people really do. It can be a real drag waking up every morning and going to a job one hates. In fact, this is one of the biggest issues many of my clients see me for. The common theme is usually, they hate their job but can't leave it because of their health insurance."

"I am blessed I don't have that issue. Part of my retirement package is that I get health insurance until Medicare starts, then the government pays all my miscellaneous coverage like medicine and so forth.

"But besides David's offer, I received this other most interesting opportunity."

"And what is that?"

"Oh, no big deal. Just saving the world and preventing World War III."

"Saving the world? That is not so important. Anyone can do that."

"Yes, but this is almost real. But I just have to quickly review that patient-psychotherapist privilege with you."

"Since you may be saving the world, I guess I can keep this confidential. Didn't you drill me on this patient-psychotherapist privilege when we first met and told me your name was John Doe or something? You probably know by now I keep what you tell me confidential."

They both smiled.

Lancaster told William a very abbreviated version of the general concept. At first, William did not believe him. Then, when he told him he was serious, William was mystified. He too had never heard of Birobidzhan or any other Jewish Autonomous Region.

William, asked Steven, "How do you say no to this? Wait a minute. Erase that. It is not for me to say, but for me to assist you in making your own decision."

"I know. The benefit of David's opportunity is that the job is right here. I would see Claire and Ashley every day, work reasonable hours ... I would make a lot more money. Nonetheless, the other opportunity I must grab. It is too much of an amazing opportunity to turn down."

William gave a little laugh. "Well, I am glad I was so much help to you in coming to that decision. That is why I love my job so much. I get to bullshit with my friends and clients on Face Time and get paid to do it."

"Well, that is what I was thinking anyway. It is a big decision for me, but I just wanted to run it by you to confirm I was not crazy for considering this. I will give David the bad news. Knowing him, if something were to fall through or fizzle out, I would think he still might have something for me.

"Believe it or not, you were helpful William. Just seeing your face and hearing your voice helps bring out my true self."

Chapter Thirty-One

AFTER LANCASTER GOT HOME, HE CALLED DAVID UP AND let him know his decision. He told him he was taking a position with an international law firm that would require some traveling. David was disappointed but understood and invited him to seek him out again should that position fall through.

"I like you, Steven. You are one of the good guys."

"Thanks, David. You are a great guy too. We will stay connected. I am not sure this position is going to be such a long-term engagement because the project I am joining is of limited duration. How long? I have no idea."

Steven always enjoyed speaking with David. His positive attitude made him feel so good. Next, he called Joe on his cell. Joe's voicemail message said he was out of the country and would not return for another five to seven days.

Steven wondered where he'd gone and what he was doing.

Chapter Thirty-Two

MICHAEL DEMSKY AND STEVEN LANCASTER BOARDED THE
El Al flight in Los Angeles that would take them non-stop to
Israel. They flew business class. The flight would take about
fifteen hours and they hoped to get some sleep on the flight.
When they touched down, a lot of meetings and appoint-
ments would begin at once. Lancaster had never been to the
Middle East. He was looking forward to seeing Israel but
knew this would not be a vacation.

Michael asked Steven during the flight, "So have you been to
Israel before?"

"No, this is my first time. I've wanted to, but never took the
time to do it."

"I think this could be the trip of a lifetime. First off, the
country is only seventy-four years old, and you will find it as
modern as any. The place is in the desert yet will seem like an
oasis. The historical monuments are like nothing else.
Jerusalem will absolutely move your soul. When you talked

with the cantor and me and mentioned something about the fact you did not consider yourself too Jewish ... I promise you, when you get off the plane, you will feel something you never felt. Just wait and see."

"Wow. I am looking forward to this. So, Michael, what is your specific position or involvement in this project?"

"Interesting question. I have several attributes that lend themselves to my involvement. I know the Birobidzhan area, including people that live there. Obviously, I was born in Russia and know the culture and people, and some think I have a sense of how to connect the two countries. I have been active in the Russian Jewish Community in Israel, plus I know a handful of politicians. I am a Zionist, and want Israel to not just survive, but thrive. The lack of space in Israel is a big problem. An apartment is expensive in Israel, especially for our young people. I have promoted and supported Israel in considering this Birobidzhan option, and want to do all I can to help make this a reality. A lot of our citizens suffer from posttraumatic stress disorder. Always in fear of another war, terrorist attack, or missile being fired from the Gaza Strip. I am kind of like a combination of liaison, interpreter, and consultant."

"Are you married? Have kids?"

"Oh, yes. I have two children. My oldest child is my daughter. She is married, has a son, and lives with her husband in Eilat, down on the Red Sea. My son, he is in the Israeli Defense Force. He is in the second of his four-year military commitment he made. He is in a tank crew, stationed up near the Lebanon border. So, both my kids are at extreme opposite ends of the country."

"Are you religious? Orthodox?" asked Steven.

"No, I wouldn't say that. I usually go to Shule on Friday night. I do not drive on Saturdays. But I do not consider myself real Orthodox. I do wear a Yamaka when I go to Shule."

"Do you work?"

"Yes, but not as much as I used to. I am what, four or five years older than you? I was in the diamond business in Tel Aviv for thirty years. I mostly cut stones and was in the wholesale business. When I wound down my business, I had just five employees. So, we were small. The only thing I do today is sell, on occasion, a diamond to either friends or customers I am referred to. I don't have to hustle anymore."

"And your wife?"

"My family dynamics are unique. My spouse is normally home. I live in a suburb south of Tel Aviv. Lately, my spouse has been staying with my daughter and her husband, helping take care of my grandson. So, tell me, Steven, your wife is not Jewish?"

"No. She would consider herself agnostic. We have a daughter who is just becoming a teenager. She was from an earlier relationship of Claire's. I adopted her when Claire and I were married. She is great. I grew up in Encino. All my friends growing up were Jewish, although I never thought about it too much at the time. I grew up less than a mile from Temple Valley Har Shalom, the place you and I met. Hardly went to services growing up. My mother was born Jewish but really was not too involved with religion. She was a full professor of Philosophy at the University of Southern California. She would say she is very spiritual."

"And your father?"

"My father died when I was in law school. He also was a professor of Business at another university. He was not religious either. So, I take it you speak not just English, but Hebrew and Russian?"

"I do. Also, I speak Yiddish and a little Arabic."

"And when you are in the United States, where do you go, and stay?"

"I have some family in Brooklyn New York and some friends in Los Angeles. During the summer months, I try to come out and visit. I am involved in a couple of Israeli charities and help promote them when I am in the States. I have a childhood friend from Ukraine that lives in the Culver City part of Los Angeles. So, when in Los Angeles, I generally stay at his house."

"Well, it is nice having you as, I guess, my guide."

"Oh yes, Steven, my pleasure. Sorry, but you are stuck with me for a while."

When they landed and were exiting the plane, they were met by a man, in ninety-degree heat, wearing a dark suit and with one of those secret service headphones in his right ear. He escorted them through a special door. They showed their passports, and without the usual questioning or inspection of bags, they were taken outside and whisked away in a black SUV.

They were driven to Ashdod, Israel's sixth-largest city, and busiest port. It was home to the largest population of Russian immigrants. As one walked the streets in Ashdod, Russian could be heard more than Hebrew. The city began to see significant population growth dating back to 1991 when Jews started leaving the Soviet Union. Russia considered Israel its "fifty-first State", with Ashdod being its Russian cultural capital.

Chapter Thirty-Three

After Joe and Paul checked into the FINCA, they hit the swimming pool before setting off to do some reconnaissance. The pool was refreshing and felt good after their long flights.

They would pose as buyers for an American Coffee retailer, visiting the region to see what product was available. After the two got out of the pool, they asked the manager at the FINCA if he was familiar with a bar in town that had a neon sign depicting a farmer walking a donkey with coffee bags on its back? The man at the desk thought about it and suggested the two of them check out the Armenia Coffee Bar.

Joe asked, "Do you know who owns it?"

"No idea," the manager smiled. "I have never been there."

Paul chimed in, asking, "Where is this place?"

"Ask any cab driver to take you to the city square. You can't miss the sign."

Paul told him, "Thanks."

The two went back to their rooms, showered, then took forty-five-minute power naps. It might be a long evening.

At around 8 p.m., they had the manager arrange to have a cab pick them up for the ten-minute drive to the city square. The two figured they would start by grabbing some dinner at the bar and have a couple of drinks. When they arrived at the square, the sign Steven described was right there—the biggest sign in the general area. They went in. The crowd was light, and a woman was singing on the stage.

Joe asked, primarily through gestures and pointing, if they could sit at the bar. They were escorted to a couple of seats and presented with menus exclusively in Spanish. Lucky for Joe, Paul could read and speak Spanish. The place was quite nice.

They ordered some food, plus a couple of beers, and tried to fit in. A conversation began between Paul and the bartender, a man who could not be older than his mid-thirties, which meant he had to be much younger than the man named Rosendo, who was the real person they wanted to meet.

Paul had learned Spanish by growing up near the Mexican border in San Diego and had refined his language skills over the years by having his food business, which delivered to Tijuana.

Speaking in Spanish, he asked the bartender, "How are you tonight?"

"Fine. How is your food tasting?" responded the bartender as he preparing a gin cocktail for another customer?

"I like my fish, especially the head part," Paul said with a smile.

"The polo is pretty Bueno," said Joe.

Paul gave Joe a look. "Oh, all of a sudden you're fluent in Spanish?" he said in English.

"Shut up, just trying to be polite."

The bartender chimed in, "No worries, guys. I speak a little English. Where are you gentlemen from?"

"We are both from the San Francisco Bay area," said Joe.

"What brings you both here to Armenia?"

"Coffee! What else?!" remarked Joe. "We work for a big coffee retailer. We are buyers. The regular buyer who handles this region just retired, so I am training Paul and getting him to know some of the farms our company deals with. I am the vice president of purchasing, and just want to make sure the transition for Paul goes as smoothly as possible. So, is this your bar?"

"I wish. No, I just work here at the bar."

Paul replied, "You do a wonderful job. Your boss must be proud of you."

"He likes me. But he is not here too much. He's kind of old?"

"Oh, really?" said Joe, as he gestured for another beer. "Old like us?"

"He is older than you guys. He does not come into the bar, until eleven or twelve o'clock. That is when things get busy. He spends his time here talking to the guests and usually stays until closing."

Both Paul and Joe went back to their meals. Both knew not to ask too many questions, at least now, as they did not want to give the impression they were being too nosy. After they finished their meals, they grabbed their beers, turned around, and walked to a small table to enjoy the entertainment until the owner arrived.

They spoke to a few other guests—some locals, and some foreigners—but they were mostly superficial conversations: What is there to do around here? Any interesting hikes, tours, that kind of thing? As the two ordered another round, Paul asked the server what time they closed?

He told them, "Generally, around midnight, but weekends no special time. Usually, when the last customer leaves, and that can be anywhere from 2 to 5 a.m."

One of the locals they were speaking with appeared to be a guy in his late sixties or seventies.

Paul, keen to seem social, asked in Spanish, "Have you been coming to this bar a long time?"

"Yes," said the local. "Probably too long. I like it. They always have entertainment here. Their food is okay too."

"So, who owns this beautiful place?" asked Paul.

"My friend, Rosendo."

That was the big bingo answer the two were happy to hear, although they managed to keep their reactions from showing on their faces.

The local continued, "I have been coming here since ... Wow, a long time. Forty years."

"Do you work around here?"

"No, I am retired. I used to be the assistant chief of police for Armenia."

Paul wished at that moment he could have a private conversation with Joe. If the assistant chief of police knew the owner and had been coming here for forty years, that confirmed further suspicions that Rosendo was tied up in some corruption, including drug dealing. It was either common knowledge or a common lie that Colombian police officers were always on the take.

Later that evening, close to 11:30, an older man came into the bar through a back door. The two at once figured this was Rosendo.

Having several beers, the older local shouted out, "Hey Rosendo," as he gestured for him to come over to meet the gringos. Neither Joe nor Paul was ready for this.

Rosendo came over, and Paul and Joe were introduced by the local as coffee buyers from San Francisco. Rosendo seemed gracious as he thanked them both for coming in and brought a bottle of Aguardiente to the table. Aguardiente was the local spirit.

"Please enjoy this on the house. This is our traditional beverage we drink here."

Joe, Paul, and the local each poured themselves a glass, and toasted to each other, Armenia, Rosendo, and Colombia. The drink was strong, but nothing a couple of former SEALs could not handle. When they finished the bottle, the place was clearing out. It was a weekday early morning, around 12:30 a.m. The two Americans left out the front door, went around the block, and waited for Rosendo to leave out the back to get some further intelligence.

Rosendo left some fifteen minutes later. Joe and Paul stood in the shadows across the street, about a half-block down. They saw Rosendo turn in the opposite direction and walk up the hill on the sidewalk. They followed him a half-mile or so. He turned right, then a house or two down, he opened a gate to what must be his house. When he arrived, there were no lights on but after he entered, the two could see lights come on for fifteen minutes before they were shut off. Bedtime no doubt. Paul and Joe walked back to the town square, where they grabbed a cab and headed back to the FINCA. The information they gathered that night was considered a success and valuable.

When the two arrived back at their room, they briefly discussed what their next move would be. They decided to do a little more reconnaissance in the neighborhood the next day to get a feel of the general area and decide to take Rosendo for a little private questioning.

Chapter Thirty-Four

MICHAEL AND LANCASTER WERE DRIVEN BY AN ISRAELI official to the main synagogue in Ashdod. Michael was obviously familiar with the neighborhood by virtue of his pointing out to Steven various places of interest. The car turned into a small lot where they parked near the rear entrance to the synagogue. Michael and Steven got out and walked inside where they were greeted by the Rabbi, along with another gentleman in a suit. Michael kissed his own right hand then touched the mezuzah hanging inside the door frame. Lancaster was the only male in the room not wearing a skullcap or Yamaka. In fact, he was the only one within five miles. This was primarily a religious community. Michael introduced the Rabbi to Steven Lancaster but did not seem to know the name of the other man.

The other man stood up and said, "I am Rudy Tzidik, the assistant Israeli minister for External affairs."

"I am Rabbi Zeitz," said the Rabbi to Steven

For the briefest of moments, Lancaster laughed to himself, thinking he had not heard so many chhhhhhhhhhaaaaas and chhhhhhhhhiiiiiiiiiiiis since watching Don Rickles on the Johnny Carson show.

"Nice to meet you," said Lancaster, as he shook hands with both bearded men.

Michael said something to the Rabbi. Lancaster was not sure if it was in Russian, Hebrew, or Yiddish. Then he greeted the minister by simply saying, "Shalom, Minister."

The minister spoke in flawless English with a British accent, and said, "I thought we would start here. Our Israeli–Russian community has deep and long relationships with our Russian counterparts. The Rabbi is also familiar with Birobidzhan, as he lived there," he turned from looking at Lancaster over toward the Rabbi, "until immigrating to Israel in the 1990s."

Rabbi Zeitz responded in English with a Russian-sounding accent, "I still have some family there: my sister, her children, along with a few childhood friends."

Steven added, "Up until a few weeks ago, when I originally met Michael, I had never heard of the Jewish Autonomous Region. I did some research on my own and was completely surprised to learn that Birobidzhan became an autonomous Jewish region even before the state of Israel was established."

A siren blasted before anyone could reply.

The Rabbi stood up. The others, including Lancaster and Michael, did the same.

The Rabbi said, "Come, we must go to the bomb shelter. I am sure they are missiles from Gaza."

The group of men found themselves in a large underground bunker the size of a high school basketball court. Other citizens from the neighborhood were also inside. Along the walls, there were gas masks, food supplies, along with several large water bottles.

"How long do we stay in here?" asked Lancaster.

The minister responded, "Until we hear the all-clear siren."

"Do missiles ever strike here in Ashdod?"

"They have, but not lately. We have a defense missile system called the Iron Dome. It is effective at destroying anything shot this way. Occasionally, there are those injured by falling debris; however, it is mostly farmers and ranchers on the outskirts of the city that don't have an adequate warning system and are too far from shelters."

"What will happen after the all-clear siren?"

The Rabbi said in a matter-of-fact tone, "We will go back to the synagogue. The IDF will bomb Gaza. Pretty typical around here."

They got back to the synagogue and Lancaster said, "So, Michael says you are the Birobidzhan expert."

"Not sure about expert. Stalin created it in 1934 to show the world the Soviets were respectful of minorities. But in the 1950s, he created some problems in the region by spreading anti-Semitism as well. That was a mistake today's Russian government regrets. In fact, the Russian parliament has issued several declarations over the years that their behavior was inappropriate and regrettable. Many of the Jews like me left the region in the 90s and immigrated here. The Russians apologized for their mistakes and have committed to do anything possible to ensure freedom of religion for the Jews. But as a Jew, we must always be cautious."

Steven responded, "And do you think Israel will want to move some of their citizens to Siberia? You have a paradise here—great weather, an ultramodern city. I read in *The Economist* last week, Tel Aviv is the third most modern city in the world next to Tokyo and Singapore. Yet you want to acquire land in some of the most hostile and chilly conditions in the world."

The minister said, "We can create an oasis there just like here. We have our 'how to build a country' learning curve down well. Piece of cake. The question is not whether someone wants to go back or simply move there, but whether Israel can expand its sovereignty beyond just this land. This land we are negotiating for is not merely the original boundaries of the Jewish Autonomous Region, but we hope a lot more. It has the potential to be much larger than Israel, with lots of natural resources. From Birobidzhan to the Pacific Ocean, this would be my goal.

"BUT WE MUST KEEP IN MIND, ANY AGREEMENT REACHED, we must be able to live in the area as an independent free country. With that said, when we combine many of these other incentives, I remain quite supportive of this project. On the other side, I would like to get a sense if there will be any restrictions on Chinese and Russian military bases nearby in the region? I do not think we would be comfortable with other military facilities in the immediate area. Just keep in mind that while the Russian government declared Birobidzhan a Jewish Autonomous region back in the 1930s, it is not considered Holy Land in the Biblical sense, like Israel."

Lancaster responded, "Well, it may not be part of the Holy Land as mentioned in the Bible today. I suggest the Bible is an ongoing story, yet to be completed, so who knows, perhaps Birobidzhan will be included in the next chapter?"

"Maybe," interjected Michael.

"So, Israel wants to further develop that area?"

"Not just develop," the minister exclaimed, "but to spread our people out, give them more land, and recognize we may no longer have the same relationship with your United States Government. The winds of political changes could be in the air but I hope that is not the case. Nonetheless, Israel's priority is to take care of itself and survive."

"And you feel this way, Minister, because you are concerned America is on the verge of political changes that are detrimental to Israel?" asked Lancaster.

The minister replied, "That could be part of it. But let us hope not. Besides that, we are experiencing a significant rise in the applications of people to immigrate to Israel. It could be credited to those DNA ancestry tests people around the world have been taking, where many families and individuals have discovered their Jewish roots. We are also extremely optimistic that the Birobidzhan region can become an amazing economic opportunity, plus it could be prudent to diversify the locations of where our people live. You Americans have Hawaii, Alaska, and Puerto Rico. We can have a remote region as well."

Steven pondered those DNA tests that he'd read about in the Wall Street Journal. There were people in the States who had taken that test and been completely surprised by their results. In fact, he thought about his neighbor in Irvine who was putting up a mezuzah next to his front door, and asked him, of all people, if it should be tilted toward or away from the house. Steven had said he did not know either; he did not even own a mezuzah! Lancaster was not even sure why there was all this excitement about this discovery but he did see it happening.

Lancaster asked, "Who do you think would oppose this deal?"

"Most of the Arabs, the United States ... Probably, everybody."

"Just remember, Steven," said Michael, "we are simply exploring our options. My parents lived in the region up until just five years ago. With the new overtures being made by Russia, the unknown political direction the United States is moving in, and the encouragement of China who wants to expand trade and friendship, this could be an important and historical opportunity."

As they were saying goodbye and has started to head back toward their car, the Rabbi said, "Mr. Lancaster, may I just have one final word with you?"

"Sure." Lancaster turned toward Michael who was walking ahead of him. "I will meet you at the car in a minute."

Walking back to where the Rabbi was, Lancaster said, "Yes?"

"Mr. Lancaster, keep an eye on Michael. I don't think he is at all dangerous, but he is not who you think he is."

"What is that supposed to mean?"

"You will find out."

Chapter Thirty-Five

At 1 a.m., he walked up the street in the direction of his home. The neighborhood was completely silent.

Paul and Joe had done a catch and grab on people so many times in the past, it was like tying one's shoes. As planned, Joe waited ahead in the shadow of a closed gas station, while Paul quietly followed Rosendo from behind. At the predetermined point of execution, Joe walked onto the sidewalk, blocking his path. Rosendo looked up at the tall American, and as he did, Paul grabbed him from behind and quickly choked him out. Rosendo was already unconscious as Joe pulled out duct tape and wrapped it around Rosendo's mouth and wrists. The stolen Nissan Sentra was right next to where Rosendo was lying, and they quickly put their victim in the trunk.

They drove the car down the dirt road to the abandoned farm they had previously scouted out, where they parked the Sentra behind the barn. Then they spread out a six-foot by ten-foot green canvas tarp on the ground. They placed

Rosendo on his back on the tarp and tied his arms and legs in a spread-out position. He was stretched in all directions about as far as any human could be. His body resembled the shape of a star. Neither Paul nor Joe was bothered in the least about what was to come next.

Daylight was still another five hours away, so there was plenty of time to do their work. The place was pitch dark. There was no moon. When the two had scouted out the area, the rural farm was about half a mile from the closest other struc-ture—a small house. The general area would resemble a thick jungle. To get to the farm where they were, one would have to travel down a dirt road. The place was remote. The sounds in the jungle of crickets, frogs, and other animals were loud enough to drown out any noises their prisoner might make.

They kept the duct tape firmly around Rosendo's mouth. Once he was securely tied up, even his loudest of screams would not be heard. Joe and Paul wanted to make sure Rosendo was awake so he could see them setting up their torture toys, which they felt would put more fear into him to ensure his cooperation.

Joe said to Paul, "Okay, let us wake him up. Here is the hypo-dermic with the adrenaline."

He handed it to Paul. Paul wasted no time injecting it directly into Rosendo's heart.

"You forgot to sanitize Rosendo's skin before you inserted the needle."

Paul responded with a smile. "Fuck you, Erect One. You want me to put a band-aid on him too?"

Rosendo at once came too with an abrupt opening of his eyes. It was as if ice water had been dumped on him. It took him no time to recognize his predicament. He tried to suck in a large amount of air, only to be restricted by the duct tape. Rosendo was able to get air in through his nose, but that required several inhales and exhales before he was able to be stabilized. Sweat beaded on his forehead and his eyes were wide with terror.

Joe and Paul went to work. Paul lit a single candle, mostly for the benefit of Rosendo. Joe knew creating fear in their prisoner was just as effective at getting information as the pain that would be inflicted. Keeping Rosendo bound, Paul and Joe used scissors to cut off his clothes until he was stripped completely naked. It was important that he had no sense of dignity.

Once they were finished, Paul said to Rosendo, "We came to get a little information from you."

One could tell from his wide-eyed stare that Rosendo was very scared.

Putting his face within six inches of Rosendo, Joe, using Paul as his interpreter, asked, "Do you know who I am?"

Rosendo shook his head.

Joe cracked a little smile, still within the same six-inch space, and, this time without interpretation, he said, "Really?"

Rosendo responded in broken English, "I think I know who you are."

"Tell me."

"You are the big guy." Rosendo paused to think of his next words. "Father of girl that died in shooting, ahhhhhh Carlos un Sr. Bellini."

Joe turned toward Paul. Paul said, "Yep, he must have heard, or someone told him about the recordings to know that."

"You big fuck. I heard it all. Funny about your daughter." He met Joe's eye. "She deserved to die."

With the faintest smile, and staying calm, Joe said, "I was going to give you an opportunity to answer some questions without further risk of injury or pain. But not now."

He slugged Rosendo ridiculously hard in the soft area of his belly button. Suffice to say, Rosendo had a breathing issue after that. Joe re-stuck the duct tape across Rosendo's mouth before grabbing the man's genitals with a tight right-hand grip that one could only imagine coming from a six-foot-seven-inch former Navy SEAL.

"I am not going to waste a lot of time with you, so let me get to my point. Remember a long time ago, you had a meeting in your bar with a guy named David (Steven's previous name), Per, and a Señor X?"

Rosendo shook his head side to side, showing no.

Joe responded, "Now you are fucking with us." He nodded over to Paul.

Paul took a can of shaving cream and applied the substance to the area around Rosendo's genitals. He then grabbed a razor and looked up at Rosendo who was shaking all over. The movements of his head and neck, however taut the ropes kept him, resembled a shaking sports car's engine that was pushing redline. Rosendo made another gesture indicating, no, don't do that."

Paul said, "Too late." He shaved his genitals completely in less than ten seconds.

"Hey, Easy, you may have just set a new shaving record. That was fast. Oh, but I see you cut him in a few places."

Paul said, "Thank you, tall one. It is dark, so shaving him with the caring attention to detail I had originally considered just could not be done. I simply said to myself, the hell with it."

Joe looked back at Rosendo. "Do you now know who Señor X is?"

Rosendo shook his head, but this time more slowly.

"Wrong answer again, dumb fuck," said Joe, as he looked over at Paul and gave him the nod.

Paul took out the two ends of a battery booster that he connected to the Nissan Sentra. He attached up only the negative end of the black cable to Rosendo's male part, using the large spring-loaded alligator clip.

"Are these battery cables helping to improve your memory?"

Rosendo just stared back at them.

Paul touched him with the red end of the cable. Rosendo jumped, but it was more the scare of the jolt than any actual shock.

"Alright, Mr. Rosendo," said Paul, speaking to him in Spanish, "now our fun starts."

Joe handed Paul a sponge along with a red plastic portable gas container. Rosendo simply watched, apparently emotionless.

"Have you ever had a sponge bath with sulfuric acid?"

Rosendo stared back at Paul in complete fear.

"And Rosendo, my buddy," said Paul, "just so you don't miss any of the experience due to fainting, passing out, or even dying, I am going to attach an IV drip to your arm, which is connected to this bottle of liquid adrenaline. The same stuff we shot you up with earlier. This will ensure your complete attention and enjoyment of this exercise. I do not want you to fall asleep and miss any of the fun. In fact, I am told that adrenaline enhances your experience. Isn't that nice of me?"

Once again, Joe asked Rosendo, "So, who is Señor X?"

Chapter Thirty-Six

THE CHARTERED EL AL FLIGHT FROM TEL AVIV LANDED IN Moscow with the Israeli delegation. During the flight, Lancaster had the opportunity to meet with many of the others. There were at least a dozen other lawyers on the flight, mostly Israeli or European. Several Russian born Israelis, who had political or business connections to Russia, were also participants. The delegation was led by the Israeli Foreign Minister.

Upon landing, they exited the plane right onto the tarmac, where they were greeted by the Israeli Ambassador to Russia, the Russian Foreign Minister, and the Minister of Internal Affairs, along with several other dignitaries. A red carpet led them to the terminal as a Russian military band performed the Israeli National Anthem to welcome their guests. Lancaster took it all in. This was pretty cool! But apart from the upbeat look on his face, no one knew his excited anticipation.

The delegation would first stop at the Israeli Embassy, where they would sleep, have a chance to get situated and freshen up, and then head over to the Kremlin, where talks of a detailed framework would begin.

Lancaster walked with Michael and a Canadian attorney. "I am somewhat in awe that we are part of these kinds of talks," he said. "I never would have imagined Israel turning to the Russians as their new best friends."

The Canadian attorney responded, "It is a bit bizarre for me as well. But I would assume they know what they are doing, and why they are doing this."

Michael joined in. "Israel has to protect itself and consider it's best interests. Keep an open mind to this project. Who knows, the both of you may change your opinion one way or the other about all this. This is just the beginning. Let us see where it goes."

Lancaster smiled and turned his head slightly in Michael's direction. "I am sure we will."

Upon arrival at the Israeli Embassy, they were briefed by the Ambassador and the Foreign Minister of any further details, including what to expect at the meeting with the Russians. Residential rooms were assigned to the members of the delegation. The embassy's architecture looked like an old castle.

Later, the delegation was picked up by a convoy of some fifteen black Mercedes vehicles, and taken to the Kremlin, where they were greeted by more cheerful Russian dignitaries. All were escorted into a large, beautiful, and primarily violet-red, room, which had dining tables set up in a huge circle. White starched linen tablecloths, fine silverware, and glasses were perfectly placed in front of each seat. On the serving plate presented to each attendee, there was expensive caviar, delicately displayed on fine china. On a small stage in a corner, two females were playing classical music on violins

while the guests entered the room. Lancaster, the other
lawyers, some advisors, and Michael were there simply to eat,
listen, take notes, and provide feedback later. Everyone in the
room had headsets at their tables to translate the conversation into their native languages.

Once seated, Lancaster saw beautiful and priceless paintings
on the walls. He wondered privately to himself how many of
them were stolen over the years? He figured probably most of
them, although the Russians would say there were acquired
through the spoils of war. There were many flags of Russia,
Israel, and the Jewish Autonomous Region, which hung from
the forty-foot-high ceiling in the expansive room.

The first speaker was the President of Russia himself, who
welcomed his Jewish brothers here for the talks. He said he
looked forward to successful negotiations and for a Jewish
homecoming to the Birobidzhan Autonomous Region. He
offered a toast to everyone with fine vodka, celebrating both
their history and the future of wonderful friends.

The second speaker was the Israeli Foreign Minister who
thanked the President for their hospitality, friendship, and for
the significant gesture of welcoming back Jews and Israel to
the Autonomous Region. He highlighted the enormous
economic impact such an agreement could have on Russia,
the far-east economies, and of course his own country, Israel.
The prospects for amazing development and prosperity for
all would be enormous. Everyone toasted with more fine
vodka.

Over the next couple of hours, the delegations would discuss
everything from proposed border areas, taxes, energy, water
rights, government, security, trading, and food. They would
discuss what land could potentially belong to Israel forever,
and what might revert to Russia after a certain number of

years. They all discussed what their vision was in trading with China whose border was right alongside the south of the Autonomous Region. The Russians proposed, financing the construction of the world's largest commercial port to accommodate this newly expected economic miracle.

All those in attendance seemed upbeat and optimistic about these prospects. The ability for Israel to expand both their region and the economy was very appealing, not to mention this "new part" of Israel would be an amazing accomplishment. The Russians knew, with the Jews returning to Eastern Siberia, this would be the new Silicon Valley, only larger. The Russians also knew that making a deal with the Israelis would be a wonderful slap in the face to the United States. They would be stealing their friend as well as setting themselves up, in the eyes of the world, as a prestigious political power.

Steven Lancaster sat there and took lots of notes, all the while enjoying his buzz from the alcohol. All the speeches and discussions seemed very conciliatory, upbeat, and suggested an amazing future for everyone. Nonetheless, there was still a little something he could not put his arms around; something that was not passing his personal smell test. He would remain open to all of this, and he looked forward to the next leg of his journey, which included visiting the Autonomous Region itself, but there was still that little unexplainable something that felt a bit uncomfortable. Maybe it was because he'd grown up at a time when the Soviets had been referred to by Ronal Reagan as the Evil Empire.

THE ISRAELI DELEGATION RETURNED TO THEIR EMBASSY. IT had been a long day. As most members retired to their rooms, Michael made sure nobody was watching him as he snuck away and entered a private administrative office, where he quietly shut the door behind him.

He pulled a cell phone from his coat pocket and dialed the same 310-area code.

A male voice answered. "Speak to me."

"It's Michael."

"I know it's you."

"Okay, things are going well. The conference today was great."

"How is Lancaster doing?"

"Good. He likes what he is hearing, but thus far seems to struggle with the idea that Russians can yet be trusted."

"Still knows nothing about the other thing?"

"Nope."

The person on the other end of the phone hung up.

Chapter Thirty-Seven

HE WAS WEARING YELLOW PROTECTIVE GLOVES THAT extended to his elbows. Paul, making sure Rosendo had a view so he could see everything he was doing, leaned the can over to pour and soak the yellow dish sponge with the acid.

He looked right into Rosendo's eyes. "Now it's Jesus time, Rosendo. Who is Señor X?" He turned to Joe, paused for a second, then nodded in the affirmative for Joe to do his thing.

Joe loosened up the duct tape across Rosendo's mouth so that he could speak.

"Please," Rosendo rasped, "I don't know."

Without any hesitation, Paul took the sponge and ran it up and down Rosendo's left leg. Joe had taken a dry rag and covered Rosendo's mouth in anticipation of the screaming.

The screams, though muted, were still intense. The skin on Rosendo's leg was immediately burned. Keeping the rag in place, Joe lowered his own head until he was nose to nose with Rosendo.

"Enjoy this," he said as he turned up the IV, causing more adrenaline to be injected into Rosendo's system.

The screaming intensified some more. Both Joe and Paul watched Rosendo until he began to calm down a bit. Then, making sure he would not scream again, Joe slowly started to remove the cloth over Rosendo's mouth.

Rosendo spat in Joe's face.

Within a nano-second, Paul had taken the yellow sponge and run it up and down Rosendo's other leg, as Joe shoved the dry rag back across the top of his mouth. More muted screaming. And if that was not enough, he took the red plastic container of acid and poured more on the same area.

"Have you had enough? Are you ready to tell us who Señor X is? Because if you do not, I am going to pour the entire can on your balls."

Rosendo responded, "Okay, okay, his name is Juan, but I don't know his last name."

"Bullshit." This time, Joe changed the location and wiped the acid over Rosendo's belly and chest area. As Rosendo's muffled screams filled the air, Joe turned up the IV again, this time leaving it on for four seconds.

"Leaving the adrenaline valve on that long is inhumane, Erect One. It is listed on one of those Conventions of International law or something, as something you cannot do? Oh well."

Paul gave Rosendo ten minutes or so to enjoy his experience and come back down.

"Are you ready to cooperate Rosendo?"

Rosendo slowly moved his head in the affirmative.

"What's his last name?

"I really don't remember, please ..."

Paul soaked his genitals with the acid, and Rosendo's screams grew louder. He was clearly in excruciating pain but the adrenaline prevented him from passing out and heightened his sensitivity to the whole experience.

As Rosendo's muted screams continued, under the pressure of Joe's hand pressing the dry rag over his face, Joe said to Paul, "I can't believe you really put it on his balls. Oh well."

Rosendo tried to speak. Joe removed the rag.

"It is Juarez. Juarez. Please, I am in so much pain."

"Well, that is a step in the right direction. Joe, let us give our friend here a little soothing lotion as a reward for his cooperation."

Joe picked up what looked like another plastic gas can, only this time it was blue. Rosendo flinched. Joe poured the contents of the container directly onto Rosendo's body, covering all areas where the acid had burned him. The thick, sticky substance did serve to soothe much of his pain.

Paul said to Rosendo, "Since you are doing such a respectable job, I expect you to continue. Where can I find Juan Juarez?"

"I don't know."

"Wrong answer." Paul poured more acid on the sponge and went to rub it on Rosendo's arm but he paused when Rosendo began to mumble something.

"Wait, wait ... If I tell you, the cartel will kill me and my family."

Paul did not hesitate. He applied more acid to both Rosendo's arms and neck. Joe covered their captive's mouth and hit the IV again. The screaming returned and lasted for a few minutes until Rosendo was so weak, he had no strength to scream anymore. He was barely even conscious.

After a few minutes, Paul said to him, now in a calm and quiet voice, "Now, Rosendo, to show my good faith, I am going to have Joe put more of that soothing lotion on your arms and neck, but I warn you, if you don't cooperate, I will take it off, and pour the entire can of acid all over you."

Joe poured more of the sticky liquid on him. His pain immediately reduced.

Joe looked over at Paul. "Let me give it a try this time. It is my turn. Rosendo, would you please, pretty please, tell me where Juan is, so we can stop doing this?" He removed the dry rag from Rosendo's mouth.

"All I know," Rosendo began weakly, "is that he is expanding the drug markets for the Cartel. He has been living on and off in China. Kashgar, China. He imports heroin from Afghanistan into Western China. He works with some Uighurs that the Cartel has established relationships with. He went there a week or so ago. Said he would be gone a couple of months."

Both Joe and Paul reflected for a moment. That made some sense.

"Well, that is appreciated, Rosendo. And as your reward, I am going to apply the lotion all over you, so you can be more comfortable."

Rosendo took a deep breath, trying to put on a grateful face and hoping that this exercise may finally be over.

He looked at Joe and asked in a weak voice, "What, what, is that sticky stuff anyway?"

Paul stood up and walked toward Rosendo's feet, as Joe replied, "It's honey."

"Honey. Really? Why honey?"

Paul pulled away the green canvas tarp that Rosendo had been lying on. "Two reasons. The first is, it helps relieve your pain. The second, the red ants that were on the ground beneath the tarp, are now crawling all over you. They like honey."

And just as Paul said that Joe placed the duct tape back onto Rosendo's mouth and completely opened the valve on the adrenaline IV. Paul and Joe stood there for another thirty seconds, watching in the candlelight, as tens of thousands of red ants swarmed from underneath Rosendo to eat up the honey—and him.

"We tied you up over a red ant hill, amigo. They will eat the honey and you in the next several hours. Want to make sure you have enough adrenaline to enjoy the experience. That is what you get when you tell me my daughter deserved to die. You never should have introduced David to Señor X. Because you did, you are now experiencing justice."

Without another word, Paul and Joe turned and walked back to the stolen Nissan. As they drove away, they could hear Rosendo's muted screams as he was eaten alive.

Chapter Thirty-Eight

THEY STILL HAD ABOUT AN HOUR BEFORE THE SUN WOULD come up. Paul was at the wheel of the Nissan, heading back to the quiet residential neighborhood where they stole the car. He pulled off onto a side street two blocks away, while Joe got out and walked over to the area where they'd taken the car from. There were no police, no people; everything was as quiet then as it had been five and a half hours prior. In fact, the same parking spot they originally took the car from, between the pickup truck and a dented white sedan, was still vacant. Joe went back to where Paul was waiting, got in, drove over, and parked the Nissan where they found it. Unless the car's owner looked carefully through the car, they would never have a clue that it had been borrowed.

The two men would head back on foot toward the center of town, grab a cab, and get to the airport. The first flight out of Armenia to Bogota was in just less than an hour.

After they arrived at the airport and had been through security, Joe said to Paul, "So, he is in Kashgar?"

"That's what he said," Paul agreed.

The two former SEALs had been to Kashgar during the Afghanistan conflict. It seemed crazy that they'd been there before. Nobody had even heard of the place, let alone been there. Kashgar, an ancient trading town on the Silk Road, was about as far west inside China as one could get. The two, along with a handful of other operators, had previously toured Kashgar as Navy SEALs, with permission and aid from the Chinese government. Their mission had been to enter Afghanistan through an "unguarded back door" to look for Osama Bin Laden. Neither of them ever thought they would go to the place again.

After arriving in Bogota, they would switch to a Delta flight a few hours later, which would take them, back to California.

Once back in Los Angeles, Joe called on an old Navy friend who had some connections with some American spooks that were stationed out of the American consulate, in the Western China capital city of Urumqi. He wanted to see if there was any intelligence on a certain Juan Juarez. The friend told Paul he would investigate and get back to him in the next day or two. Paul went back to San Diego, dropping Joe off at his house in Long Beach on the way.

Three days later, the friend called Joe back, He'd learned that Juan was suspected by Chinese authorities as a person of interest associated with importing heroin from Afghanistan. The friend told Joe, "Let me see if I can get you some additional help with this."

THE TWO WOULD HAVE TO FIGURE OUT A WAY TO GET there. Then the next problem would be how to avoid being the center of attention. The place was seventy percent Uighur, thirty percent Han Chinese. There were not a lot of white people there; certainly not six foot seven ones.

Chapter Thirty-Nine

THE ISRAELI DELEGATION FLEW FROM MOSCOW TO
Birobidzhan. The Russian delegation would meet them there.
Lancaster told Michael he would have preferred taking the
famous Trans-Siberian Railway but he knew this was not a
sightseeing trip. Nonetheless, the excitement continued in
anticipation of what would be next.

Birobidzhan was the administrative center of the Jewish
Autonomous Oblast. While the city was established in 1928,
it officially became the Jewish Autonomous Region in 1934,
some fourteen years before Israel became a state. Today Birobidzhan's population was around eighty thousand, less than
half of what it used to be in the early 1960s.

Upon their arrival, they were greeted by members of the local
Jewish community, whose numbers had dwindled since the
1990s when they could emigrate elsewhere, as most did to
either the United States or Israel. There are about two thousand Jews living in Birobidzhan today. The delegation took
buses around and was shown much of the central city.

Michael pointed out to Lancaster that every street name was in Yiddish.

Lancaster thought Birobidzhan smelled like a blend of mold and burned coal. The air around the city looked gray, and he was not sure if it was fog or smog. He did not see any heavy industry or smokestacks, at least in the part he was in. It felt and looked much more third-world than Moscow. It was old and tired. Turning a corner in the bus, he saw an old man with a clarinet, playing a piece from Fiddler on the Roof. Skeptical, Lancaster wondered if it was staged.

Their buses drove by the menorah near the city's main square and they were told it was the largest in the world. They were taken to the main synagogue in town, for a PowerPoint presentation of the city and surrounding Autonomous Region. Lancaster was fascinated. Two months ago, he had never heard of this place.

There was lots of open space on the outskirts of the city, including several farms. The landscape looked a little bit swampy with the earth uneven and wet. There were lots of mosquitos and bugs flying around. The inner city looked like it needed a major power wash. The buildings, most of which were gray-white or tan in color, had accumulated dust and dirt over the years, but it seemed like it would be a simple enough task to clean things up. The architecture was of the classic Stalinist box design. The main boulevard seemed in decent shape. It was wide, lined with trees, flowers, and benches. The three or four public parks the buses drove past looked quite beautiful. The side streets, by comparison, had many potholes and were not well cared for. A few restaurants were seen, along with a variety of shops. Nothing fancy. The city needed some investment, but there were bones in place that gave Birobidzhan the potential to be an incredible place.

"And you lived here, Michael?" said Lancaster.

"Yes, I did. I was actually born here, but most of my child-hood I lived in Ukraine."

"When was the last time you were here?"

"Let me think ... Besides last year as part of an exploratory committee, it must have been the 1980s."

"And you still think this is all a promising idea?"

Michael smiled proudly. "Israel is a wonderful place. But living there, we are always on guard for an attack. There are new missiles and weapons being developed by some of our neighbors. I would prefer not to be around that. Besides, our Russian community in Israel is different culturally from the Jews that were born or who have had generations of family there. If this became an actual part of Israel, I would feel more comfortable living here—not weather-wise, of course. It gets below zero in the winter. I speak Russian, and a little bit of Yiddish. Most of my close friends have mixed feelings. Israel is, and will always be, their home. So, to move here, I do not think you are going to see a lot of non-European Israelis do it. The infrastructure today in Israel, wages, and lifestyle is exceptionally good. I see mostly new immigrants, those seeking a sense of adventure, entrepreneurs, young people who want a lower cost of living, being the ones to make the move here.

"Jewish people are pioneers. Like your old west. Plus, there is the excitement that there will be tremendous financial incentives to encourage those to come. What stimulates me most, is the vastness of open space, something we never experience in Israel. Plus, China. China borders this region. The economics of this place is going to explode, and it would be nice to participate in that."

"I see your points."

The delegation was driven to their hotels. The next morning, they would drive back to the city's main Jewish synagogue for a presentation by the Chinese to discuss trade, followed by the Russian government on their plans to supply abundant energy and build the largest shipping port in the world. The Chinese invited the delegations from both Russia and Israel to come to Beijing next week, where they would present their own ideas for a modern highway and rail system to Biro-bidzhan, plus tax-free zones along the Chinese border.

Lancaster could not argue with the fact that everything he heard seemed like a tremendous opportunity for all in the region, yet he was still bothered. Russia was a communist country, even a dictatorship, not too long ago. China still was. The earlier Jews that lived here had left in droves. But then he thought, had Russia changed? He was glad his job was only to consider legal issues and that he was not the one who took part in policy decisions or the direct negotiations. He trusted that the Israeli's knew what they were doing.

It was at that moment, he felt, for the first time, a personal connection to the Jews, and that he was legally and techni-cally Jewish. These were his people and felt an affinity he never had experienced before. Lancaster realized he had a vested personal interest. If a deal was to be made, he wanted to make sure it would be a durable one. Michael's talk to him on the plane had something to do with the awakening of his Jewish heritage.

The next day, both the Chinese economic trade and Russian harbor proposals were presented and were well received by all those who attended. There were lots of vodka toasts. Lots of smiles from Chinese, Israelis, and Russians. It seemed almost surreal to Lancaster. They were in the middle of nowhere, creating a monumental change to the world.

Lancaster wondered how Claire, Ashley, Joe, and Paul were doing. He missed them all, especially Claire.

The members of the entire delegation would take a short break, starting the day after tomorrow. Lancaster would take the day off and walk around Birobidzhan with Michael. He would then return home to California for a brief vacation and to be with his family. Then it would be back to work again—this time in Beijing.

Chapter Forty

LANCASTER AND MICHAEL TOOK A WALK TO GET A SENSE OF Birobidzhan from the viewpoint of some of the local population. Something that would not have been staged ahead of time. *Trust but verify the Russians*, Lancaster thought as Ronald Reagan said.

The two walked down from their hotel along a commercial street named, Hetzel, which took them in a direction they had not traveled while on the bus. They saw normal city activities—police directing traffic, garbage trucks picking up trash, road crews tearing up the streets, merchants running around, mothers walking their babies in strollers. There were no signs of poor or homeless people around. Nobody was begging or asking for handouts. Everybody just seemed busy, tending to his or her own affairs.

The two entered a small coffee and pastry shop. There were five or six small tables and a counter for ordering. Lancaster noticed on the wall, a large black and white photograph, depicting a nighttime scene of the Brooklyn Bridge, with Manhattan lit up in the background.

Why did that end up here? he pondered.

They both ordered little white cakes, along with Americana coffee. The coffee shop's host, and most likely owner, was a proud gray-haired gentleman, either in his late sixties or early seventies.

Michael had done the ordering, while Lancaster observed. He could not figure out if they were speaking Russian, Yiddish, or a little of both. During the conversation, Demsky mentioned they were both part of an Israeli exploratory delegation to the area, and that Lancaster was an American from California.

As they received their coffee and cake, Michael said something to the pastry shop owner that, combined with his gesture, suggested he should join them at their table. Their host was honored by the invitation, poured his own coffee, and sat down with them.

The host spoke no English, so Michael was the interpreter for both.

"What brings you both to Birobidzhan?" asked the host, as Michael translated into English.

Michael responded in mixed Russian and Yiddish on behalf of both Lancaster and him. "We are simply here on a fact-finding mission. We want to get a sense of the Jewish history here, the city today, and what it is like to live here."

The host responded, and Michael interpreted for Lancaster. "I was born here in 1952. Many things have changed throughout the years. Most of the Jews have left after the Soviet Union was dismantled. I had many Jewish friends. They left for Israel, at least most of them did. It was a mistake by the Soviets, not controlling better the anti-Semitism. The Russian government knows they made a mistake. Everyone in town feels the same way. The city no longer has the same feel it used to. Up until the late 1980s, the Jews helped create a wonderful place. We had the best university, certainly in this part of the country, one of the best in the Soviet Union. That is no more. We had many more businesses. More doctors. The place was thriving. Then the Jews left."

Lancaster asked Michael if he could interpret a question he had for the host and Michael, of course, agreed.

"So, if someone could wave a magic wand and bring back, say, a hundred thousand Jews into this area, would they be welcomed here?"

The man responded as Michael interpreted, "Well if we could have the infrastructure to accommodate them, absolutely; one hundred percent. The Jews were always loved here. It was the Soviets after World War II, not even from this area, that stirred up trouble. The Jews were very warm people. They were good citizens. When I read about what Jews have done today in Israel, I think, wow. They could have done that here if we gave them the chance."

Michael replied to the host. "And you think most residents of Birobidzhan feel this way?"

"I do. I certainly feel this way. We still have around two thousand Jews living here today, only about two percent of the population. Our earlier mayor was Jewish. One of the biggest factories in town, a furniture factory, employs many people and pays good wages. The family that owns it is Jewish. But even more than that, most of our current citizens, including my family, are of Russian Cossack descent. Many feel the way I do. When the Jews left, so did the soul of our community.

Most people here still speak Yiddish. It is still taught in our schools, as are the Jewish holidays and their culture. Every year at Chanukah time, there is a big ceremony in the center of town, where our large menorah is lit up. Some of our Jewish residents recite Jewish prayers in Hebrew, and everyone present, hundreds, clap after the ceremony. Let me show you something else you may not have noticed."

He got up and gestured for Michael and Lancaster to follow him as he walked just outside the front door. Once again, Michael interpreted for Lancaster.

"See all the stores in the neighborhood? Mine included? Every place has a mezuzah on its door, and most of those people are not even Jewish. The Jews were a particularly important cultural piece of this community. The entire region misses them dearly."

"Thank you," Michael told the host as he and Lancaster left to continue their walk and exploration.

Lancaster said to Michael, "I don't know what to say. Unless this is all a fake set-up by the Russian government, which I doubt it is, this absolutely feels like a Jewish community; and by the way, yes, I think my eyes may have opened up to something, I never would have foreseen."

The delegation was going to start a short five-day break. Lancaster would return to California.

Chapter Forty-One

Joe got a call from the Chinese consulate in Los Angeles.

"Mr. Reid?"

"Yes."

"My name is Wong Sim. I work at the Chinese consulate on Wilshire Boulevard in Los Angeles. I received a phone call from someone in your State Department. Would it be possible for you and your friend to come over here for a visit? We would like to speak with you about a mutual interest."

"Who called you? How do you know about any friend I might have? What is this about?"

"Come down and have some tea with us. We have some thoughts on your Juan Juarez issue."

"What do you know about any Juan Juarez issue I have?"

"Come down, you will be with friends."

Joe was very suspicious, but he called Paul, and then called the consulate back and set up an appointment for two days later.

Chapter Forty-Two

"HELLO."

"Claire?"

"Speaking. Who is this?"

"It's Joe."

"Hi, Joe. How are you? How is Sheila?"

"We're fine. Is Steven around?"

"No, he is out of town right now."

"I see. I left maybe four or five messages on his voicemail."

"He has a new job. He has been gone for quite a while. He didn't take his cell phone with him."

"Really?"

"Yes, let's just say his new employer forbid him to bring it."

"Are you kidding me? Why is that?"

"Joe, you of all people should know this. When you went on missions before, did your employer allow you to bring your cell phones with you when you went out of town?"

"No, but I was in the military."

"I can't tell you what Steven is up to exactly. You know he worked for the Justice Department for thirty years. It is related to that. He will not tell me much, and I understand. He wasn't allowed to even speak to me about cases he had ongoing in those days, and I am his wife and a lawyer."

"Yes, I am sorry. Can you have him call me when he is available? In fact, you know what, you are a lawyer too. How dumb for me to forget. Can I ask you a legal question that I was going to ask him?

"Sure."

"If someone I know was invited to a foreign embassy or consulate here in the United States ... that person goes inside that building, can the foreign country arrest him? I ask you this because I have always heard that foreign embassies are the soil of the other country."

"I have no idea. That question is way above my pay grade. I tell you what though, I will research it if you hold on."

She sat down at her little desk below the wall-mounted phone in the kitchen, turned on her computer, and brought up her *Lexus* online law library. In the online legal library business, there are two main companies—*Lexus* and *Westlaw*. They are both good.

"I am not seeing anything. The Julian Assange case, which is mentioned, would not apply because his facts are different. He was a non-British citizen who walked into the Equator Embassy in London and was given asylum for several years.

The Equator Embassy staff later called in the British to come in and arrest him. So, he was not arrested by Equator, Joe.

"I see no laws or cases. I do not see how they could. More importantly, unless the embassy had the consent of the hosting country, or some extradition ordered, the person arrested would not be forced to go to the country's home soil. So, I can't see a visitor being arrested."

Joe responded, "Makes sense to me, but I'm thinking now if my friend could meet with a consulate representative at a neutral location like a restaurant, then a hundred percent for sure, nothing could happen to him, right?"

"That's right, Joe. Nothing could happen to you. I mean your friend."

"Okay, thanks smartass. I mean, Claire. Bye."

"Bye bye, Joe."

Chapter Forty-Three

PAUL AND JOE DECIDED TO CHANGE THE LOCATION OF THE meeting from the Chinese consulate to the Full House Restaurant, found on Broadway in China Town. They preferred the neutral turf.

The two headed north up the Harbor Freeway in Paul's Ford Explorer. Joe had on a dress shirt and tie. Paul wore a Hawaiian flower shirt.

"Why didn't you wear a tie?" asked Joe.

"I don't own a tie. Plus, even if I did, I forgot how to tie them."

"How will we know who Mr. Sim is?" asked Paul.

"He will be the Chinese guy," Joe smiled.

"Great," said Paul. "A Chinese guy in a Chinese restaurant. That will be easy."

The traffic was stop and go. Paul pressed his Bluetooth button, called Mr. Sim, and told him, "We are going to be a little late. We are just passing the University of Southern California. I figure another twenty-twenty-five minutes."

Mr. Sim told him, "No problem."

THEY ARRIVED AT THE RESTAURANT. THERE WAS A CHINESE man alone in a booth wearing a blue suit, with a pin of the Chinese flag on his left collar. Sim raised his right hand, signaling for the two former SEALs to come over.

Mr. Sim stood up, shook both their hands, and said, "It is nice to meet you both in person." He had a Chinese accent but seemed to speak English very well.

Paul and Joe sat down in the booth as Joe commented, "You speak pretty good English."

"Thank you. I grew up in China watching Bugs Bunny Cartoons. Then I went to Vanderbilt in Tennessee."

The server brought tea to the table and asked the three if they had decided on what they wanted to eat.

Mr. Sim asked his American guests, "Do you like fish?"

Paul nodded, as Joe answered, "Yes."

Sim proceeded to order in Mandarin, pointed toward the large fish tank along the back wall as he did. The server took abundant notes and then, finally, walked away and entered the kitchen door.

"What did you order?" asked Paul.

"I will surprise you. I promise you won't be hungry."

The three of them looked in the direction of the fish tank and saw the server come out of the kitchen with a cook, dressed in white attire, along with a fishing net. The server pointed to a large gray and black fish. The cook caught it then retreated behind the door with the fish squirming and flipping around in the net.

"We are going to eat that," asked Paul?

"Oh yes. Very tasty; very fresh."

"It probably is," said Joe.

Joe continued. "So, tell me what you know about this Juarez character, and who told you?"

"A call came to our Washington D.C. Embassy. I guess from someone who works for your State Department. He gave us a little background, and we suggested maybe our government could help you get him."

"I am confused," Joe admitted.

"Juan Juarez. We know who he is. He is a Colombian cartel member who we consider a significant importer and drug trafficker of heroin into China. He lives in our western city of Kashgar, an old Silk Road trading post. He has dark features and blends in well with our Uighur population.

"He has a pretty sophisticated system of drug importation from Afghanistan. He surrounds himself with the Uighurs, and every time we, or should I say, a Han Chinese comes close to him, his Uighur friends warn him, and he vanishes. That is our biggest challenge. As you may or may not know, most Uighur's don't particularly like us Han Chinese."

"I gather that," said Paul.

Sim added, "We also know that during your Afghanistan conflict, both of you visited western China and our government cooperated in assisting you in entering Afghanistan through our backdoor."

"This is true," agreed Paul.

"So, getting back to Mr. Juarez, we both have a common interest in capturing him," said Sim. "Would you like some more tea?"

Paul said, "Yes, please."

Joe said, "No, thank you, not right now."

"So, Mr. Sim, how do you know what our interests are?"

"We all know who this guy is, along with what he does for a living. You are both former Navy SEALs. Your State Department contacted us. We can, as you say, connect the dots pretty well."

"Why do you need us then?" asked Paul. "Why not just grab the guy yourself?"

"Because of his fear of Han Chinese people. Again, he knows ahead of time when we are in the area. Kashgar has underground tunnels where he can escape or hide. We think our Uighur community protects him."

"So, what can we do, that your government can't?" asked Paul.

"Probably get closer to him than us. Neither Juarez nor his guards will suspect a couple of white round-eyes of going after him in China."

Paul and Joe both chuckled. The food was served. It was an enormous feast.

Joe asked, "Do you have a plan for how we can infiltrate?"

"We do. But before I get to that, there is one important warning my government requires you to obey. We do not want Juarez dead. You must capture him and bring him to our authorities alive."

"What?!" Paul exclaimed. "What does China care if we kill him? We would be doing your government a favor."

"Because he must stand trial for his crimes."

"A trial? In China? Ha. You got to be shitting me. What is that, a ten-minute exercise?!" asked Joe.

"We have to do it this way. Primarily, so we do not offend the Uighur community who always are suspicious of us."

Joe asked, "So, with a ten-minute trial and a guilty conviction, your Uighur population will feel that fair and equal justice has been achieved?"

"I don't make the rules," Sim said.

"So, what if he shoots or tries to kill us?" asked Paul. "Aren't we allowed to defend ourselves?"

"We don't care about his bodyguards, but you must return him to us alive."

"Oh brother," muttered a confused and irritated Joe.

Paul said, "Okay, tell me about your plan for us to get close to him and not attract a lot of attention."

"You might even have some fun with this plan. Every week at this time of year, an Austrian company hosts tourists taking a motorcycle adventure along the Silk Road; our Highway 314. They begin the tour in the city of Urumqi, with stops in Turpan, Korla, Kuqa, Aksy, and finally, Kashgar. About eighteen hundred miles (about twice the distance from Florida to

New York City) of mostly paved, some dirt, highway through our Taklamakan Desert."

"Eighteen hundred miles?!" asked a surprised Joe.

"Yes, eighteen hundred miles. A very scenic and interesting area. Very historical."

Joe said, "That's a long ride."

"Yes, but you will have an enjoyable time, and nobody will suspect anything because this motorcycle tour is a weekly event. Plus, a lot of round-eyes do this. We will have both a Uighur agent to go with your group who will serve as your assistant tour guide, along with a Han Chinese agent as well. Your trip leader will be an Austrian who will merely think you are both Americans traveling on holiday."

"When is this next trip?"

"You will both fly out in two days. You'll take a flight to Beijing, then a domestic air carrier to Urumqi."

Paul responded in a positive manner, "We got some packing to do."

Chapter Forty-Four

AFTER A TWENTY-FOUR-HOUR JOURNEY, THEY FINALLY landed in Urumqi. As the two exited, they were greeted by Hans, the Austrian tour guide, along with his assistant guides Ray Fong and Ahmed, the Chinese Uighur. They drove Paul and Joe to their hotel. There were six other motorcycle riders: four were already at the hotel, the remaining two would arrive in a couple of hours.

Hans told Joe, "Get a good night's sleep. The long ride starts tomorrow. We have about five hundred kilometers to the first destination."

The next day, at 8 a.m., the six riders and three guides met outside in front of the hotel. Each rider was supplied a 650 cc Enduro-style Chinese brand bike, called Jialing.

Joe said to Hans, "Will I fit on this thing-a-ling?"

Hans responded, "You mean, Jialing? Well, you are tall. Let us see."

Joe straddled the motorcycle, and it was clear he was too big. He would not be comfortable for the eighteen-hundred-mile ride ahead.

"Let me call my office and see what we can do," said Hans.

Within an hour, a small Chinese pickup truck pulled up with what looked like a brand-new red 1200 cc BMW Adventure tied to its bed.

"Now you're talking," said Joe.

Paul, standing next to Joe and Hans, responded, "That is not fair. Joe gets a new BMW, and I must ride this piece of junk. The Jialing is maybe a $5,000 bike, the BMW around $23,000."

Joe told Paul, "This is China. It's not a fair country."

While Joe would ride his Harley Fat Boy back at home in Long Beach on occasion, Paul had not ridden a motorcycle in at least ten years. His reintroduction to riding would be pulling out of the downtown Urumqi Hotel, a city of three and a half million people, then being thrown into the fire by dealing with the crazy traffic right from the get-go. But if he was nervous or concerned, he did not show it to anyone in the group.

The group rode for five days in the hot Taklamakan Desert and finally reached what was supposed to be the final destination, Kashgar. The group stopped along the way and stayed each night at moderate western-style hotels. They saw Buddhist monasteries, Uighur villages, oil drills, a nuclear power plant, and several other historical sights commemorating the history of the Silk Road.

While Joe and Paul knew there would be work up ahead, they enjoyed the sights along the way, the challenging ride, and the

Uighur culture. Virtually every day, they ate lunch in small family-operated restaurants along the road. They were always the traditional lamb meals cooked on a Mongolian-style barbeque grill, served with a Nan-type bread. Toilets, except for in their hotels, were not nice. Other than the one female rider in their group, when any of the guests needed to relieve themselves by going number one, it was preferable to find a bush and take care of business that way.

The group would go out to dinner each night at a local restaurant in the town of their daily destination. All the hotels they stayed at served American-style bacon and egg breakfasts each morning. The traffic along the Silk Road, outside the cities, was light, consisting primarily of trucks shipping various goods and products in both directions.

Upon their arrival in Kashgar, the group was given a tour that included the main mosque, central bizarre, and fairgrounds where livestock, fruits, and vegetables were sold at what appeared to be some sort of auction. Kashgar was not the typical "China" most Americans would see on their televisions. Most of the people were not of Han Chinese descent.

Unlike most Islamic countries, the Uighur men were forbidden from wearing beards, the women from covering up in their traditional ways, and the call to prayer with loud-speakers was also prohibited.

The center of the city of Kashgar, where the group's hotel was, had more of a mix of Han Chinese in the population. Outside of the center of town, it was exclusively Uighur. The billboards seen in and around the city were written in both Chinese and Arabic. Ahmed told the group of riders that the Uighur language was most like Turkish.

While Joe, Paul, and the rest of the group could not sense it, tensions between the Uighurs and their Han Chinese "co-citizens" were said to be high. The Uighurs claimed they were exploited, denied jobs that were given to Han Chinese, and were restricted in their movement within the country. Not to mention, of course, there were limitations placed on the practice of their religion. Many Uighurs were sent to "re-education centers" that looked more like prisons than schools. Their high walls, barb-wire fences, and guard towers were out of place and inappropriate as a center for "learning how to blend better into Chinese society".

Hans was never told or appeared to be aware of Ray and Ahmed's secret role in aiding Paul and Joe with going after Juarez. Once the city tour of Kashgar was completed, Ray and Ahmed met back at the hotel privately with Joe and Paul.

"We just finished speaking with our contacts here on the ground concerning Juarez," said Ahmed.

"Juan Juarez, we are informed, took off last night to the city of Tashkurgan with some of his Uighur bodyguards. We think he is going to enter into another part of Afghanistan to import some more heroin," said Ray.

Joe asked, "Where is this Tashkurgan?"

"In the mountains," Ray told him.

"What mountains?" Paul asked. They had seen nothing but desert the last five days, and he certainly didn't recall seeing any mountains when he was in Kashgar years ago.

"Way up in the Himalayas. About two hundred and thirty kilometers south of here," said Ahmed.

"Can we get there," asked Paul?

"Yes. There is a brand-new highway—The Karokaran Highway."

"Is it paved?"

"Oh yes. It is beautiful. Brand new. Twists and turns. An ultramodern road. As nice as any mountain road in the world. Perfect fun for a motorcycle. The road reaches heights of over five thousand meters, or sixteen thousand feet (about half the height of Mount Everest). It will be a bit chilly there, and in the adjacent Afghanistan Mountains," said Ahmed.

"When can we go?" asked Paul.

Ray responded, "We need to make arrangements with the Chinese Army that controls the road. We also need to tell Hans we are going to take you on a private side trip."

"The only way up there is through Uighur villages we think are controlled by Juarez. He will have lookouts with cell phones. I suggest we do this under cover of darkness. Once we get to the Army checkpoint along the road and start heading up, most of the people we will see will no longer be Uighurs," Ahmed added.

"Will we be okay?" asked Paul.

"Hard to know for sure," said Ray. "They probably have Uighurs along the road up to the security point, but after that, we don't know if Juarez has created any relationships with the locals in the mountains, called Tajiks. We should assume he does unless we are able to get some intelligence that says something different."

Joe asked, "If the only way up is through this Karokaran Highway, and then there is the Chinese Army checkpoint you mention, how do Juan and his people get through that?"

"They are either smuggled in through the back of trucks or they walk along old goat trails."

"So, you think they are doing a deal up there?" asked Paul.

"Tashkurgan is right near where the Pakistan, Chinese, and Afghanistan borders converge. I suspect they are using new routes to import the drugs."

"Guys, do what you need to do to get us there," Joe said. "Can we leave tonight?"

"Let us plan on meeting at sundown behind the hotel. I will have your AK-47s and ammo ready by then."

Chapter Forty-Five

CLAIRE WAS PICKING UP STEVEN AT LOS ANGELES International airport. Traffic on both Century Blvd. and at the airport was surprisingly light. He was waiting on the curb with his suitcase out in front of the Thomas Bradley International Terminal.

Claire saw Steven up ahead and drove up to where he was standing. She hit the trunk release button for his suitcase and hugged and kissed him to welcome him back as the recording over airport loudspeakers said, "The white zone is for immediate loading and unloading of passengers only. No parking is allowed."

"Hi, Honey. Welcome back," said Claire. She was glad to see him. She had missed him dearly.

"Thanks, Claire, it is good to back. Long flight. Want me to drive?"

"Are you tired?"

"A little."

"In that case, yes you drive. Just kidding."

The two got in the car, she pulled away from the curb and drove off toward the 405 Freeway.

"How is Ashley," asked Steven?

"She is fine. She got an A on her history report about the missions of California."

"I had to do one of those reports when I was a kid too."

"Me too. I remember building a model of the Santa Barbara Mission."

"And work, Claire?"

"A little slow. I have a petty theft trial starting tomorrow."

"Are you ready?"

"As much as I will be. The client is a sixty-year-old woman. Clean record. No priors of any kind. She walked out of a *Bed Bath and Beyond*, without paying for a showerhead."

"Over a showerhead? And they are making you go to trial?"

"As usual, in a case like this, it will most likely settle at the last second. Stupid case. She said she just spaced out and forgot to pay."

"Have you spoke with Joe or Sheila lately?"

"Joe a few days ago. He left the country today for China. I am not supposed to know that, but Sheila told me. He actually called you and wanted to ask you a bizarre legal question."

"What was his question?"

"He wanted to know whether if he, I mean according to him, some friend of his, went inside a foreign consulate office here in Los Angeles, could that foreign government arrest him?"

"Arrest him? For what?"

"No idea but guess that is a moot point—something about the soil of a foreign embassy or consulate as being part of that country."

"Anything else?"

"He said he stayed at the FINCA you stayed at in Armenia a long time ago, and that it was still there. They loved the pool."

"Joe and Sheila went to Colombia?" Lancaster was surprised.

"No. Joe and Paul!"

"And Paul? What the hell?"

Chapter Forty-Six

WHEN STEVEN AND CLAIRE ARRIVED BACK AT THEIR HOME, it was around noon. Due to the jet lag, Steven decided to take a rest until Ashley got home from school. The house seemed recently cleaned and smelled like vinegar. The house cleaner must have just been here. Because it was Friday, not a school night, and because Steven had not been home for close to a month, Claire and he decided to surprise Ashley and take her to Disneyland later in the afternoon.

At close to 5 p.m., they all jumped into the car and headed up the 5 Freeway toward Anaheim. Disneyland was less than fifteen miles from their home.

Disneyland was always fun, especially for adults. They did rides in Fantasyland, Adventureland, and Tomorrowland. Disneyland was always nostalgic for Steven. His parents took him there ever since he was a little boy. He recalled the old ticket ride books, which were divided into A, B, C, D, and E tickets. He could even remember which rides required which tickets. The best rides were the E tickets. The Bobsled, Small World, and Pirates of the Caribbean were E's. The People

Mover and Submarine were D's, Utopia cars a C. He even remembered that the GE Carousel of Progress was free and did not require a ticket. Even more bizarre, he even remembered the theme song:

"It's a great big beautiful tomorrow, shining at the end of every day, oh it's a great big beautiful tomorrow, and tomorrow's just a dream away. Man has a dream to reach the stars, he follows his ..."

He laughed to himself and smiled. The more he thought, the more he remembered. He even remembered the songs from Small World and Pirates of the Caribbean. But his favorite ride, back in the day, was the Haunted House. The guests would ride in cars along this track, moving from room to room in the large house. As the car moved, the ride would put this kind of digital monster or ghost in the seat beside you. The ride would travel in front of giant mirrors, and guests would see these scary characters laughing while sitting next to them. Lancaster loved that.

But the most infamous Disneyland memory for Steven was during the traditional "Grad Night" he'd attended, his last night of high school. That would remain with him for the rest of his life.

After Ashley, Claire and Steven got off the Small World ride, Ashley blurted out to her mother the question they'd known she would someday ask:

"Mom, who was my real daddy before Steven?"

Claire looked at Steven. They both heard what she asked loud and clear. They had rehearsed how they would respond to this uncomfortable but important question. Their biggest concern was just how many of the details Ashley might want to know. They didn't really want to tell their thirteen-year-old kid that her mom was previously a promiscuous sex addict who went to swinger parties often and accidentally got pregnant. To this day, she still didn't know who the biological father was. Claire and Steven knew that, having been brought up by two lawyers, Ashley had developed the skills to conduct a thorough and sharp cross-examination! They were both fearful of the probing questions she might ask.

"Ashley, Honey, come with me. Steven, I will call you when we are done. We can meet somewhere in Fantasyland," said Claire.

Steven thought to himself, *Oh fuck! Glad I won't be involved in this discussion.*

"I will see you guys in a bit," he said as he walked away from the two in the direction of the pellet gun shooting range, over in Frontierland.

"Bye, Daddy," Ashley called as she waved to him.

"Honey," Claire said to Ashley, "I am glad you asked me this question." Little did Ashley know her mom's stomach was churning and had started to cramp so that she wondered if she might have to run to the bathroom. "Mommy made some bad choices in her life, but sometimes out of these choices, good things can come. In this instance, I made a mistake of judgment, but I was blessed by having you. Both Daddy and I love you very much."

"Yeah, but who was my real daddy?"

Claire's cramps got worse, and she could feel perspiration developing in her hair and on her hands.

"Ashley, Mommy was going out with several men at one time. It was not something I should have done. One of those men, no doubt, is your biological father. But sorry, Honey, I really do not know which one it was. But the good part is, that's when you came." Claire held her breath in anticipation of the next question.

Ashley said, "Okay, Mom. Can we get ice cream now?"

"Yes!" exclaimed Claire. Let us find Daddy first." Claire wanted to say, "Oh my God!" as the stress she was experiencing dropped dramatically.

IN JUST THREE DAYS, STEVEN WOULD HAVE TO HOP BACK ON an airplane. This time he would fly to Beijing for the next round of meetings. There, the Chinese would present their ideas of an economic zone along the Russian border, and how they planned to develop their new infrastructure in the region.

Chapter Forty-Seven

JOE, PAUL, RAYMOND, AND AHMED, STILL BEHIND THE hotel, completed the final details associated with getting their motorcycles prepared for the journey up into the mountains. It was getting dark. Ahmed was looking around to see if any lookouts were spying on them.

The group stuffed their motorcycle side bags with supplies they would need for their journey: ammunition, Kevlar vests, extra water contained in canteens, knives, warm clothes, and some communication equipment. They each affixed AK-47s to their motorcycle frames and placed wood around each of the rifle's circumferences to create a camouflage so they would be difficult to detect.

Ray and Ahmed's roles now changed from assistant tour guides to Chinese agents aiding the two former SEALs to bring this wanted drug trafficker to justice.

They each started up their motorcycles in anticipation of their journey toward the Karokaran Highway. Using their feet, the four slowly maneuvered the noses of their bikes into a circle for a final briefing.

As they got together, Paul looked over and said to Joe, "I love this stuff."

Joe grinned back. "Me too, Easy."

Raymond spoke and said, "We have probably a little more than a one-hour ride to the Army checkpoint. The Army knows we are coming. They were given the orders to simply wave us through, and not ask any questions. There are three Uighur villages we need to ride through before the checkpoint. I will go first and we will be keeping our speed down in those areas. Absolutely no stopping at all prior to the checkpoint. If you need a rest or must make an equipment adjustment, hold off until then. Once we get past the Army checkpoint, we will not stop until we get to Tashkurgan. Keep your eyes open.

"While our latest intelligence suggests Juarez is in Afghanistan, we do not know this one hundred percent. We also do not know if he has any lookouts along the route. Neither Ahmed nor I know the Tajiks tribal language, but many of them speak Chinese. My preference is to drive just past the town. You will see an old Mongolian fort atop a hill on our left, and just past that, there is a dirt road toward Afghanistan. The international border is only about three miles from that point. I expect to stop before that. The border on the Afghanistan side sometimes has, sometimes does not have, a manned checkpoint. I do not want to deal with that. There is a goat trail about half a mile off the road that will take us to the general area we want to get to. That is the more safe and secure way. Any questions?"

Paul asked, "You have a detailed topo map of the goat trail and the area inside Afghanistan?"

"I do," said Ray, "and we will go over that after we park the bikes. Oh, and just another reminder: you are to capture Juarez. You are not permitted under any circumstance to kill him."

"And if he comes at us with a machine gun blasting away or a knife?"

"Deal with it. He comes back alive."

Joe looked over at Paul, and without saying anything, shook his head as he mouthed, "This is so fucking stupid."

"And then you are going to give Juarez the five-minute trial, take him outside and hang him?" asked Joe.

Ray smiled at Joe. "Almost. We give him a ten-minute trial, then take him out and shoot him."

They all smiled.

Chapter Forty-Eight

THEY ARRIVED WITHOUT INCIDENT AT THE CHINESE ARMY checkpoint at the base of the Himalayas. Ray Fong spoke very briefly with the commanding officer. The group of four motorcycle riders was expected. The group each added an additional layer of clothing, plus switched to warmer down-type jackets. Joe and Paul were eager to ride this brand-new Tashkurgan Highway, even though it was pitch dark and they knew it would be cold.

Before they took off from the Army checkpoint, Joe, teasing, said to the other three riders, "Well, people, it is time for me to turn on my heated grips and seat warmer. Too bad your thing-a-links, or whatever they are called, don't have them."

Ahmed, who had been incredibly quiet, smiled at Joe and gave him the bird through his right-hand glove.

"Yea, I know I am number one," said Joe.

The four twisted their throttles, and with Ray still in the lead, off they went. Paul and Joe found this new highway to be a flawless, ultramodern state-of-the-art design as it cut through the Himalayas. Joe, who had previously ridden his Harley through much of the west, felt this road had both Highway 1 in California, and Interstate 70 in Colorado beaten easily. He only wished it were daylight so he could appreciate the twists and turns more. He thought how much fun this would be on the way back, assuming it was daylight. Assuming, in fact, they came back.

Arriving in the mountain town of Tashkurgan, in the middle of the night, they saw a handful of Tajiks walk around. Their clothing was completely different than what the Chinese and Uighurs wore. The Tajiks' clothes, as illuminated from the town lights, appeared colorful. They only saw men walking around, but those they saw wore funny looking hats that looked a bit like a wool scalp cover sewn into a Cracker Jacks sailor hat. They also noticed the men were wearing some sort of necklace beads. The temperature felt like it was in the low forties and very dry.

As the four rode past Tashkurgan, they reached the Fort. It was officially known as Stone Tower fortress, considered in academia to characterize the place where invaders from Pakistan and Afghanistan were fought off hundreds of years ago. About one or two miles past the Fort, Ray pulled over to the side of the road. At that point, there was a Chinese Tajik agent waiting who spoke briefly to Raymond in Chinese. The other three had stopped in single file behind him, everyone kept their engines on. Raymond shook his head up and down at the agent, then gestured to the other three to move on out.

About another mile up the road, the group made a right-hand turn at an unmarked dirt road. Small to medium size rocks were present, but the suspensions of the bikes handled the hazards quite well. There were no structures in the immediate area. One could tell from the moonlight, there was a single, dim light some distance ahead, and a narrow, jagged canyon between two mountains just beyond that. Another mile or so on, Ray made a right turn onto a trail that sloped slightly uphill. It had short shrubs on both sides. There was very little other vegetation in the area since they were well above the tree line here. They rode the bikes slowly, using mostly first gear, cruising under five miles per hour. Up ahead, another couple hundred yards, Ray turned his bike's ignition off, cutting the noise and headlights. The others followed and did the same. Ray took his bike and walked it up an even narrower trail to his left, as the others pushed their machines single file behind. They all stopped next to a small flowing creek some a hundred and fifty yards after they turned onto the trail. Paul was pleased with how well the Enduro bikes seemed to work in this harsh environment. A street motorcycle with a different suspension and ground clearance would not have made it up this terrain. Everyone dismounted, set their kickstands down, and gathered around Ray.

"The Tajik agent I spoke with near the Fort gave me the latest Chinese intelligence, including the possible whereabouts of Juarez. Our satellites appeared to have picked up Juarez along with ten of his associates in this general area. Intelligence reported they continued traveling on the same goat road. We will transition to walking from here. That is Afghanistan over there." He pointed toward the southeast. "The actual border is at the base of that canyon, and as we enter, you will notice a marker in both Chinese and Arabic, which signifies the international boundary.

"Ahmed is going in there with you two. I have been instructed to ride my bike back into town and return with a van and get as close as I can to this location. I will not be able to drive up this far, so keep walking the way we came up, and I will meet you as close as I can get. The plan is, after you capture Juarez, I will transport you all back to town in the van. You guys can then grab the bikes and ride them back later. Do not kill him."

"Aye aye, your greatness!" said Joe.

Paul chimed in. "We hear you loud and clear." He gave Joe a sideways glance.

The three put on their Kevlar vests, stuffed their pockets with the clips of AK-47 ammunition, attached the canteens to their belts, and confirmed their communications equipment were in working order.

Then Paul, said to Ahmed and Joe, "Time to lock and load, gentlemen."

They each pulled back on their charging handles and chambered their first round.

"Let's move out." Paul led the way with his topo map stuffed under his vest.

Just before daybreak, the three warriors entered the border of Afghanistan and came upon the steep narrow corridor or mini canyon. It was about ten feet in width with straight-up walls that were twenty to thirty feet high. Paul figured this would be a wonderful place to set up an ambush.

"Let's do one final communication check."

Joe began. "Erection one."

Ahmed followed Joe. "Unhappy Uighur one."

Paul responded, "You're an unhappy Uighur?"

"No, not really," said Ahmed, "but out here with nobody listening, I can call myself what I want."

"Are you sure your Chinese bosses aren't listening in?" said Joe.

Ahmed clarified, "No, I said Happy Uighur one. There must have been a radio malfunction on that broadcast." Ahmed and the other two smiled.

"Okay," responded Paul. "Ten-four. Happy Uighur. This is Easy One. All good?"

Ahmed and Joe both gave the thumbs up.

Paul, talking to Joe, said, "I want you to take the extreme-forward position. You will also be the highest up. Ahmed, see that rock over there halfway between where Joe will be and here?"

Ahmed shook in the affirmative. "You will be atop that. I will be just up above here. Erection, you broadcast on the COM system when you see them, including distance, what size force they have, weapons, etcetera." Joe gave the thumbs up. "Nobody shoots until I give the order. I want to make sure they are all in the kill zone, and most importantly, I want to identify which one is Juarez. Hopefully, we can distinguish him from the others. Juarez should look different from the people he is with. Joe, you got the binoculars?"

"I do, Sir."

"Fuck you with the sir shit," said Paul.

Ahmed asked, "What is that about?"

"Don't worry about it, Happy Uighur; just a personal joke. We should not have a problem with crossfire, as we are all on the right. Watch out for ricochets. These rock walls are pretty solid."

"Stupid question, Mr. Easy," said Ahmed.

"You can just call me Easy or Paul. What is your stupid question?"

"What if we can't identify Juarez for some reason?"

"That is a problem, Ahmed. A particularly good question. We can't shoot until we figure out which one he is."

"What if they shoot first?"

"They will only shoot first, Happy Uighur, if they see us. If this happens, and we have not identified which one is Juarez, we will have a problem, and I will deal with that later."

All three took their positions.

BY LATE MORNING, JOE GOT ON HIS COM. "I HAVE contact."

"What you got, Erection?"

"Well, I don't have an erection?"

"What's an erection, you guys?" asked Ahmed.

Joe and Paul, even in the face of an enemy coming toward them, could not help but chuckle.

"We will explain by Joe's example later after the mission, Ahmed. So how many targets do you see, Joe?" asked Paul.

"I see one, two, three, four, five, six, seven, eight … nine people all with automatic weapons, about four hundred yards out, headed this way on the goat trail. They also have one, two, three … four, no three mules or donkeys with them. It looks like they have packs on their backs, carrying something."

"I am sure that is heroin," said Ahmed.

Joe asked, "I assume we can shoot the donkeys."

"Hell yes, unless Juarez is disguised as one."

"I don't think identifying Juarez is going to be much of an issue," said Joe as he peered through his binoculars. "In fact, stupid Juarez may actually be an easy I.D."

"Tell me more, Erect One."

"Is Erection a good thing," asked Ahmed?

"Shut up, Ahmed. Until you complete BUDs you are not allowed to be funny unless we give you special permission," said Paul. "What about Juarez, Erect One?"

"There is a guy in the middle of the pack. His skin is darker than everybody else. He is the only one with facial hair. Everybody else is in white; this other guy is wearing orange. And he walks with an overconfident swagger of a seasoned drug dealer. No doubt guys, this is Juarez. How stupid is he?"

"We like stupid," said Paul. "It makes our job much easier."

"Okay, now about two hundred yards prior to entering the kill zone. They are still walking, not much space apart. They don't look too concerned about encountering any danger."

"Where are the donkeys relative to the people?"

"All three of them are toward the back."

"If they are still walking in that single-file line, what number in the line is Juarez?"

"He is ... one, two, three, four. He is four."

"How much space per man?"

"They're pretty tight. Maybe two feet or so."

"Everyone switch to single shot," said Paul. "No automatic fire. I do not want Juarez hit by mistake. They are too close. I imagine, once the shooting starts, they will spread out, but they will not have much cover down there. If after the shooting starts, Juarez distances himself significantly away from others, I do not care if you go to automatic or stay on single shot. Just do not shoot near him. Accuracy is especially important. Wait for me to fire first. You guys get all that?"

"Roger," said Joe.

"Yes," said Ahmed.

"Silence on COM now. No shooting until after me. I am waiting until all are in the kill zone."

Moments later, the caravan of drug smugglers entered the zone. The men in front were scanning the walls, but they were sloppy with their weapons, simply not predicting any problems. Most of the men in the caravan had them slung over their shoulders. A couple of them held their rifles toward the dirt. There was one guy, immediately in front of Juarez, who was the only person at any ready position. Paul had decided he would be the first to go since he was the greatest threat.

Paul lined up his first shot, wanting to make sure the bullet would not exit his victim in the direction of Juarez. He waited until there was a bend in the trail so Juarez would be at a slightly different angle, and away from any exit bullets. Paul fired the first shot. It worked. A clean headshot. The guy in front of Juarez was down. Then Joe and Ahmed started shooting. Ahmed and Paul quickly took out the three unsuspecting victims in the front of the single-file line. Joe took out the one behind Juarez. The remaining three behind him seemed to struggle but there was nowhere for them to hide. Realizing their dilemma, instead of fighting back, they merely prayed, and then it was over for them in seconds. Juarez also knew he was dead as well. He had his AK at the ready and was firing randomly, but he had no idea exactly where his attackers were. Juarez knew there was no cover and he expected to die shortly. Then, suddenly, Juarez shouted to his attackers, speaking in the Uighur form of Arabic, at least what little he knew:

"Please stop. Please stop."

Ahmed translated for Paul and Joe. The three of them were just sitting on top of their positions. Paul considered his next move.

In fluent Spanish, Paul yelled down to Juarez, "Put down your weapon immediately!"

Juarez's eyes lit up with surprise. Who knew he spoke Spanish? The guy yelling Spanish certainly did not have a Chinese accent of any kind.

Juarez called back in Spanish. "I will give you lots of money; just don't shoot me and let me go."

Playing with Juarez's mind, Paul responded, "How much money?"

"I can get you as much as you want."

"How much you got on you? I am not a bank. I don't give out credit for future payments."

"Please, please. I have $50,000 with me, plus another couple of million dollars' worth of heroin. You can have it all."

"Well, it seems to me, I could have it all anyway. I just kill you and take what you have. Why should I accept that?"

Frustrated, and realizing his captors were right, Juarez said, "I have several million dollars in both American and Chinese money back in Kashgar."

Ahmed whispered on the Com, "Ask him the location in Kashgar, so we can seize it."

Paul whispered back to Ahmed, "Why are you whispering to me? I don't think it matters, plus I don't even think this guy speaks English."

Ahmed responded in a normal voice, "Okay, is this an appropriate time to tell me what an Erection is?"

Joe and Paul couldn't hold their laughter. Joe doubled over, laughing and crying.

Meanwhile, Paul shouted back to Juarez, "What is the address of where the money is?"

The dialogue was interrupted by Joe firing a single shot.

"What was that?" asked Paul on the Com.

"Oh, one of the guys we shot earlier started to move. He wasn't quite dead."

Ahmed got on the COM "Well, Erection Person, I think the boss wants you to shoot more quietly."

They laughed some more.

Paul shouted out again, "Juarez what is the address where the money is?"

"I have it in two places. There is a place in the Kashgar Bizarre where they sell donkey saddles. There is a rug under the desk in that booth. Remove the rug, there is a tunnel there. Go inside the tunnel, you will find several million dollars."

"And the other place?"

"The other place is buried in the desert. I do not know how to describe it exactly without showing you, but I will do as best as I can. You know the three villages between Kashgar and the Chinese Army checkpoint before you go into mountains?"

Easy looks at Ahmed, who shook his head in the affirmative.

"Yes."

"The first village on the Kashgar side—not halfway between that village and the next village—there is a billboard on the left advertising pitta bread or something. Past that, plus maybe two hundred or three hundred yards further away from the road, there is a buried hole. A bunch of rocks with an X on it."

"An X. As in Señor X?" asked Paul.

There was a long pause ...

"What are you talking about?"

You are also known as Señor X?"

Another long pause ...

"Maybe a long time ago I was."

"Remember your buddy Rosendo from the Donkey bar in Armenia? Remember a deal you did with an American named David?"

Yet another pause ...

"Not sure."

"You do. A coke deal where you wanted this young eighteen-year-old, and some Swedish guy to sail up to California. And guess what, Señor X? We are his friends and that is why we are here. So, throw your weapon behind you, and we will have a little meet and greet."

Juarez knew he had no other options. He threw down his rifle and followed the order. He knew that David was the son of the college professor he'd ordered to be executed.

———

AHMED TIED JUAREZ'S HANDS BEHIND HIS BACK WITH plastic handcuffs he'd brought with him.

Joe asks Ahmed, "Aren't you going to read him his Miranda rights?"

This bust Paul up, but Ahmed seems confused.

"What's that?"

"Oh nothing," Joe replied, "just some bullshit American Civil rights thing. That wouldn't matter for his upcoming ten-minute trial."

Ahmed did not understand, so he just ignored the response.

Joe asked what they should do about the donkeys and the merchandise on their packs?

Ahmed responded, "We'll take the bags off, get some pictures of the inventory, then burn it. As to the donkeys, we will just let them go."

"Let them go?" said Paul. "I thought we were supposed to shoot them?"

"Shoot them?" responded Ahmed. "That would be cruel and inhumane"

"So, all of a sudden, China is interested in the concept of animal rights?"

Ahmed responded, "Animal rights—that is a moral question. What do I look like, an Inman?"

They chuckled. They took an inventory of the heroin, estimated the weight, took pictures, then they completely burned it. They let the mules go. The mules did an about-face and headed back in the direction of Afghanistan.

They started to walk back toward the exfil location, with Paul escorting the prisoner, while Ahmed and Joe walked behind with the guns at the ready, just in case Juarez had any other friends around.

As they continued further down the goat trail and approached the Chinese border, the blast was loud and created a huge dust ball of debris that could be seen for miles in each direction—a black and gray mushroom cloud, spiraling clockwise as it reached out for the heavens.

Joe, who was walking the furthest back of the four, had been thrown backward and, apart from some superficial cuts and scrapes, escaped unharmed. Ahmed, who was closer to the blast than Joe, was also thrown backward. He also received some cuts but was remarkably less banged up than even Joe.

Juarez took the bulk of the IED blast, and his body parts were spewed out all over the place. Head, chest, a left leg, and foot were seen in various directions, forty to fifty feet away from the epicenter of the explosion.

Paul was heard moaning. His left leg and right hand were missing ... but he was alive. Joe rushed over with Ahmed and applied a tight tourniquet to the two affected areas. Joe was not sure if Paul would survive. He would be carried out back to the exfil spot, which was still probably three and a half to four miles away. Hopefully, the Chinese military and Ray had heard the explosion and would be coming toward them.

In so much pain, he almost passed out, Paul told Ahmed to take pictures of the blast area and Juarez's body parts, as evidence there was nothing they could have done to prevent his death.

As they headed down the goat path, about a mile further, Ray and five Chinese soldiers, including a medic, greeted them. They cleaned Paul up as much as possible and retied his tourniquets. Joe asked if they could get a helicopter to get Paul to a hospital. The commanding officer apologized but said there were no helicopters in the area that could help.

An hour later, they got Paul and the others to an Army hospital on the outskirts of Tashkurgan. Paul was rushed into surgery. Joe and Ahmed were seen by an emergency nurse, and their cuts and bruises were cleaned up. Ray remained with Joe and Ahmed for the next couple of hours when the commanding Chinese officer of the Army base asked to speak privately with Ray.

The two of them walked down the hospital hallway, some twenty-five feet away. The officer was speaking quietly to Ray, and suddenly, Ray started yelling and screaming. Two other Army personnel rushed to where the argument was occurring, pulled Ray away from the commanding officer, and escorted him in another direction further down the hall.

Ahmed couldn't hear what the officer was saying, but he heard Ray yelling back at him, essentially saying, "You can't do this. These people are heroes!"

With no context, he was not sure what it all meant ... until a couple of minutes later.

The commanding officer came over to where Ahmed and Joe were, and in English announced, "Gentlemen, under the powers given to me by our government, you are both under arrest for violating an order of the Chinese government."

"An order? What order?" asked Ahmed.

"You were ordered to bring Juarez back alive."

"We couldn't. He was killed, not by us, but by an IED blast nobody knew was coming. Look at the other American, he lost his leg and hand due to that same blast. It's a miracle he is not dead as well."

"He is being arrested too. You two will be held here at the base jail. When Paul is stable, all three of you will be transported to our Western Region main military base in Urumqi, where you will stand trial for this violation."

Ahmed and Joe look at each other, astonished. They could not believe it. Two Chinese security soldiers handcuffed them both. What would their penalty be after their expected ten-minute trial?

Chapter Forty-Nine

LANCASTER ARRIVED AT THE BEAUTIFUL BEIJING HILTON with Michael Demsky and Lin Chow, a Chinese lawyer who attended Southwestern Law School in Los Angeles, not too far from his alma mater, the University of Southern California. While Lancaster was five years older than Lin, they both thought they knew some of the same people, including professors, but were not one hundred percent sure. Lin knew many of the same streets, restaurants, and sports teams from his days back in Los Angeles. So, there was this sort of loose connection, even though Lin had returned to China, and had been practicing law here for over twenty years.

The Chinese assigned a government attorney to each member of the Israeli legal delegation, and Lin filled that role, being assigned to Steven Lancaster. They had just finished their third day of Chinese presentations on what their proposals were to support the Birobidzhan plan. Today was an overview of the proposed dam China would build, which would supply electricity to the greater region.

The three were dressed in business suits. They were a little tired from information overload, but still all excited and optimistic about the real possibility that this project could become a historic reality. They had just been seated in a booth and were going to have dinner. Steven could not believe he was going to eat at the hotel's Oklahoma Steak House, some six thousand miles from Oklahoma.

"May I bring you gentlemen cocktails?" the waiter in this mostly westerner-visited establishment asked."

Lancaster and Demsky thought it was funny that the Chinese staff in the restaurant wore cowboy hats, shirts, and boots. The typical cowboy song describing a broken pickup truck and a dead dog was played in the background on the restaurant's speakers.

Michael ordered a rum and coke, Steven a wheat IPA, and Lin a dirty martini, with Tang Ten, straight up, no ice, with two olives.

After the waiter went off to fill the drink orders, Michael said, "Lin, every presentation seems to get better and better. I am extremely excited about all this."

"I have to say I agree with that too," said Steven. "The proposals by your government have been very well thought out. The highway and railroad systems should make the transportation of goods and people extremely efficient."

"And the international airport, plus the harbor the Russians will build—amazing," said Michael.

Lin added, "We want this to work. With the influx of Jewish people into the region, along with Israel's scientific and business expertise, I don't think anyone can feel anything other than total optimism."

"I am no economist," interjected Steven, "but am glad neither your country nor the Russians have the enormous amount of debt that many other countries have. If either of your countries did, this project would not be able to get any financing. If we looked anywhere else, I could not see myself recommending such a project. Hell, Africa, South America, Mexico, Greece, Turkey, and Brazil are for all practical purposes, bankrupt and could all default on their debt at any time it seems."

"Those countries are out of control. No fiscal discipline," said Lin.

"Who would have thought even Russia, through Putin, would be in as good a shape as they are? In all the years I had lived there, it certainly was not. I will move back to Birobidzhan, and just keep a winter place in Israel," said Michael. "I can't believe all this."

Lancaster took it all in. His earlier skepticism, that Russia and the U.S.S.R were always considered the evil empire, the bad guys, the enemies of the United States, was shifting. Maybe they really were legitimate.

Michael asked Steven if a deal were to be made for the Autonomous region, who would regulate civil liberties there, the Israelis or the Russians?

Lancaster paused, put his right elbow on the table, and brought his hand underneath his chin. "Good Question. I would assume Israel, but I would imagine that would be part of the negotiations. I just cannot see Russian police enforcing laws inside Israeli sovereign territory. Do you have any concerns?"

A pause. Michael had a lump in his throat. "Thinking about women's rights, LGBTQ that sort of thing."

"I see your point. The Russians haven't completely embraced those liberties."

Lin said, "They certainly haven't here in China. I wouldn't worry too much about that, Michael."

"You never know these days," said Michael.

All three smiled.

The three continued their conversation as the drinks, and later their meals, were served. As they were finishing, a Chinese man in a tuxedo, who was not wearing a cowboy hat or cowboy boots, walked up to their table carrying a cell phone. The Maître D' spoke first to Lin Chow in Chinese, but Steven was able to pick out his own name.

"STEVEN, YOU HAVE AN IMPORTANT PHONE CALL. IF YOU would be so kind as to take the phone," said Lin.

"Phone call? Who knows I am even here?"

"Certainly, my government does. They know I am hosting you. They know exactly where I am."

The Maître D' handed Lancaster the phone.

"Steven Lancaster."

"Mr. Lancaster, my name is Arthur Fields. I work for the United States Secretary of State. I am attaché with the United States Consulate office here in Urumqi."

"Urumqi," said Lancaster, "Where is that, and how did you know where to find me?"

"Urumqi is in Western China. A couple of thousand miles west of Beijing. My office knew you were somewhere in

China because when you entered the country with your passport. The international database system informed us you were here. As to your specific whereabouts, we contacted the Chinese government, and they knew exactly who you were and where you were located. Modern science I guess."

"I say, big brother knows everything these days," added Lancaster.

"Look, they do, but I don't want to focus on that now. We have a situation here and your help is needed at once."

"What could you possibly need me for? I don't work for the U.S. government anymore."

"You have a couple of friends here that are behind bars in a Chinese military prison. They are requesting your help."

"Is this supposed to be a funny joke? I don't know anyone else here in China, especially in 'A-room-key' or whatever you say is the name of the city."

"It's Urumqi"

"Okay, Urumqi. That isn't part of a project I am working on."

"This isn't a mistake. The Chinese military has your friends Joseph Reid and Paul Dos Santos in custody. Mr. Paul Dos Santos is in a military hospital and is in critical condition. They are both awaiting a trial by the Chinese military. It is not clear what the specific charges are, but my office is concerned they are going to be charged with murder."

"I am at a loss," said Steven. "I don't know what this is about, but yes, I do know both people."

Next to Steven, Lin Chow was on his cell phone, learning more about the nature of what was going on. He was speaking to the commanding military officer in Urumqi to get more information. Michael Demsky knew something serious was happening, but he remained silent.

Meanwhile, Steven said to the U.S. consulate attaché, "Let me get your name again and contact information. I will see what I can do and will call you right back."

Steven hung up the phone, and seconds later, Lin hung up too.

Steven looked over to Lin and said, "That was our U.S. Consulate office in Urumqi."

Lin was ahead of Steven. "Yes, I know. It seems a couple of your associates are in a military prison there, awaiting trial on some charges that they violated Chinese orders. One of them has lost a leg and a hand due to an explosion. Both men are requesting your immediate help."

"What can we do?"

Lin picked up his cell phone, spoke in Chinese to some person on the other end of the call, and within three or four minutes, hung up.

"We are flying to Urumqi right now. There is a Chinese government jet that is waiting. We will be at the airport in twenty minutes."

"What about Michael?"

"He will have to stay here. We need to get there now!"

Chapter Fifty

PAUL WAS RECOVERING AT THE URUMQI CHINESE MILITARY hospital in their version of the Intensive Care Unit. He had just completed his fifth surgery in four days. Joe and Ahmed were locked up in a separate area of the prison, both in solitary confinement cells. Being an American, Joe was treated better than Ahmed. He had decent food delivered to him three times a day; his cell had a window, a small black and white television, and a western-style toilet that flushed.

Ahmed, on the other hand, was in a windowless cell, had a gaping hole for a toilet, canned soup twice a day, a mattress on the floor, and no television. Neither of the two was informed of any specific trial dates, other than it would be "quite soon". They were being held for violating a Chinese order to bring Juarez back alive even though they had nothing to do with his death. That did not matter. Joe and Ahmed had no idea about how Paul was. None of the three had spoken with any lawyers. Joe did not even know if he would be entitled to one. What they also did not know was that

Lancaster was now aware of their predicament and was on his way.

A government car met Steven and Lin Chow at the military airbase in Urumqi in a black, made in China, GMC Denali SUV. Arthur Fields, the U.S. consulate attaché, was waiting for the two at the reception area inside the prison. Lin Chow knew nothing more than what was said on the phone to Steven and himself. Consistent with Chow's effort to make the Birobidzhan deal a success, he wanted to accommodate Lancaster as much as possible, and keep China on his good side.

As they walked through the reception doors, Fields was there and greeted them both. Also present was a Chinese military officer, who, in English, directed the small group to an adjacent conference room where they could have some privacy.

When the three were seated, the military officer who remained standing spoke:

"Mr. Reid, Mr. Dos Santos, and one of our Uighur agents working with them, a Mr. Ahmed, were arrested. They were assisting our people in a narcotics operation, including the apprehension of an important drug trafficker near our border with Afghanistan."

Steven asked, "Why were they assisting in a Chinese drug enforcement operation?"

The officer responded by saying, "I assume it is to do with their military background. It is something you can ask your government. This trafficker was a Colombian cartel member. He was smuggling heroin into our country. The Colombian used a lot of locals to aide him. The locals are primarily Chinese people of Uighur descent. We Han Chinese have a difficult time penetrating this kind of cultural roadblock and had a plan put together that white Americans traveling into the area would not be suspected by the cartel, but merely considered tourists, allowing us to get close and shut down their operation."

"But why Joe and Paul? This is your country's issue. Why did you need them? I am still having difficulty following all this."

"Joe and Paul wanted to go after him as well. We did not really ask, as we just assumed it was your government that wanted him, and they were your agents. Your friends were given specific orders by Chinese officials that the main drug suspect was not to die. We demanded he be brought back to stand trial. Your friends violated the order since he died. Because of that, our government is prosecuting them."

"And Paul is in critical condition. What happened to him?"

"Things are a little unclear. Your Joe said Paul was walking the prisoner down a goat trail and claims an explosion blew the two up. Paul was hurt badly and has lost a leg. The Colombian was blown apart and died at the scene."

"And they are responsible because he died in an explosion caused by someone else?"

"We are looking into all this. But they were ordered to bring him back alive."

"Oh, come on. Really? A man lost his own limbs in the same explosion, and you have him in prison? Who was this Colombian trafficker?"

"His name was Juan Juarez."

"Who is that?" asked Lancaster.

"Your man Joe said you know him. He also goes by another name: Señor X."

Steven paused and immediately felt a little dizzy. He eased back into his chair. In shock, he was quiet and conscious of his every breath as he realized they were talking about the man who had forced him to smuggle drugs when he was just eighteen. The man responsible for killing his father. Now he was dead, while Paul had lost two limbs. Paul and Joe went after Señor X for me? They got retribution, and now they are in prison? He sat there, holding back angry tears. He had to get his friends out.

"May I see them now?" he asked.

"We will let you see Mr. Joe Reid only. We will give you and Mr. Lin Chow five minutes. Wait and I will have him brought in here."

The two waited.

As Steven was taking this all in, Lin Chow said quietly in his ear, "I am deeply sorry about all this."

Steven merely looked at Lin and slowly nodded his head once. His furious facial expression said it all.

Joe was brought into the room and was immediately at a loss for words to find Steven there. The two men hugged, both holding back tears. "What in the hell are you doing here?" said Joe.

Lancaster said, "What am I doing here? What are you doing here? On second thoughts, do not answer. I kind of found out."

"I don't know what to say," said Joe, "except it would be nice if you could get us the hell out of here. They may try to charge Paul and me with murder."

"I am trying to get you out," said Lancaster, who then turned toward Lin Chow and said, "I am so fucking pissed at your government." Lancaster turned back toward Joe, "And that Paul lost his hand and leg in the explosion that killed Señor X."

"Yes. And you need to get Ahmed out of here too."

"Who is Ahmed?"

He did the mission with us. He is a Chinese agent of Uighur descent. The Uighurs are treated like second-class citizens. He will not have a chance in here. He also won't have a future in this country, given how they treat the Uighur people."

Steven was quick to think. "Okay, Joe. I got it. I have a plan. Our time is limited. I want to get you guys out of here today. I want to go outside with Mr. Chow here, along with an American State Department official in the reception area, I need to speak with them both."

"Do what you need to do. I am not going anywhere."

Lin opened the door and spoke to someone down the hallway in Chinese. A soldier came to the door and went inside to be with Joe. Steven and Lin left the room and walked briskly back toward the reception area where Arthur was sitting. Lancaster was extremely angry yet focused on the task at hand.

"Let's go outside for a few minutes," Steven said to Arthur.

"Yea, sure."

The three went outside and Steven spoke to Arthur. "I have two Americans and one Chinese Uighur national who assisted our guys in an important mission. Long story short, they are all innocent, but I am afraid a Chinese kangaroo court could make matters worse for all of them, certainly the Uighur. I want to go back in there and see if the Uighur would be willing to request and accept political asylum in the U.S. If he does not get asylum, even if he were to be released by the Chinese military, his life will most likely never be the same."

"Let me see what I can do and make a call," said Arthur.

Steven looked back to Lin, and said, "Let's go back and see if we can meet with this Ahmed."

They headed back to the conference room, where Joe and his soldier guard were still there.

Lin told the soldier in Chinese, "They want to speak with the Uighur Ahmed that was with them."

The soldier excused himself and told Lin he would ask his commander. The door was shut.

Joe chimed in, "We need to get Ahmed out of here."

Lancaster said, "Damn right."

Lin responded, "We know. Otherwise, Ahmed will be in serious trouble."

Some ten minutes later, Ahmed was led to the conference room. There was a quick introduction and then Lancaster told Ahmed he was familiar with what had happened, that he was friends with Paul and Joe, and that he knew Ahmed was a Uighur even though he served as a Chinese agent. He knew they were being charged and asked Ahmed whether, if they could get him amnesty in the United States, would he be interested?

Ahmed's eyes lit up. Without any hesitation at all, and with a smile on his face, Ahmed said, "Yes. I am not married. My parents are gone. I have just one sister here. I would be in danger, not only from the Chinese government, but if I were released from prison, by my own people. It would be my dream to come to the United States."

"Okay, stand-by, Mr. Ahmed. Wait here, Joe." The soldier entered the door as Steven headed back toward reception, followed by Lin. Steven gestured for Arthur and Lin Chow to go back outside, which they did. Immediately, Lin picked up his phone and made a call to someone.

Steven asked Arthur, "Could we get him asylum?"

"The answer is yes. My people spoke to some guy from your old office. A Mr. Jones?"

"Jones?" said Steven. "I don't know any Jones."

"No, I am sorry, a Smith. Anyway, the recommendation is, if you say yes and can pull this off with the Chinese government, he can get asylum."

A minute or so later, Lin pressed the mute button on his cellphone and looked over at Lancaster two feet away.

Lancaster raised his chin slightly to ask what was up.

"I am talking to my supervisor in Beijing," Lin said. "They have promised to look into the matter more carefully."

"More carefully?" Lancaster was thinking of an idea he'd come up with on the flight over from Beijing to Urumqi. "Tell your boss bullshit, and use that word. If they do not agree to release all three right now, I will do everything I can to blow-up the entire Birobidzhan deal."

Lin was taken aback. He told the person on the other end of his phone to hold for a moment, considered further what Lancaster just said, went back to his cell, spoke some Chinese for a few more minutes, then hung up."

Lin, with a slight smile on his face, told Arthur and Lancaster, "Let us go back inside the prison and get these guys out of here and on a plane now. The Chinese government has accepted your demand, including not opposing Ahmed's request for asylum."

They walked back to the conference room and Steven told Joe and Ahmed, "We are getting all of you on a plane right now to the United States. Ahmed, you are offered asylum in the United States of America."

Joe and Ahmed were completely elated and teared up. Everyone hugged each other. Lancaster had Lin summons the guard and they asked to see Paul to tell him the news.

As Ahmed, Steven, Lin, and Joe were escorted over to the hospital wing, Steven turned to Joe and Ahmed. "I hope this doesn't interrupt any plans you have."

Joe just smiled. Ahmed had not stopped smiling since he got the news.

Ahmed turned to Joe, and with a huge smile said, "Okay, big man, tell me now what Erection is?"

Lancaster spun around to face Ahmed and Joe. "What?!"

———

LANCASTER MET WITH PAUL. HE WAS AS SURPRISED TO SEE Lancaster as Joe was.

Lancaster told Paul, "We cannot speak about anything now other than you are leaving for the United States as soon as possible, along with Joe and Ahmed."

About an hour later, Paul was being taken out of the military hospital on a gurney, followed by Joe and Ahmed walking behind. Arthur, Lin Chow, and Lancaster were waiting to make sure they got into their transportation to the airport.

As they were loading into the van, Ahmed walked by Lin Chow and handed him an envelope. Lancaster noticed this but did not think much about it. It was probably just some Chinese government formality. Perhaps just a thank you note.

Chapter Fifty-One

STEVEN WAS GRATEFUL FOR LIN'S COOPERATION AND efforts to help get the three released. He told him he was sorry for getting mad at him earlier. In hindsight, he felt he could not have done this without his help. Paul, Joe, and Ahmed were now in the United States.

After a couple more days of meetings back in Beijing, Lancaster and Michael flew to Tel Aviv. Lancaster would have a few days there to meet with other attorneys of the Israeli delegation to review documents, relevant information, consider the legality of it all, and make recommendations to both the Israeli Parliament and Prime Minister. His optimism about the Birobidzhan deal returned after he was able to compose himself again.

Michael and Steven both had rooms at the Hyatt in Jerusalem. They agreed to meet for dinner at 7 p.m. The Hyatt Italian restaurant was recommended to them by other members of the delegation. Michael told Lancaster in the afternoon that a friend from his past would be joining them.

"Fine," Steven replied, thinking nothing of it.

When Steven arrived, Michael was already seated enjoying a glass of white wine. There were three places set and three glasses of water on the table.

"Greetings Michael," said Steven, "how was your afternoon?"

"Oh, it was fine. A cousin of mine drove up from Ashdod, met me at the pool, and visited for a couple of hours. After that, I rested a bit, then reviewed a draft of an education curriculum for elementary schools in Birobidzhan. And you?"

"After calming down from getting my friends out of jail, I went over some legal things: proposals for border crossing protocol, weight limitations for trucks on highways, a lot of important, but not all that stimulating stuff."

The two ordered cocktails. They both had a little toast to Birobidzhan. Steven noticed Michael's eyes start to water. Tears began to trickle down his cheeks. He grabbed the napkin from his lap, and gently wiped them.

"Is everything okay," asked Steven?

There was a brief pause as Michael composed himself. "Remember when we first flew over to here from Los Angeles, and I told you my family dynamics were somewhat complicated and unique?"

"I do."

Steven considered his own family dynamics. His daughter Ashley not knowing who her biological father was, his own mother and father; the stories he learned over the years as a prosecutor. Frankly, there was nothing that Michael could say that would surprise him. Besides, Michael seemed a generally calm and a grounded kind of guy.

"Oh, go ahead and tell me."

"You asked me on the flight if I was married or had kids, and I told you one kid is in the Army, lives up north, and my spouse spends a lot of time down south in Eilat, with our daughter, her husband, and grandson." Michael appeared nervous and uncomfortable.

"I remember."

"That is all true, but probably not exactly what you might have envisioned. I hope this doesn't change our nice relationship, but Steven my spouse is my husband."

There was a slight pause. "Well, that's okay. I don't mind if you are gay."

Another slight pause as more tears trickled from Michael's eyes. "That is not it. Steven, I used to be a woman."

Lancaster stared. Never at a loss for something immediate to say, this time was different. He picked up his wine glass and took a long gulp.

After he set his glass down, he said, "I'm not sure how to respond."

Now Michael's facial expression changed a little, reflecting a tiny smile. "My previous name was Michele. I am the birth mother of my two kids. About fifteen years ago, I could not be myself anymore. I had known for a long time, I never felt right being in a woman's body, so I began my transition."

"Ah, okay," said Lancaster, still searching for something meaningful to say. He felt empathy for Michael and was accepting of what he was saying, but he did not understand everything. "And your husband?"

"He is a champ. He has stayed with and supported me. He is the biological father of my kids."

Michael considered what Michael had just said. He was thinking what a brave person Michael was for telling him this. A couple of other things suddenly made sense. Michael peeing in the bathroom stall as opposed to the urinal; what the Rabbi told him in Ashdod—that he was not who he appeared to be; his questions about civil liberties in the Autonomous Region.

They both paused for a minute, each hoping the other would take over the conversation.

"Michael, I want to apologize in advance, as I am not real knowledgeable about this subject matter or trends. So, forgive me if I do not say the right words. I do not wish to hurt you or make you feel bad. Does this mean you are really a girl?"

Michael smiled some more, which gave Lancaster some comfort so he could smile back.

"I don't consider myself so. I underwent hormonal therapy, that is why you see my beard. I had my breasts removed as well."

"Thank you for trusting me and telling me this. Does this mean you are your kids' mother, father, what are you?"

"We have to continue this conversation later, as here comes our surprise guest."

"Oh yes, I forgot."

Michael smiled a little bit. "Here he is," said Michael. "Please don't mention anything about this to him."

Steven looked back over his left shoulder to see who this mystery person was. "No shit," said Steven, as he saw him walking briskly toward the table with a huge smile.

Lancaster got up. He smiled back. It was true that he had not seen him in twenty-five to thirty years, but frankly, this was not his favorite person in the world. Lancaster had invited his old law school roommate, Stephen Weinstein, to attend his wedding to Claire just a few years ago and remembered he did not even receive the courtesy of a response.

"Steven, I think you know Stephen."

Stephen Weinstein said, "We absolutely do. We were roommates in law school for all three years. A lot of memories with this guy. In law school, he was David, not Steven."

Michael said, "You were David, not Steven? What does that mean?"

"It means I had a name change. I had an unfortunate incident during finals week, my last semester in law school. In the mid-1980s my father was murdered. They thought it was organized crime that did it. My mother was also threatened. Because of that, I changed my name to Steven Lancaster from David Miller. I don't speak about it much because it was such a horrible experience for me."

"Oh, Steven, I am so sorry to hear that. How did you end up picking the name of Steven Lancaster," asked Michael?

"I wanted to name myself after Stephen here." He pointed to Stephen Weinstein.

"Oh bullshit," said Weinstein. "Although, if that were true, it would have been nice of you. How is married life this time around? Sorry I wasn't able to make it."

"Make it?! You didn't even respond!"

"You know, David; I mean, Steve … Back then, you know that I know that you know, your then employer the Justice Department was investigating me. So, I was uncomfortable. I wasn't even sure if it was you that was heading the investigation."

"They asked me about you. I knew you were doing some bankruptcy, and I told them, since we were roommates previously, I could not get involved and had to recuse myself from any part of your investigation. So, I am sorry. I can see your point, but you should have just sent a declination to the wedding invitation. Common courtesy. Anyway, obviously, they found no evidence of any wrongdoing because if you were ever prosecuted, I would have heard about it."

"That is true. I was always clean."

"Really?!"

"I don't deny being aggressive and taking things to the limit, but I never crossed any lines."

"Are you still practicing in the Beverly Hills area?"

"No, I retired a couple of years ago. It is nice not having to deal with clients anymore. I assume you know about that guy I helped write that fictional book on pulling off a bankruptcy fraud?"

"Yea I know, and it turned out he committed a fraud on you because he was merely picking your brain on how to get away with a crime. Then he acted out on it. Our office briefly looked at that to see if there was some conspiracy between him and you, but concluded you got taken as well."

"Exactly. Was he ever caught?"

"No idea. Were you really helping him with a story?"

"I thought I was. After he left my office for the consultation, I learned he was a guy that quit a hedge fund, and that is when I suspected he'd used me. He was a complete con artist. On top of that, the guy never even paid my author-consulting bill. He stiffed me."

"So," Lancaster turned toward Michael Demsky, "how do you two know each other?"

"From a fundraiser in Los Angeles," said Michael.

"I have known Michael for maybe two or three years. We met at a Zion Federation of Los Angeles charitable function. I was on their board; Michael was a member visiting from Israel. I think sometime during the event, he started talking about this Birobidzhan idea."

"You did?" Lancaster looked at both Michael and Weinstein. "How come this is the first I have even heard of this?"

"I didn't want you to know," said Weinstein. "I told Michael not to say anything. Somehow, Michael knew the cantor from that synagogue in Encino. We were looking for an experienced attorney to become part of the project. Someone with knowledge of United States Federal Law. I'd heard nothing but good things about you and I knew from law school days you were smart. I knew you worked for the Justice Department after that. I figured you might be a good fit, so I had the cantor and Michael try to recruit you."

Lancaster turned to Michael. "Why didn't you tell me this?"

"The truth is, he said I shouldn't. He wanted to keep this quiet. He felt that if you knew he was involved, you might not want to do this because maybe you felt he was dirty." Now looking at Weinstein: "True?" Weinstein nodded in the affirmative. Michael continued, "Which he wasn't, and we simply wanted the best person for this, and felt you would be a great candidate."

Turning now toward Stephen Weinstein, Lancaster asked, "I have been on this project for maybe a couple of months now. We are almost done with it. I have never seen you around. Never heard your name. Nothing. If you are involved with this project, why am I only hearing about you now for the first time?"

"I thought you might ask me that. The best way to describe it is thinking of me as part of a layer of people that independently reviews the work of your delegation to supply impartial comment to the Israeli leadership. I report directly to the Prime Minister, and they asked our small group to keep an arm's length distance from your delegation to ensure our impartiality. The Prime Minister has me review reports, give him feedback, and he insisted that we be separate from the actual delegation."

"So, you have known everything all along?"

"As much as I could. I knew eventually I would have to let you know. Since the project is almost over, I figured this would be as good a time as any to break the silence."

"Wow, said Lancaster. Well, I am glad you did. Would you gentlemen like to order dinner?"

Lancaster, who now supported the Birobidzhan project could not help but feel he had been had or used. He did not know how or in which way, but thought this was weird. Conversely, Lancaster knew of himself to be quite skeptical of everything, including his occasional overreaction to things he heard. Was this simply another overreaction? It could be. He could understand the Israeli's desiring a neutral in-between advisor to the Prime Minister; someone who did not want to be influenced by people directly affiliated with the delegation. But why Weinstein? What did Michael Demsky know? Lancaster felt that while Weinstein was never convicted or indicted of any criminal wrongdoing, there was still something a little shady about him. He did not completely trust him. The Israelis should know this. This was a bit weird. While Lancaster had only known Michael a brief time, he seemed like a nice enough guy. Certainly sincere in his work and desire to see Birobidzhan succeed. Maybe Lancaster really was overreacting and unnecessarily skeptical?

Michael said, "So guys, tell me some stories about your law school days?"

"There are lots of stories," said Lancaster.

"Yes, there are," said Weinstein. "Well, let me start. If you've never been to the University of Southern California campus, it is in a lousy area. High crime. The campus is nice and safe, but we had to live off-campus. Our first year we lived in the neighborhood next to the university. We got broken into ... what do you reckon, Lancaster? Two or three times?"

"I remember, let me think. Twice. The burglary when we were both in class. They stole a small Sony television and your microwave. But the second time, we were there and sleeping. Someone tried to break into our front door. We both got up, and you said to me, 'Give me that gun,' and I said, loud enough so the intruder could hear us, 'Here you go, and I have my shotgun too.' Even though we did not have any guns. That worked and the guy took off."

"Then there is the greatest story of all time," said Weinstein. "I would not have believed it if I weren't there. You and I went to Vons Grocery store on Olympic in Santa Monica.

You had your white Honda Civic. We picked up some groceries, left the store, went into your car, and started driving home. No big deal. We drive about a mile or so, I asked you when did you get that crucifix hanging from your rearview mirror and that little Jesus statue on your dashboard. You said 'What?' looked up, and something like, 'I didn't put that there.' Then you looked around the car and saw some clothes or something in the back seat and said, 'Shit! This isn't my car.' And it was not. We drove back to Vons, parked that Honda, and found yours in another isle. Your key fit both Hondas. And the cars, both white, looked identical"

"Yes, that was the most ridiculous experience I ever had. We just locked up the one Honda, took our groceries out, jumped into mine, and left. I wonder if that other guy ever found out?"

"Another thing we would do, Michael, was take Weinstein's old Chrysler, and go cruising Wednesday night up in the valley."

"Yea. We would cruise Van Nuys Blvd."

"But what you did was pretty sick, Weinstein."

"You mean the ignition thing?"

"Of course. Check this out, Michael," as he looked over at Demsky, then back to Weinstein. "We would cruise in this rusty old Chrysler ... whatever it was. Weinstein had a Jimmy Carter for president and Steve Garvey is #1, bumper stickers on the back of his car."

Weinstein smiled over at Demsky. "I actually did!"

"Anyway, we would cruise alongside someone, say some girls, maybe walking on the sidewalk. Then Weinstein would go to his ignition on the column and, as we were driving, he would turn the ignition off, then back on, and do you know what would happen when he did this, Michael?"

"I have no idea."

"When you turn the ignition back on, it creates a large bang, like an explosion in your exhaust system, and it would scare the hell out of everyone around."

"It does?" asked a smiling Michael.

"Yea, and it was hysterical, until maybe the tenth or fifteenth time we did it. The car's muffler blew up."

Michael said, "That's what you guys did for fun growing up in Los Angeles?"

"We also went to a bunch of University of Southern California football games, including that Notre Dame game in the rain. That was fun. We weren't too far from where the Dodgers played and did that a few times."

"Yes, but that is before we moved closer to the beach. That apartment was great. Two blocks from Santa Monica Pier."

"And it was rent-controlled. We paid less there, then our dump near campus. And there were always beautiful women around, rollerblading in bikinis. I loved that."

"Me too."

"Remember that girl you went out with Weinstein? You brought her back to the apartment, and she got undressed in the bathroom, then walked into my bedroom naked?"

"Kim was her name. And you always said she went to your room on purpose and that it wasn't a mistake."

"It wasn't. She wanted me."

"Right. Dream on."

"I did her."

"No, you didn't."

Michael interjected, "So, did you guys ever talk about practicing law together?"

"We did," said Weinstein.

"That's true," added Lancaster. "He was interested in personal injury law. I was thinking about Workers' Compensation. We thought since they were both injury-related law, one would complement the other well."

"So why didn't you do it?"

Lancaster looked over at Weinstein. "I think we both considered it for a while. I worked for a Workers' Compensation firm. You worked for a personal injury firm. We talked about each working at separate firms for a couple of years, getting some experience, then maybe starting our own firm."

"So, what happened?" asked Michael.

"It just never materialized. I did my two years, went out, and opened my own doors. In fact, my office was across the street from Valley Har Shalom. The place I met you. I then kind of had that unpleasant experience with ... the cantor told you the story, Michael, of Dr. Schlomo."

"Oh yes, I heard that particular story. And then years later you caught him smuggling drugs into the U.S. using dogs or something."

Weinstein said, "I knew you took a job with the Justice Department but never heard that Dr. Schlomo story before. Anyway, after you went to work for them, at some point after that, I switched to bankruptcy law. We both kind of did our own things."

"That's true."

The three continued to talk for another hour or more. It was nice, but Lancaster still had an odd feeling about this coincidence. He just could not get his arm around it.

AFTER DINNER, LANCASTER WENT FOR A WALK BY HIMSELF up to the main outdoor market area of Jerusalem. He came upon the booth he was looking for. They were selling disposable cell phones, and Lancaster wanted one. He wanted to call the states and he needed to make sure nobody would be listening to his call.

After buying the phone, and on his walk back to the hotel, he called his friend in San Francisco.

"Smith," the person on the phone answered.

"Smith, Lancaster."

"Hey, what are you doing?"

"I am in Israel and need your help."

There was no small talk or catching up. Smith was always smart enough not to ask or question Lancaster over the telephone for any nosy details. If Lancaster wanted to tell him something on his own, that would have to come from him.

"Something is fishy here," said Lancaster. "Between you and me, I am working on a project that involves the state of Israel and this Jewish Autonomous Zone in Siberia, called Birobidzhan. Take down these names: Stephen Weinstein from

Santa Monica, and Michael Demsky from Ashdod, Israel. In fact, add to that a cantor named Eric Weinberg from the Encino, California area." Lancaster pauses for a moment.

"Something may be up. See if these three guys have any connection, economic interests, anything at all associated with the Birobidzhan region of Siberia."

"Why would you say that?"

"Not sure. But things lately have happened, and I am always the last person to find out, usually after the fact. This time, I want to be a little more proactive, and not behind the ball. I might be out of my mind and on a total fishing expedition, but ... I am not sure of anything anymore."

"Let me look into this. I'll have something for you in a day or two."

"Try to keep this to yourself. I am going back to California, day after tomorrow. I am going to assume you will discover something, although I am not sure what. We can meet at the Peking Duck Palace we used to go to in Chinatown, San Francisco?"

"About 12:30 Friday?"

"Works for me."

Chapter Fifty-Two

LANCASTER HAD BEEN BACK HOME IN CALIFORNIA FOR JUST twenty-four hours when he grabbed the 9:45 a.m. Southwest flight out of John Wayne Airport to Oakland, for his 12:30 p.m. China town lunch with his former forensic investigator Smith.

After landing, he took the BART right from the airport, rode it to the Oakland Coliseum station, changed trains, and grabbed a San Francisco bound train. He would exit at Montgomery Street for his short walk to China Town and the Peking Duck Palace. Flying into Oakland was much easier than directly into the San Francisco Airport. The weather in San Francisco was always hit and miss with fog. When it was foggy, they would either circle around in the sky for a while or be forced to fly somewhere else. Oakland did not have the fog risk of San Francisco, and using BART was just as quick into the city center. But his favorite reason for flying into Oakland instead of San Francisco: Rapid Reward Miles! There are a lot more flights into Oakland on Southwest than San Francisco, and Lancaster loved his Miles.

Lancaster arrived at the restaurant around 12:15, fifteen minutes before their meeting. Smith arrived some ten minutes later. They greeted each other with hugs, as they had not seen one another for several months. After they'd both ordered, they got down to business.

"Find anything out, Sergeant?" Smith had three of his four limbs blown off, but with his clothes and his prosthetic devices on, most people would not have a clue. He had been with the Justice Department for the last ten years. He was well-liked by everyone. Smith had won the Justice Department Award for Administrative Support Staff, twice.

"I did find something," said Smith. "It is weird. Then it gets weirder."

Lancaster smiled and shook his head in a, "I can't believe this" sort of gesture, as he wondered, yet again, how Smith always managed to find information.

"Great, another surprise. At least I am learning about this on my own, or at least with your help, rather than finding out the hard way. What'd you get?"

"Let me get the easy part out of the way first. This Cantor Weinberg, I do not see anything at all. But Demsky and Weinstein are a different story. It seems both have purchased options to buy real estate in the Birobidzhan region. Mr. Michael Demsky of Ashdod, Israel—the equivalent of five hundred acres, all within the city limits. Stephen Weinstein, an attorney from Santa Monica on the other hand, over two hundred thousand acres (about the area of Austin, Texas)." Smith paused.

Lancaster thought. *He knows that a real estate option is a mechanism to buy land at a certain price, within a limited amount of time. If they knew the land would go up in value because of a special announcement, they could purchase these options to buy, ridiculously cheap, and after the announcement, the value skyrockets, the owner of the land must sell it to them at the previously agreed cheap price. A way to make a large profit if you know what is going to happen ahead of time. And they did.*

"So, Smith, it sounds to me as if they would have a big payday if this deal goes through," said Lancaster who realized he just said something he should not have. He'd never mentioned anything about an Israeli-Birobidzhan deal to Smith before.

"What does that mean?" said Smith, who knew virtually nothing about the Israeli deal that was being worked on.

"Oh nothing," said Lancaster, wishing he hadn't said it. "I will tell you later, I promise."

"Then it gets weirder," said Smith.

"Weirder? Yes, you said that. Okay, tell me the weirder part."

"They both have even more options to buy real estate somewhere else."

"You're kidding me," said Lancaster. "Where?"

"Mexico. Specifically, Baja California"

"Mexico? What the fuck?"

You tell me, boss."

"I'm not your boss anymore. Just your friend now. I wonder what this is all about. Are you sure?"

"I am sure about the options these guys own. I have no clue about why they were acquired. You do what you want with this," said Smith.

"Oy vey iz mir."

"What does that mean?"

"It means I have been in a place where they speak a lot of Yiddish. It also means, 'Oh, my woes'."

"What are you going to do next, Lancaster?"

"Speak to my ethics attorney."

"What about?"

"Buying international real estate based upon inside information."

"We did those kinds of cases didn't we?"

"Not exactly these specific types of cases. We did cases based upon the buying of stocks and securities with inside information. I do not think this is in the same category. This is real estate. This also is more complicated for other reasons; like, it is not in the United States. That is why I want to meet with my ethics lawyer. Frankly, Smith, I have no idea if what they did is legal. I need to see Roger Goldman over at Briar and Watson"

"Can you afford Briar and Watson?"

"Not sure, but it doesn't matter. The Israeli government will pay my bill. Not sure even they can afford Briar and Watson. But not my problem."

Lancaster thought to himself, *What bothers me, is not the Birobidzhan real estate options, but the Mexican ones. Birobidzhan is easy to figure out. I can see that motivation. But Mexico? What the hell is going on here? Why am I not surprised Weinstein is somehow connected?*

Chapter Fifty-Three

LANCASTER WENT TO THE DOWNTOWN LOS ANGELES OFFICE of Briar and Watson, where Roger Goldman was expecting him. Goldman was the independent ethics attorney he hired at the advice of the Israeli government before he accepted the position.

Lancaster stopped at the reception desk, and half-jokingly asked, "Do you guys validate parking? I only have $100 with me?" In Los Angeles and, especially this building, a visitor needed to take a loan out to park here for more than an hour.

"Mr. Goldman will see you now. Do you know where his office is?"

"If he hasn't moved, yes I do."

"Hi Roger," said Lancaster. "Is this the same office I met you in last time I was here?"

"Well look out my window. Dodger Stadium still seems to be up on the hill."

"Guess I didn't notice last time." He looked at Roger's clothing. "Does your wearing an expensive suit allow you to bill me more?"

"Not you. Israel. We bill them directly. How are Claire and your daughter?"

"I forgot you knew Claire. She was once on a case with you?"

"Yes, she brought us in on a government fraud case we were defending. We were co-counsel with her."

"Great. I hope you both made a lot of money and lost the case." The former prosecutor felt a certain bias that most of these companies that were charged with fraud were guilty as hell.

They both smiled. "I don't remember what happened on that."

"So, what is going on Mr. former Prosecutor?"

"Something very strange is going on with this Israeli deal."

"Like what?" Goldman said in a tone that suggested he had heard every combination of "strange" that ever existed during his legal career.

"So that deal I mentioned to you previously in Siberia. Two people I know working on this project, have secretly bought options to buy real estate there, I assume in anticipation of the deal being made."

"Like insider trading, but with real estate?"

"Yes, exactly."

"Are the insiders Americans?"

"One is for sure. Not completely sure about the other."

Roger thought about this for a few seconds, and then said," My gut is, since this is not a stock, and this does not involve a corporation, I am not seeing any violation of U.S. law."

Lancaster considered his response. "This is still dirty, but you are probably right. What about Israeli or Russian law?"

"That, Sir, is outside the scope of my brilliance. Let me get one of my young crack international lawyers in here and see if she has any clues."

Roger hit a button on the phone atop his desk. "Melissa, it's Roger."

"Hi, Mr. Goldman"

"My father is Mr. Goldman, not me. I have told you a hundred times to call me Roger. Could you please come back here? We have a bar exam question for you on Israeli and Russian law."

"And Mexico," said Lancaster.

"Mexico?" said Roger. "Why Mexico?"

"The two also bought land options in Mexico and I have no idea why. I have a guess, but it is only a long-shot guess."

Melissa walked in the door.

Roger said to her, "Remember that former federal prosecutor client I was telling you about that is doing this special job for the Israeli government?"

"Yes."

"This is he, Steven Lancaster."

The two acknowledged each other with pleasant smiles, but no handshakes. You want to tell her, Steve, or do you want me to?"

"I don't know how much she already knows. So, you tell her."

"Melissa, this guy is a legal advisor for Israel. He is serving in the role of an American lawyer to make sure a potential land deal between Israel and Russia is legal both here and under international law. The deal involves Israel acquiring some land in the middle of nowhere, deep inside Siberia. Two guys Mr. Lancaster works with on this deal, in anticipation of the deal being made, and with their inside knowledge, have bought options to purchase real estate in the area and make a ton of money."

"So you want me to tell you if there is some Israeli or Russian insider trading violation being committed?"

"Exactly," said Roger.

"That's an easy one Mr. ... Roger. I was working on the same fact pattern yesterday!" she began sarcastically. "Are you out of your mind? I have no idea. Do you want to know if there are civil and criminal violations in both Russian and Israel? And I assume there are no securities involved?"

"True," said Roger.

"I am going to have to research this."

"And while you are at it, research the same facts, but use Mexico instead."

"Mexico. I thought you said this was an Israeli and Russian deal?"

"Let's assume, for simplicity, there is also an Israeli and Mexico deal."

"Let me look into this. I would assume there is no harm in Mr. Lancaster reporting this to the FBI, Russian, Israeli, and Mexican authorities just to cover his ass."

"That's a wise idea but check into both criminal and civil liability as well."

Melissa left the room.

"Give me a call in the next day, Roger, and think about whether I should really report this to law enforcement. I would prefer not to if possible. I am going to hold off on doing that part for now."

———————

STEVEN DROVE BACK HOME TO IRVINE. WHEN HE GOT there, neither Claire nor Ashley was home. He went into the den and turned on the television. The show that came on was *Cramer's Mad Money*. Steven was only half-listening to it as he simultaneously read the Los Angeles Times.

"So, you want to make some *Mad Money* next week?" came the voice from the television. "Let us look at who is coming out with earnings. Monday is General Motors and Pfizer. Tuesday is WhoWeR. Wednesday is Amazon and Apple, and Thursday is Kraft Foods. These are the ones to watch."

Steven's sat up straighter at the mention of WhoWeR, the company that had come up in conversation several times since he started working on the Birobidzhan project. He was not a big individual stock investor. He had a 401k and pension from when he worked at the Justice Department, which were mutual funds. He knew how stocks worked because those were the types of cases he prosecuted. But for his own account, he rarely invested or traded in individual stocks. He owned only the stock of one company now.

Lancaster turned up the volume on the television. "So, WhoWeR trades in this new ancestor DNA space. Kind of a high-tech biosciences data company. The company has been growing at an incredible rate of seventy-five percent per year. They still have not shown any profit, but then neither did Amazon for fifteen years. The street is predicting revenue growth of between another seventy-five to eighty percent, and a loss at somewhere between nine and eleven cents a share. If their revenue growth were to be reported higher, this stock will soar."

And then it hit Lancaster: the Israelis were being bombarded with inquiries about immigration. Many in the delegation were talking about how this new wave of DNA technology was shocking people throughout the world, that their blood showed significant Jewish heritage. More than likely, these people were the offspring of those that survived the Spanish and Portuguese Inquisition. And suddenly you have millions, tens of millions of people thinking, could I be Jewish? And these people are excited and want to learn more. How do they learn more? By spending the $250 each on WhoWeR tests.

And they would come out with Earnings Tuesday? That is the same day the Israeli Prime Minister is addressing the United Nations for an important announcement. Birobidzhan. Could one have something to do with the other?

He thought further, and for one of the first times in his life, it hit him over the head like a ton of bricks. He was ahead of the curve on what was about to happen, and he wanted to share what he knew with his friends. He was not a WhoWeR corporate insider. He was going to invite his friends over for a surprise breakfast party.

Chapter Fifty-Four

LANCASTER ARRANGED A MEETING OVER AT STEPHEN Weinstein's home in Santa Monica. He made sure Michael Demsky would also be in attendance. Neither Weinstein nor Demsky knew why Lancaster called for this meeting. The work of the Israeli Delegation on the Birobidzhan option was completed. It was in the hands of the Israeli legislature and Prime Minister. An announcement would be made at the United Nations in six days—next Tuesday.

Demsky had arrived before Lancaster and was visiting with Weinstein in the family room prior to his arrival. When Lancaster got there, he noticed Demsky sitting in a large comfortable leather chair, left leg crossed over his right, with the elevated foot moving back and forth quickly. He had never seen Demsky act in this matter. Obviously, he was nervous.

"It was nice catching up with you, Lancaster, in Tel Aviv," said Weinstein.

"It was nice, Weinstein. Those were good memories."

"Some of your stories were pretty wild," said Michael.

"So enough small talk. You would not tell me over the phone. Lancaster, why did you want this meeting?" asked Weinstein.

"You both seem a little nervous. I think you both know why. You guys used me."

Weinstein replied, trying to appear a little surprised. "We used you?"

"Yes. I worked, I guess now, with the both of you on this project, yet there were many secrets you both kept from me."

"Wait Lancaster, I was with you for virtually every minute. What secret, other than knowing Weinstein was involved, could I have kept from you?"

"Not mentioning Weinstein to me before was certainly a secret. But both of you had other concealed motives you kept secret." Demsky and Weinstein who were looking at Lancaster, turned to face each other with confused, and slightly worried, expressions.

"You both had options to purchase real estate in Birobidzhan."

There was silence for several seconds as Weinstein and Michael looked at each other again. They knew they'd been caught.

"And what if we did, Lancaster," said Weinstein. "So what? It is not illegal. Besides, I did think of telling you, but then you would have interpreted this the wrong way. Frankly, if you would have thought this project through, seen the potential for a real estate price explosion, you would have figured this out on your own, and done the same thing."

"No, I wouldn't. Contrary to your motivations, it's not always just about the money."

"Lancaster, you are such a righteous hypocrite. How can you of all people judge Michael or me? Look at yourself. You are the sneaky person here. How could you have even worked for the Justice Department? Why would they have hired you? They obviously never did a background check. You and I both know you did something you should not have between high school and college. You never told me the specifics, but I have enough pieces of your puzzle put together to create a clear picture of what you did.

"You told me you were in Colombia. Something bad happened to you. During law school, I saw you have many nightmares. You were always nervous—seemed to be constantly looking over your shoulder to see if someone was following you. You never had money issues—always paid your bills in cash, whether it was rent, going out, groceries, gas, everything. I never once ever saw you go to the bank. I'm not even sure you had a bank account. Where did all that cash you had come from?

"One time when we got drunk, you started to tell me you went to some meeting at a bar in Colombia, you never should have gone to. I asked you why, and you responded to me, something like, 'Oh, it was nothing,' then changed the subject. *Really?* I wondered. Then in the last week of law school, your father was murdered, in what was obviously a professional hit. You and your mother immediately changed your names. Your mother quit her position at the university. She moved out of her house. You told the police investigating your father's murder, you knew of nothing that would be of help to them in trying to solve the crime. Yea right. So, what does this suggest to me? It suggests you were involved with drug trafficking in Colombia, and something went wrong."

"You have it all wrong, Weinstein. You are trying to deflect your bad deeds, not by addressing the merits of your wrongdoing, but simply attacking me."

"As I said earlier, Lancaster, I considered mentioning this real estate option opportunity to you. This isn't illegal, and you are just pissed because you aren't included or weren't able to figure out this opportunity on your own."

"Really?" said Lancaster. "Well, I am not as smart as you, Weinstein. And, Demsky, I especially cannot figure you out on this? I thought you were a straight-up person who was only interested in doing the right thing. I didn't think it was about money for you. But even if I were to have figured that out, there was another little detail you thought I was not in the loop on. Another secret. You both also have options to purchase real estate in Baja California."

This was not something Weinstein or Demsky expected to hear from Lancaster. Now Michael and Weinstein looked at each other and both froze. They knew very well Lancaster was a retired financial fraud criminal prosecutor. Lancaster knew about Mexico, but what, specifically, did he know, and were they suddenly going to be somehow criminally prosecuted?

"What do you know about Mexico?" Weinstein asked Lancaster aggressively.

"Not going to tell you what I know."

It was becoming a bit of a poker game. Lancaster clearly understood the motivation to buy Russian real estate options but he could only guess about Mexico. But he was confident about one thing: both Demsky and Weinstein did not know what *he* did not know. Lancaster was making the ultimate bluff, playing this little scrap of information, and was going all-in.

"Then who told you?" said Demsky.

"Let's just say I know."

"So, go ahead and buy Birobidzhan and Baja options yourself."

"I could, but unlike the both of you, that's not why I worked on this deal."

"So why are you here? What do you want us to do? We want to make a deal for Israel as well. At the same time, neither of us has a problem with also making a few dollars on the side. There is nothing wrong with that. Nobody is getting hurt."

"Yes, Lancaster, that is the only reason I did it," said Demsky. "I wasn't out to screw anyone; certainly not you."

"Michael, I am disappointed. The Prime Minister's announcement is next Tuesday. I came to tell you there is something neither one of you knows about. There is actually a third option?"

"Really?" said Demsky.

"There is?" said Weinstein in a surprise.

"Surprised, Weinstein? Using your words, you should have figured this out on your own. I'm surely not going to tell either of you the specifics about it."

What do you think will happen to the both of you if this third option happens?" Lancaster chose his words carefully, knowing this other option he was speaking about had nothing to do with Israel. He wanted to watch them both struggle and question the speculative investments they had made.

"In light of all this, you may wish to question your Russia and Mexico purchases. It might be prudent for both of you to sell out your options before the Prime Minister's speech. Yes, you fools, because there is another option that will also become known on Tuesday ... and neither of you is even aware of it."

There was a pause for a few seconds.

"So, are you going to tell us?" asked Weinstein.

"No, you boys figure it out for yourselves."

"Get out of here, dick head!"

LANCASTER LEFT THE HOUSE. BOTH WEINSTEIN AND Demsky were completely baffled and flabbergasted. They were nervous and scared too.

"What could this other option Lancaster is talking about possibly be, Michael? Did you tell him about Mexico?

"Of course, not. I just followed your directions, Weinstein. I know little about Mexico. Only you do. Hell, on top of that, I know next to nothing about real estate options. I just followed your lead. You told me I was going to make a lot of money and could not lose. I do not know anything about any other deal."

Weinstein said, "Apparently, if there is another option Israel is considering, I am not as high up the food chain as I thought. Is there another land deal being worked on that I was not brought in the loop on? Did they tell Lancaster about it, but not me?"

"I certainly don't know of any, if there was," said Demsky. "Hell, other than what you told me, I wasn't even aware of the Baja deal."

"And if there is another option, and if the Russian or Mexico deals are rejected, all our options will expire—worthless. We will be screwed. But there is no other deal. Is there? And if we sell our options now, and he is lying, we will both take a bath, plus lose out on the missed land values going up."

"So we might lose everything?"

"We couldn't lose if it were just Birobidzhan or Mexico being the place Israel does the deal with. We both knew that even if we lost out on one side of the real estate deal, whatever real estate option hit, that land would have blasted off so much in appreciation that it would not matter. The profits on the winning land deal would have been greater than the losses on the other. Now, if Lancaster says there is a third option, assuming he is truthful, and that one wins out, we are both screwed."

"I told you, Stephen, I can't afford to lose on this deal. My money will be all gone."

"The more I think about it," said Weinstein, "the other option may not even be an Israeli land deal at all. The other option he is talking about, maybe is his option to get us prosecuted."

"But I thought you said this was legal?"

"I thought it was. I think it is. But he is the expert. Now an angry expert. Over the years he always suspected me of bankruptcy and securities fraud, but his office never prosecuted me. This has to be some sort of personal payback on his part?"

"So now you are saying, not only will I lose all my money, but also go to jail?"

"I don't know anymore," said Weinstein. "I can only speak for myself, but I am going to sell out all my options now. If I do not own any options at the time of the Prime Minister's announcement to the United Nations, I can't get criminally prosecuted."

"But we only got six days. We are not going to get much money for those options if we must sell them quickly. Who would even buy them right now? We got to do this quickly."

"Sometimes you just got to cut your losses and reduce your risk. I am just going to have to face the situation, sell everything out at once, and get what I can."

"I have no choice either. This other unknown option he talks about scares the hell out of me."

"Me too."

As Lancaster walked back to his car, he still was not sure what this Mexico thing was all about. Were the Israelis considering doing a deal in both or either Birobidzhan or Mexico?

Chapter Fifty-Five

AFTER LEAVING WEINSTEIN'S HOUSE, LANCASTER GOT ON the southbound 405. He felt bad for Michael and so, figuring he had left Weinstein's house by now too, he gave him a call on his cell phone.

"This is Michael Demsky."

"Michael it is Lancaster. Are you still at Weinstein's?"

"No. I left about twenty minutes ago."

"Look, I'm sorry. I did not mean to come down so hard on you. That was a mistake. I have no doubt this was all Weinstein's idea, and I kind of put you in the middle of things."

"Well, I am not sure what I am supposed to do right now," said Michael.

"Want a suggestion?"

"Sure."

"Only if you promise not to speak with Weinstein until after the Tuesday Israeli announcement."

"I promise."

"Okay, don't sell any of your options."

"Don't sell? But you said there is a third option."

"There is."

"I don't want to be prosecuted, nor lose my money."

"You won't be prosecuted."

"But if prosecuting isn't the third option you were referring to, then I assume there is another country that Israel could make the deal with."

"There could be, but I am not sure."

"So, what then, is the third option?"

"I can't tell you right now. You will have to trust me."

"But what if there is another country Israel is negotiating with, and they are the winners of the deal?"

"Then, yes, you more than likely would lose everything."

"And that is my concern. I cannot risk losing all this money. It is my entire life savings."

"I see your point and concerns."

"Yes. So, I am considering jumping on a flight tonight and heading back to Siberia."

"I will be home in twenty-five minutes or so. Let me ponder this for a little bit and call you back."

———————————

LANCASTER CALLED HIM BACK AFTER ARRIVING HOME.

"So here is how I see it, Michael. You can choose to do nothing, and as you previously planned, if one of the two deals are made, you will make a lot of money. Second, if you are worried about that, you can go back to Russian and Mexico and try to sell them back to who you bought them from or whoever else might buy them. Third, and you do not have to do this, but if you wish, I will buy half of your options from both Mexico and Russia and reduce your risk by half. Of course, by doing this, if a deal is made, you will lose out on some of your upside."

"I am happy to sell you half my position. Do you think Weinstein will have any chance to sell out his positions before the announcement?"

"He has such large positions. At this late in the game, if he does, he will only be able to get pennies on the dollar."

Chapter Fifty-Six

THE NEXT MORNING, JOE PICKED UP LANCASTER AT HIS home, and the two headed down to La Jolla to visit Paul. They entered his Scripps Hospital room; Paul was receiving physical therapy on his leg.

"They gave you the freeway view instead of the ocean view?" said Joe.

"Hey, dudes," said Paul. "I thought you weren't going to be here for another hour?"

"The traffic wasn't too bad," said Joe.

"Must be all the people moving out of the state, due to what they say on Fox News, either too many homeless people or high taxes," said Lancaster.

"Either that or more people are getting their cars repossessed," said Joe, now changing the subject, "which reminds me, Paul says Claire has, not one but two, sex dolls?"

Lancaster turned from Joe and gave Paul a piercing stare, "You told him this?"

And before the recent double amputee had a chance to respond, Joe added, "... and one is male, the other female?"

"Thanks, Easy, you big mouth."

There was a slight pause as Paul thought about what Lancaster had said.

"Maybe it was the drugs I've been on." He extended both arms (one missing a hand) and shrugged, and for once, his eyes were wide open.

Joe chimed back in. "You're with friends, Lancaster. Besides, I like the fact they are both hers, and that one is a girl. I think it is a compliment to you. You're a lucky guy."

Lancaster stared at Joe, trying to look unfazed. He was pissed at Joe and Paul for butting into his private life, but he could not forget that both men had risked their lives to get justice for him.

"It's not just the dolls," he said after a moment. "If I give you both an itemized list of all her toys, and the complete details of their usage, would you each agree not to ask me any more questions on this subject?"

Joe and Paul turned toward one another, giving careful consideration to Lancaster's offer. They each nodded their chins toward one another.

"Okay," said Joe.

"Okay, is your answer."

The other two nodded. Lancaster couldn't believe they'd taken his offer seriously.

"Are you both out of your mind? This is none of your fucking business."

The room was silent for a good thirty seconds.

Changing the subject into a less interesting one, Lancaster said, "How are you feeling Paul?" It was, after all, the reason they were there.

"Thought you would never ask. Better than anyone predicted. The prosthetic devices are working out well. I expect to be jogging by lunch today."

"Uh ah," said Joe.

"Actually," Paul looking at Lancaster. "I spoke with your buddy Smith in San Francisco. He was encouraging. And he lost a lot more limbs than me."

"Yes, he did," answered Lancaster. "Smith is a great guy. I am glad you spoke with him."

Now in a serious and heartfelt tone, "Listen, both you guys," said Lancaster, "I didn't have much time to speak with either of you at the prison in Urumqi. Even if I did, I could not speak freely given where we were. I have been spinning too many plates lately. But I got to tell you how grateful I am to both of you. You guys somehow tracked down Señor X and took care of business. You both got justice for my father, and I am in debt to both of you."

"We didn't take him out. An IED did. Hell, we got in trouble, as you know, for him dying. But I will tell you, your buddy Rosendo is out of the way too."

"Thanks, you guys. I really appreciate it."

"Is Ahmed somewhere around here?"

"He is staying at my house," answered Paul. He does not know anything about our motivation to go after Señor X, whose real name, by the way, was Juan Juarez. He just thinks it was some type of U.S. government mission."

"Fine with me. So that will be our story. Does he have a cell phone number?"

"No, if you need him, just call him on my house phone. Why you ask?"

"I am having a surprise breakfast party next Tuesday morning at my house. A few friends will be coming over. I wanted to invite you guys along with Ahmed. Party starts at 6:30 a.m. Be there on time."

"6:30 in the morning?" said Joe.

"You never been to a surprise breakfast party?"

"No," said Joe.

"Me neither," said Paul.

"Well, this will be a first then," said Lancaster

"A surprise party? For whom?"

"I could tell you, but that would ruin the surprise."

"Do we need to bring gifts," asked Paul?"

"Nah," said Lancaster, "just bring yourself, Ahmed, and Sheila. But do not be late. 6:30 a.m. sharp!"

Both Joe and Paul said, "Okay."

Two days later, Lancaster got a call on his cell phone.

"Hello. Steve?"

"Yea. Hi, Paul."

"I got Ahmed here. He wants to ask you a question."

"Okay. Put him on."

"Hello, Mr. Lancaster."

"Hi, Ahmed. Call me Steven or Lancaster."

"Okay. Mr. Steven. You know the upcoming surprise party at your house on Tuesday at 6:30 a.m.? Can we start with some of the guests at 6 a.m. instead?"

"What do you mean, Ahmed."

"I have a little surprise myself. I just want to have you, Paul, and Erection there. Oh, and your wife can be there too."

"I guess so. What is this about?"

"You have your surprise; I have my surprise too."

"Okay, 6 a.m. You want me to tell Joe?"

"I already told him. He will be there."

"See you guys then."

Chapter Fifty-Seven

LANCASTER, DEMSKY, AND WEINSTEIN WERE ALL INVITED by the State of Israel to attend the Prime Minister's speech Tuesday morning at the United Nations.

Lancaster declined because he was hosting a surprise party that morning. Weinstein declined, for reasons unknown, but Lancaster presumed he was out of the country selling his real estate options.

Demsky initially agreed to attend, but later declined as well, as he was also invited to the surprise party. Demsky was invited by Lancaster to come down Monday night so he would not have to wake up too early Tuesday morning to drive down. Besides, Lancaster wanted to speak with him privately.

IT WAS MONDAY NIGHT AT THE LANCASTER HOUSE AND Demsky and Steven finally had a chance to speak.

Michael told Lancaster, "Thank you. You didn't have to buy my options."

"You didn't have to sell them to me. But I must say, Michael, if Mexico or Birobidzhan work, then I will feel bad that you lost out."

"That is the least of my concerns. I would much rather give you half than take a chance on losing everything."

"Any word from Weinstein?"

"No."

"And getting back to our previous conversation about your transition, do you mind if I ask you some, I don't know, naive questions?"

"No, go ahead. Ask me anything you want."

"I don't understand a lot of today's sexuality issues. By going through this transition, does this mean you are attracted to women? Are you gay? Do you still have sex with your husband?"

Michael shrugged his shoulders and smiled. "I think I am what they call a flow. I do have relations with my husband, but that part of my life is still a work in progress."

Michael sat back in his leather chair. Lancaster smiled too then, and asked Michael in a sarcastic and joking manner, "I take it you never had a bris?"

AT 6 A.M. TUESDAY, THE DOORBELL RANG AT THE Lancaster residence. Steven opened the door. It was Joe,

Sheila, Paul, and Ahmed. They all came in. Claire and Ashley were cooking in the kitchen. Michael, who was standing next to Lancaster, was introduced to the other guests.

Steven said to Ahmed, "Okay, Ahmed, it is 6 a.m., what is your surprise all about?"

"You will have to wait until 6:15 to find out."

"I could have slept for another fifteen minutes?"

"At precisely 6:15, the doorbell rang again."

Lancaster opened the door, as the others followed to see his reaction. "What the hell are you doing here Lin Chow?"

"I had a Southwestern Law School reunion, so thought I would stop by. No, just kidding! Ahmed told me about your early morning party and I have a little surprise for you. Do you remember when all of you were leaving the military prison in Urumqi, and Ahmed handed me an envelope?"

"Come to think about it, yes I do recall something like that," responded Lancaster"

"Do you know what was inside that envelope?"

"No idea."

"Your friends, Paul, Joe, and Ahmed, got valuable information from Juan Juarez, also known as Mr. Señor X. Specifically, the location where he was hiding just over $52 million in drug money."

"They did?"

"They did. And in appreciation for providing this information to my government, along with putting Mr. Señor X out of business, the money was seized, and was earmarked for two projects, one of which is half-completed already."

"What projects?" said Ahmed. "This was a surprise to Joe, Ahmed, and Paul as well, even though they were tipped off ahead of time that Lin Chow would be surprising Lancaster with something."

"In anticipation of the Birobidzhan project becoming a reality, the main highway that is going to be constructed between Beijing and the international border with Birobidzhan, a bridge is going to be built to cross the Yee River. This bridge is going to be called the Peace and Justice Bridge. As one travels in both directions and crosses over the bridge, two iron statues reflecting the four of you standing side by side with your arms on the shoulders of one other will be welcoming the visitors. One of the statues is completed. Here is a photo of it. It is made of iron and stands atop a pedestal. While it is hard to get a perspective from the picture, each one of you is standing here at your actual heights. On the pedestal below are words written in English, Chinese, Arabic, and Yiddish, which translate to: "With friendship we can achieve Justice and Harmony.""

"I don't know what to say," said Lancaster. "I am not even a hundred percent sure, the Israelis are going to do the Birobidzhan deal."

Ahmed, Joe, and Paul were equally as surprised and humbled and told Lin Chow how much they each appreciated it, and that they were so very honored.

Lin Chow responded to Ahmed, "I know you have been given amnesty by the United States. The Chinese government, after learning of all the facts and circumstances surrounding the death of Señor X, wants to extend to you the opportunity to come back to China where you will receive a promotion with the Chinese Security Agency. In addition, the Chinese Communist Party has issued a proclamation honoring your courage and loyalty in both bringing this horrible drug dealer to justice and providing your country with the information, which led to the confiscation of the money. Please consider your invitation to come back to Mother China."

Ahmed was not able to decide now as to whether he would return to China or not and told Lin Chow he was very appreciative and honored but would want to take the next week to think about it.

In the next ten minutes, the other guests began to arrive: David Berman and his wife, Per Dennis and his wife, Juan Sanchez, Sergeant Smith and his girlfriend, Steve's mom, and Claire's parents. The only other person who was invited but could not attend was Lancaster's coach, William Weidemann.

As each entered the Lancaster home, they were presented an envelope with the instructions not to open it until Steven told them. Before their arrival, Steven gave Michael Demsky an envelope too.

He asked his guests to please go into the kitchen where a buffet of eggs, bacon, ham, bagels, fruit, orange juice, and coffee had been set up atop the kitchen counter for them to help themselves to. An envelope was not provided to Lin Chow, as Lancaster had not known he would be there. Nonetheless, he was welcomed to help himself as well.

Lancaster told Chow, "Sorry we don't have any chopsticks."

Standing behind Lancaster, Joe heard and, as he was drinking a hot beverage and found the comment so funny, he was forced to give a few people a demonstration of what it was like to have coffee coming out of one's nose. Lancaster had put aside an envelope for Weidemann holding the same thing as everyone else, but he would have to give it to him later.

"This is informal. Everyone grab some food, then come back into the family room where the T.V. is."

"Hey, I am tired," said Per, who had shown up to the party wearing, as a personal joke, Los Angeles Kings hockey pajamas. It was a reminder to Lancaster of their adventure years before when they had met in Colombia, and then throughout their subsequent sailing voyage of smuggling drugs to the United States, the only shirt Lancaster ever saw Per wear had been a Los Angeles Kings t-shirt.

David Berman said, "Your right, Steven, this was a long drive from Thousand Oaks."

Everybody gathered in the family room after getting food. Steven let them dig in for a few minutes, then at five minutes before 7 a.m., he said, "Okay, everybody. Those envelopes I gave you at the door—open them."

Everybody opened them, and, apart from Smith and David Berman, nobody understood what the contents meant. The paperwork was marked with the letterhead, "Morgan Stanley". Below that were printed some numbers nobody could understand and each of their names.

"Anyone know what this is?" said Lancaster.

"Smith raised his hand, as did David Berman."

"All right, Smith. I know you know what this is. Tell them."

He looked at his paper and described what it was and what it meant, but he was still confused as to what this was all about:

"This is a document from the Stock Brokerage Company, Morgan Stanley, that reflects the ownership of ten thousand stock option contracts to buy the current month stock of

WhoWeR at $25 a share. That is what it says, but I don't get it."

David Berman adds, "I agree with Smith. I have the same thing but I have no idea why."

"Well, let me tell you," said Lancaster. "In about an hour, the Israeli Prime Minister is going to make a major announcement about the acquisition of some land. The Israelis have gone through a tremendous amount of population growth in the last few years, and most recently the last few months, they have received millions of applications for either residency or citizenship. They need more land. Why? Because people have discovered through WhoWeR that they are Jewish, and never knew it.

"The conclusions are based on theories that they are decedents of people who fled after the Spanish and Portuguese Inquisitions. Many of these people want to take advantage of an Israeli policy of the Jewish People's right to return. These people are from all over the world. In the next fifteen minutes, WhoWeR, the publicly traded company that was behind the DNA discovery, is going to announce earnings, and because of this, I predict their stock price is going to explode. How much the stock price will go up by, I have no idea. The stock is at about $22 a share as of the close yesterday. You have options I bought on your behalf that have a strike price of $25. If the stock goes to $26 for example, since you have ten thousand contracts you will each make $10,000. $27, you make $20,000 and so on. I know stock options are hard to understand and I do not expect my brief example to be that helpful. Do not worry about it for now. We are all going to have a good morning." Then Lancaster turned and spoke directly to Michael. "This was the other option I referred to when we were at Weinstein's house."

Demsky had no idea.

At 7:10 a.m. earnings for the company were announced. They were off the charts. The stock jumped up to $45 a share, something even Lancaster could not have foreseen.

Everybody at the Lancaster residence was hooting and hollering. They could not believe it.

"This is amazing," said Ahmed. "Is this a typical thing in America?"

Joe said, "No Ahmed, but you know that Erection thing I previously defined for you?"

"Yes," said Ahmed.

"Well, I got a big one right now."

"Don't look at me, Joe, your wife might get mad."

"This is fun," said David Berman. "Why did you do this? And why did you think of me?"

"Because, David, as you would say, 'It's fun'!"

"Thanks, boss," said Smith.

"Maybe we go to the world cup," said Per to Lancaster in his Swedish accent.

"Okay, Per. But only if the United States makes it."

Each of Lancaster's guests had options worth around a quarter-million dollars. Not a bad gift to give a bunch of friends. Not a bad earnings play of WhoWeR by Lancaster either.

About an hour later, the Israeli Prime Minister took the podium in front of the General Assembly. This too was on Lancaster's T.V. The world knew Israel was going to make a major announcement. The world knew the country's population was exploding, and he was going to address that situation. Many people predicted something to do with land. Some thought a deal with Jordon, the Sinai with Egypt, but nobody seemed to know for sure, except the Prime Minister himself.

The Prime Minister spoke to the assembly in English, with his perfect American accent:

"Members of the General Assembly, Citizens of the World, thank you for providing me the opportunity to address this body.

"As many of you are aware, Israel is a small country with enormous population growth challenges. We do not have a lot of space. Our challenges in this regard are going to continue at, we believe, an astronomical rate of growth. Just an hour ago, the Santa Clara based company, WhoWeR verified our challenge by putting out a statement during their earnings release.

"They said, and I quote, 'The percentage of people in the world we are discovering to be of Jewish descent, is tantamount to the new Black Swan of the century.' This finding by WhoWeR of so many Jews in the world, nobody saw coming.

"Due to our country's limited size, Israel has become one of the most densely populated areas in the world. In less than three years, absent getting new land, we will be the most densely populated country in the world.

"To this end, the State of Israel has considered assorted options to expand its size. We first looked at trying to work things out with Egypt and mutually determined with our Egyptian friends, that would not be practical."

As the Prime Minister took a brief break from his speech, due to some sort of glitch in the teleprompter, members in the assembly, from all over the world were seen discussing this situation with other country representatives sitting near them.

The general observation by one British reporter was, "They all look stunned and nobody seems to have expecting anything like this."

The Israeli Prime Minister continued, "I am pleased to say that an amazing opportunity by our dear friends in Russia and China was proposed. Over the last year, and even more so the last sixty days, representatives from these countries have been discussing and negotiating, in detail, a beneficial opportunity for all of us.

"Many of you are not familiar with the Birobidzhan Oblast; a Jewish Autonomous Region in Siberia, along the northern border with China.

"Established before the State of Israel in 1934, the land area we have negotiated would expand the current land size of Israel from eight thousand six hundred and thirty square miles (about the area of New Jersey) to over fifty-five thousand square miles (about twice the area of South Carolina). Our friends, China and Russia, have offered wonderful incentives, including infrastructure additions, such as a new highway system, new railroad, brand-new ultramodern harbor on the Pacific coast, trade incentives, low-cost energy, and the availability of important natural resources.

"Moreover, Ladies and Gentlemen, if you can see the slide up here on the screen of this magnificent area, and how it hugs the northern border of China, it is wonderful to consider the enthusiasm the Chinese also have for this project as well. They too will add substantial resources to improve the infrastructure, including roads and railroads as well. China has also offered to build new cities in the region to help what some expect could be tremendous manufacturing opportunities.

"Quoting the President of Russia, 'I see this region becoming the new Silicon Valley of the East.'"

"Ladies and Gentlemen of the United Nations Assembly, the people of Russia and China have offered the State of Israel one of the greatest opportunities this planet has ever seen. We are so grateful to these wonderful friends.

"At the same time, Israel has also received another wonderful option. This option is from both Mexico and the United States of America. This project was referred to as code-name, 'triple play'. A three-way deal between the United States, Israel, and Mexico.

"The United States has offered the opportunity for Mexico to become part of its country. As an important aspect of this deal, the United States will absorb all of Mexico's debt, their crime would be marginalized, plus Mexico would receive a legal system free of corruption and create laws that would be fair to all their citizens. These advantages would allow Mexico the opportunity to thrive economically and enhance the lives of all its people.

"In exchange for Mexico's commitment to agreeing to the 'triple play', the United States will benefit by reduced labor costs, resulting in the lowering of many consumer goods, new natural resources, and a young population that will allow them to strengthen and support a more fiscally sound Social Security and Medicare system for its current senior citizens.

"By the United States and Mexico agreeing to these terms, Israel will receive and become part of their new homeland, the entire Baja Peninsula. This new creation will have an enormous positive economic impact on trade in the area. The idea of Israel being next door to their best friends, the United States is extremely comforting. The weather offered in Baja, with all due respect to our Russian friends, is much more moderate."

The United Nations Assembly members were now talking to one another so loudly that even with the translator headphones many were wearing, those that wanted to hear more details from the Israeli Prime Minister were having a challenging time listening.

The same British reporter commented that "The conversation between Assembly members is even more active. The problem for this reporter is, I cannot get a sense of what people are saying. Whether they support or don't like this other proposed deal."

"So, it is with both a combination of sadness to our friends in Russia and China, and joy to our friends in the United States and Mexico, that we must reject the Birobidzhan option, and hereby accept the trilateral 'triple play' option of Baja California. We look forward to beginning its implementation at once."

Watching this unfold on television, with his friends all around him, Lancaster turned to Smith and who were sitting near him. "So that is what they were up to. I guess no Peace and Justice Bridge?"

"It appears that way," said Smith. "You kind of predicted that after you realized there were Mexican land options as well."

Michael Demsky, sitting to Lancaster's left on a separate chair, looked over at Lancaster. He did not say a word but a tear dropped from his right eye as he nodded and gave Steven a big thumbs up.

Chapter Fifty-Eight

ABOUT AN HOUR AFTER THE ANNOUNCEMENT, LANCASTER'S guests started to leave. It was still a workday for some. Everybody had a great appreciation for Steven Lancaster for sharing his gift of knowledge, which translated into the money they all made from the stock options.

Lancaster's house phone rang. Claire picked up the phone.

"Steven, it is for you."

"Who is it?"

"Stephen Weinstein," responded Claire.

An ear-to-ear smile lit up Lancaster's face. "Smith and Michael, follow me to the kitchen. You guys got to hear this."

Lancaster, Smith, and Demsky all walked into the kitchen where he took the wall phone from Claire.

Lancaster said, "Hellllllllllloooooooooooooo," in an extremely overconfident and sarcastic tone that was quite rare for him.

Weinstein said, "You told me there was another option. I called to tell you, that if that option was to somehow cause me to get criminally prosecuted, you can forget it all putz. I dumped all my options last week."

"Oh, so sad to hear that," said Lancaster. "I have a question for you, Weinstein. If you held on to the options and weren't criminally prosecuted, how much would you have made?"

"Net of everything, over $65 million. I do not know about Demsky. I don't even know where he is."

"Did you have a tough time selling them?"

"I took a bath on them. It was hard to find anyone to buy them. I ended up getting only pennies on the dollar. Whoever bought the Mexican ones from me hit it out of the park and made a fortune."

"Oh, you are making me feel bad," said Lancaster as he looked over at Demsky and Smith, as all three were smiling.

"And why is that?"

"Why?" said Lancaster. "Because if you would have kept the options, you could have gotten away with it." Then, in a whispering slow voice, Lancaster said, "Your buying of the options wasn't illegal."

"What are you saying?" asked Weinstein. "You told us there was this other option you knew of besides Mexico and Russia, and your veiled threat suggested to me, it was to get us prosecuted. It had to be that. Either that or you somehow knew about some third deal Israel was working on that I didn't even know about."

"There was no criminal case there, Weinstein. I certainly was not aware of any other land deal. Quite frankly, until I heard the Prime Minister's speech, I was not a hundred percent sure there was even a Mexican deal working. The only reason I suspected that, was the purchase of the real estate options by the both of you.

The other option, Weinstein, was not criminal prosecution, or even a real estate option, it was a stock option. The stock option to buy WhoWeR. I bought a ton of them. Too bad you couldn't figure that out on your own."

"That was the other option?!"

"Yep, and all my buddies made a large profit. You were too greedy, Weinstein, and ended up losing money."

"You are such an asshole. Have you heard from Demsky?"

"Oh yes, he is here, celebrating the money has made on his WhoWeR stock options and his Mexican real estate options. One more thing, Weinstein, then I got to let you go: you know the options you sold for pennies on the dollar and that somebody else has made a fortune off of?"

"Yes."

"That buyer was me. I contacted agents before you went back to both Mexico and Birobidzhan, told them to be on the lookout, and that I was interested."

"You bought my options?"

"All of them, my friend. They were a bargain."

"You bastard, Lancaster. And Demsky kept his Mexican options?"

"Ask him."

Weinstein just hung up the phone.

Epilogue

THREE WEEKS AFTER THE ISRAELI ANNOUNCEMENT, CLAIRE, Ashley, and Steven drove over to Balboa Island in Newport Beach to eat breakfast at Billy Boys, one of the family's go-to places for a Sunday. After breakfast, they put their car on the Balboa Ferry for the three-minute ride over to the Peninsula, where they would park, walk down to the Wedge at the end, and see if any daredevils were riding their Boogie boards on the big waves. There were none that day, so the family headed over to the Balboa Pier to allow Ashley to fish for a couple of hours. Fishing poles for rent and bait were available at the tackle shop found at the pier's end.

Once Ashley's pole was set up, and her line in the water, Claire and Steven had a chance to speak.

Steven pulled a piece of notebook paper from his rear jean pocket, on which he had scribbled a list of topics he wanted to speak with her about. He began to read from his list.

"You have a checklist?" asked Claire.

"I do. It is been so long since we have been able to catch up. You remember Lin Chow?"

Claire nodded.

"He got back home to China and called me yesterday when you were working with Ashley on her homework."

"What did he have to say?"

"You are not going to believe this, but China has still decided to build that highway, bridge, and put those statues up, even though the Birobidzhan deal wasn't finalized."

"Really? Why?"

"Lin said, even though Israel had said no, both the Chinese and the Russians think there is still a chance to put the Birobidzhan deal back together. Plus, he also said, China is happy for not just what the delegation did, but also what Ahmed, Paul, and Joe accomplished; that our combined efforts somehow reflected the spirit of the Birobidzhan project."

"So, does this mean there is no Mexico deal?"

"Lin said, no, it would be on top of Mexico. They still think their plan was sound and makes sense for all. That reminds me of something not on the list. I need to contact Michael and find out when those Birobidzhan options we have expire. Who knows, they may become valuable too!

"Lin said the bridge, highway, and statues should be completed and in place by next summer. The Chinese want all four of us and our families to fly out for the unveiling ceremony."

"That would be exciting. We should."

"Next item," continued Steven, speaking slowly and respectfully. "Michael Demsky, it turns out, used to be a woman named Michele. Michele gave birth to two children."

Claire was taken aback. "He was? I didn't know that."

"I'm sure you didn't know that. And he or she—I guess he is a he—is still married to the original biological father of his children. Claire, I really don't understand this kind of stuff."

"It's a little difficult for me to understand as well. Whatever; he is a nice guy. It doesn't really bother me."

Lancaster responded, "I don't have any problem with it. I wish them nothing but happiness. Kind of cool he is still with his husband. Doesn't mean I understand it."

"Mom, I got a fish," screamed Ashley from a few feet away. Claire and Steven ran over.

"Honey," said Claire, "I think you're snagged."

Lancaster said, "Here, I will untangle it." He cleared her line, put on fresh bait, dropped the line back in the water, and continued his conversation with Claire.

"Steven Weinstein. I am not sure what to think. Did I wrongfully screw him? Part of me still feels he deserved what he got."

"Maybe you worry too much about what you told him?"

"I'm not sure. Let me give you an example. I know you are familiar with the Child Burn Victims' case."

"Vaguely!"

The Child Burn Victims case was Claire's greatest moment in the practice of law. She worked out a complicated criminal defense of a charitable fraud scam. She represented several ex-felons accused of stealing over $200,000,000 from unsuspecting senior citizens and was able to finesse her legal skills so that none of her clients spent any time in prison. It was also because of this case that she formally got to know Steven on a personal basis, leading to their marriage.

"On that case, when David Berman threatened your boiler room clients with criminal prosecution unless they returned the money to their victims, that gave you the leverage you needed for your defense. Remember, a lawyer cannot use the threat of criminal prosecution for a civil advantage. In this situation, for Berman's class action. You were all over that."

"Yes? So?" said Claire in an overconfident kind of manner. "Steven, at least they were forced to return the money."

"No problem with that part, Claire. But I think I have the same thing going on here with Weinstein. I hinted that if he were to exercise the real estate options, he might get prosecuted. Was I not doing the same thing as Berman?"

"And what was your civil advantage?"

"I did end up buying his options and making a killing off them."

"Oh yes, I forgot! What else is on your list?"

"Thanks for your emotional support and legal defense, Claire."

"Okay, your legal defense? You never specifically told Weinstein what the other option was, except on the phone after the fact. The other option you were hinting at was the WhoWeR stock options."

"True. That makes me feel better, Claire."

"But then, of course, you did buy his real estate options."

"That is enough!" He smiled. "I feel bad for Paul Dos Santos. I did not even know him for awfully long. Without even asking me, he goes off with Joe after Rosendo and Señor X on my behalf, kills them, loses two limbs, and was up on charges in a Chinese prison."

"Yes, that true."

"Then on top of that, when Israel moves some of their citizens into Baja, that will put him out of business and probably bankrupt him."

"You may be right. Any thoughts?"

"He made the money from the WhoWeR options. I also gave him some Birobidzhan real estate options as well in case that works. Plus, I gave him an ocean view lot next to ours in Scorpio Bay in Baja."

"We have an ocean view lot?"

"I forgot to tell you. Michael Demsky and his husband are going to be flying out there in a couple of weeks. He wants us to join them and consider building the lot we have next door to his. He says there is a great ocean view. I told him I would speak with you.

"Finally, do you recall that envelope Ahmed gave Lin Chow before departing China?"

"Yes. The one with the locations where the drug money was buried."

"When I was leaving Israel for the last time, an attorney from the African Union also gave me an envelope and told me not to open until I got home."

Did you?"

"I forgot about it until yesterday."

"Did you read it?"

"No, I will open it now." Lancaster pulled an envelope out of his inside windbreaker jacket pocket, opened it up, and read it out to Claire: "'We need your help urgently in Ethiopia. They have recently built the largest dam in Africa, called the Grand Ethiopian Renaissance Dam, and Egypt is threatening to bomb it. Please contact the African Union office at the United Nations. They are expecting your call and will fill you in on all the details.' ... I guess I better call and see what my next save the world project is all about!"